SEARCH & DESTROY

SEARCH & DESTROY

METAL LEGION™ BOOK SEVEN

CH GIDEON   CALEB WACHTER   CRAIG MARTELLE

DISRUPTIVE IMAGINATION

LMBPN Publishing
PMB 196, 2540 South Maryland Pkwy
Las Vegas, NV 89109

First US edition, June 2019
Version 1.01, June 2019
Print eBook ISBN: 978-1-64202-347-3

DEDICATION

We can't write without those who support us. On the home front, we thank you for being there for us.

We wouldn't be able to do this for a living if it weren't for our readers. We thank you for reading our books.

SEARCH & DESTROY TEAM

Thanks to our Beta Readers

Micky Cocker, James Caplan, Kelly O'Donnell, and John Ashmore

Thanks to the JIT Readers

Misty Roa
Dave Hicks
Peter Manis
James Caplan
John Ashmore
Peter Manis
Jeff Eaton
Micky Cocker
Jeff Goode
Kelly O'Donnell
Paul Westman

If we've missed anyone, please let us know!

Editor
Lynne Stiegler

ACRONYMS

AP = Armor Piercing
APC = Advanced Personnel Carrier or Armored Personnel Carrier
CAC = Command And Control center
CIG = Commander Intercept Group
CIP = Combat Interceptor Patrol
DIE = Durgan Industrial Enterprises
ER = Extended Range
FGF = Fleet Ground Force
FOB = Forward Operating Base
HE = High Explosive
HQ = Headquarters
HUD = Heads Up Display
HPC = Heavy Plasma Cannon
HVM = hyper-velocity missile
HWP = Heavy Weapons Platform
ILPF = Illumination League Peacekeeping Force
KPH = kilometers per hour
LRM = Long-Range Missile
LZ = Landing Zone

MIRV = Multiple Independently-targetable Reentry Vehicles
MRM = Mid-Range Missile
P2P = Point to Point
PD = Point Defense
PDF = Planetary Defense Force
POI = Point of Interest
RAP = Rocket Assisted Projectile
SAM = Surface-to-Air Missile
SOM = Surface-to-Orbit Missile
SOP = Standard Operating Procedure
SRM = Short-Range Missile
TAC = Terran Armor Corps
TFMC = Terran Fleet Marine Corps
THCG = Terra Han Colonial Guard
TRMC = Terran Republic Marine Corps
ZOC = Zone of Control

PROLOGUE: MANDATORY FUN

"I still can't believe I let you talk me into this," Xi Bao grumbled, fidgeting with her excessively flattering formal gown as their vehicle neared its destination.

Lee Jenkins chuckled, taking no small pleasure in her self-consciousness. "Trust me, in a room filled with aspiring and actual trophy wives, *you'll* be the only one turning heads."

"I should have stuck with my formal black-and-browns," she hissed as the vehicle slowed, their destination now in view.

"Probably," Jenkins agreed, causing her to deliver a straight left into his shoulder hard enough to send a bolt of pain down his arm. The aircar drew to a stop, and an actual red carpet stretched between it and the ostentatious façade adorning the skyscraper's front. A white-gloved gentleman with striking coal-black skin and platinum hair approached and opened the vehicle's door, prompting Jenkins to exit before the major could get in a second blow.

She cursed him in Mandarin, offering a fairly pointed criticism of his lineage while he stood outside the vehicle and extended a hand to her. He knew that normally she would have not accepted the offer of assistance, but the physical restraints imposed by her corseted, form-fitting garment and stylish but uncomfortable pumps made it necessary.

Glaring at him while she accepted his hand, she stepped out. The press of journalists, videographers, paparazzi, and others produced dazzling flashes that stabbed Jenkins' eyeballs.

Make that "eyeball," he thought, once again reminded of his recent loss. As his lone remaining orb acclimated to the near-blinding intensity of the flashes, Xi somehow managed to look equally stunning and intimidating. Her curved, muscular physique was exaggerated and laid bare by her chosen evening-wear, and she kept a winning smile on her face as she turned to each of the cameras vying for their attention.

"You act like you've done this before," Jenkins muttered as they began to walk up the carpet.

"If you looked like I do," she quipped, "this wouldn't be *your* first time in the spotlight, Colonel."

He laughed. "Is that a dig at my appearance, Major?"

"People have been taking my picture since the lunar op. That was uncomfortable enough to give me all the education I needed on social exposure," she said, all while keeping that model-perfect smile on her face and maintaining pace with him as they headed down the red carpet. "But like Darwin said, adapt or die."

"I'm not sure he ever said that," he muttered as they approached the glittering ten-foot-tall solid ruby doors leading to the building's interior. Those doors had been manufactured using a relatively new form of molecular assembly, pioneered by Terran scientists decades earlier, and stood as a testament to the human need to impose order on a chaotic universe and create beauty in an often ugly one. "But at least you didn't wear sky-high heels," he added as they passed through the scarlet doors, leaving the press and paparazzi to mob the next car's arriving VIP.

She flashed him a mischievous smile. "I would have if you weren't short an eye."

Jenkins laughed. "You're a cold-hearted bitch, Major."

"I had good teachers, Colonel," she retorted.

"All right." He held up his hands in mock surrender as they received their paper passes to the first showing of the holovid *Major Metal*, based only in the loosest sense on the events of Operation Antivenom and starring none other than Major Xi Bao. "You win this round. Let's see how you do on Luna."

Her triumphant smirk turned to a scowl as they made their way to their reserved balcony. "I just hope this is better than that digi-porn I've seen floating around with my likeness. I'm flexible, but not *that* flexible."

"How close did they come to depicting the reality of combat, Major?" pimple-faced Thucydides asked in the post-premiere gala. He was barely fifteen, but he was surrounded by a trio of seemingly-identical buxom women whose roles Xi couldn't quite pin down. They were either extraordinarily attractive bodyguards or incredibly overqualified escorts. Given that the young man before her was one of the twenty wealthiest living Terrans, Xi expected they were a combination of both.

"I'd say," she began diplomatically. "that the artists captured the essence of our missions, and that's a rare thing. Usually, art like this is nothing but explosions and dismembered body parts, which the creators think represents warfare. This was a little different. It was a pleasant surprise."

"Oh, come on." He grinned, flashing gapped teeth. "If I wanted to suffer through self-serving doublespeak, I'd tell my lawyer to stop fighting off those government antitrust inquests and actually appear at one."

She couldn't help but find his plain approach refreshing after suffering through a full hour of post-vid questions from the polite society of New America. "All right, you want blunt? I'll give you blunt: vids like this one make people think they've got a handle on what combat is like, but the truth is, nothing can prepare you for the reality of going tracks-down on some hell-hole, surrounded by an enemy who only wants to see you dead, with only the people and metal in your unit to keep you from turning into a name on a wall somewhere."

"It scares you?" he pressed. "Being in combat, I mean."

"Of course," she said dismissively. "But that doesn't mean you don't push through it. And sometimes you can even use that fear to your advantage. It sharpens things, and makes you realize what's important and what isn't."

"And all the dark cross-talk?" He cracked a grin. "That can't be real. *Nobody's* that witty under life-and-death pressure."

She chuckled. "Hate to burst your bubble, but that's the one part they absolutely *nailed*. When every word might be your last, you tend to say what's on your mind. And a simple fact of combat is that the quick-witted have better survival rates."

He cocked his head, his eyes suddenly alight with comprehension. "I never thought of it that way! Thank you, Major," he said, proffering his hand, which Xi accepted while the trio of seemingly-identical porn stars-slash-bodyguards exchanged muted looks of surprise. "You've given me a rare gift: a thought which had not previously occurred to me." He snapped his fingers immediately after releasing Xi's hand, and one of the buxom women produced a slip of paper, which Xi accepted. "Since donations to the Terran Armor Corps are tax-deductible, I've decided to allot my entire remaining offset budget to your organization for this fiscal year. Have your people get with mine to go over the details."

"Thank you, Mr. Thucydides," she said graciously, unconsciously tucking the slip into her bra, which only served to broaden the young businessman's grin. She shot him a withering look. "Unless you'd like a lesson on the finer points of hand-to-hand combat—"

He threw his head back and laughed. "You might be telling the truth after all. You Metalheads really are quick-witted."

Just then, Solar Marine Colonel Cao made his way over to where Xi was standing. He looked out of place in his all-white bodyglove, its pristine surface marred only by the minimalist rank insignia on his shoulder and left breast.

"Colonel," Xi greeted him, relieved to have a fellow serviceman to talk to, even if he *was* a Solarian.

Sol had increased its number of delegates to Terra following War God's conclusion, and military servicemen who had fought alongside the Metalheads were heavily represented in this second batch of dignitaries.

"Major," Colonel Cao acknowledged. "I must admit, the pomp and theatrics of this event are both amusing and perplexing."

"I can see the 'amusing' part," she said, noticing one of the holovid's actors successfully juggling five prop grenades for a small crowd. That actor had played an over-the-top-silly version of Podsednik. Podsy's name had been inexplicably changed to Kostelnik, which wasn't even of the same etymological root since the former was of English-Irish origin while the latter was Czech.

To say that Xi wasn't a fan of his role would be an understatement, although she recognized that actors could only go where they were directed.

"But what do you find perplexing?" she continued.

"I can understand the need for literary license to be taken with real events," Cao replied. "but I thought our respective governments would be reluctant to release what could reasonably be viewed, at least in part, as a documentary rather than a work of pure fiction, especially so soon after such a highly-sensitive and rightly-classified operation while its effects are still being cataloged."

"That's a difference between us Terrans and you Solarians." Xi shrugged, barely conscious of the dozens of eyeballs that clung to her every nook and cranny now that she had someone interesting to talk to. "Your One Mind makes Solarians think everything is open, giving the illusion of no secrets."

The Solar Marine scoffed. "We know there are secrets, Major."

"That's the nature of limited cognitive capacity," she said dismissively. "Some things you have to take on faith, like the idea that a wheel is probably the most efficient traction system you can use on land-based vehicles. It took us thousands of years to develop that wheel, and there were a lot of boneheaded alternatives bandied about before we finally settled on it. But on the *core* philosophical issues? The *really* important ones that are still up for debate? Those you absolutely *must* investigate to the best of your ability before adopting them as central tenets. You can't let a catchy slogan, attractive spokesperson, or, if you'll forgive me, a social trust mechanism like the One Mind reorder your entire life's priority tree for you. Abrogating your individual agency is dangerous, and we both understand how high a price that abrogation can carry," she finished with a knowing look.

Cao chuckled. "You never fail to disappoint, Major. You might be wrong more often than you suspect," he chided before sighing in resignation, "but you might also be right more often than my people would care to admit."

"I wouldn't be worth listening to," she replied sincerely, "and you wouldn't be worth my time to talk to unless both those statements were true, Colonel."

Major Trapper made his way over, wearing his new black-and-brown dress uniform. He looked nothing short of heroic in the new threads. His formal transfer to the Terran Armor Corps had taken some in the Metal Legion by surprise, but not Xi. She had known for a while that he belonged in TAC, and his appearance at the gala was yet another cog in the Legion's public relations machine, which was desperately fighting to keep the branch solvent.

"Major," Trapper greeted her, his handlebar mustache immaculately groomed and having a distinctive twirl at each tip. "What'd you think of the show?"

"About like porn or soft-serve 'ice cream,' I prefer the real thing," she deadpanned, drawing snorts from both men.

Trapper threw back a glass of something that looked suspiciously like whiskey. "As far as state-approved media masquerading as entertainment goes, I've seen a *lot* worse."

Colonel Cao smoothly interjected, "Major Xi and I were just discussing the often-conflicting social priorities of maintaining information security versus having a well-informed populace. Which side do you favor, Major Trapper?"

"I think those who can make you believe absurdities can make you commit atrocities," Trapper replied, flashing a mischievous smile beneath his bushy mustache.

Cao gave him a withering look. "Yes, Major Trapper. We Solarians are taught our Voltaire during secondary education."

"Secondary education?" Xi and Trapper blurted in tandem. "We Terrans cover Voltaire in first grade, Colonel," Xi said, returning Trapper's grin.

"This can't be good," Colonel Jenkins declared in a raised voice as he walked over with Alice close to his side. Xi legitimately felt bad for the colonel over the loss of his eye, but the eyepatch suited him. Made of black-and-brown embossed leather, it was barren of the rank insignia Jenkins was permitted to display when wearing his dress uniform. Apparently lost eyes had been such a frequent occurrence in the Legion's earliest years that eyepatches were specifically addressed in the regs. "Seeing the three of you huddled together makes me want to call in air support."

"They'd never get us all, Colonel," Trapper drawled.

"Probably right," Jenkins agreed. "So, have we made it past Voltaire yet?"

Xi sighed irritably before reaching into her dress and producing a fifty-sovereign coin. "Not yet," she said as Jenkins plucked it from her fingers.

"But it was close," Trapper said in conciliation.

"How much longer do we have to stay here, Colonel?" Xi asked, producing a thin stack of papers detailing the contact information for the various tycoons she had mingled with thus far. "I've already glad-handed at least fifty of these fat cats, and frankly, I need to find the ladies' room."

"Maybe it is time for us to call it in," Jenkins casually replied, appropriating the slips of paper and tucking them into his breast pocket. But his use of the phrase 'call it in' meant he had received an update from Podsednik regarding Jem's calculations. Xi felt her heart skip a beat at the dual prospects of getting the hell out of there and of finally hearing Jem's theory now that its calculations were complete.

"We will continue to persevere in your absence," Alice assured Jenkins, and again Xi thought she detected something more than mere professional courtesy when they made eye contact. However, thus far, despite the Legion's best efforts, no one had produced anything beyond water-cooler gossip regarding that particular front in Terran-Solar relations. It was juicy, so the colonel and Alice were under the microscope.

"Indeed." Colonel Cao nodded as a gaggle of media suits came their way. "For the sake of diplomacy, I must publicly endorse the self-evidently ludicrous notion that Sol's fate hung on a thread, and if not for a band of rabble-rousing self-described 'Metalheads,' we would have fallen victim to our own self-confidence."

Jenkins and Xi shared mildly surprised looks before Jenkins said, "But Colonel Cao, that was exactly what happened."

"That it happened does not make it any less ludicrous, Colonel Jenkins," Cao retorted. "In fact, to my mind, it makes it more so."

"Fair enough," Jenkins agreed before gesturing to the exit. "Majors first."

She glared at him, knowing that an army of paparazzi awaited them on the other side of those doors.

It was a small price to pay to see the social gala in her rearview mirror.

1

FALLING INTO ORDER

"Your language appears insufficient to the task of conveying my appreciation and gratitude for your forbearance," Jem began when Xi and Jenkins arrived at the TAC HQ planning theater. General Moon, General Pushkin, and Captain Podsednik awaited them at the far end of the long, slender table at the theater's center, the vacant trio of chairs overlooking them from the Command Dais.

"We'd be lying if we said it was nothing," Moon replied. "But you've been instrumental in many of our efforts to date, and that earned you some leeway we wouldn't have otherwise been inclined to grant."

"Agreed." Jenkins nodded firmly as he took his seat beside Xi and Podsednik.

"Then I will offer no further delay," Jem declared, its ruby-red crystalline cylinder pulsing with light as it spoke. "After examining the information gathered from artifacts recovered at The Pearl, and incorporating what I know of Vorr history and psychosocial makeup, I calculate a high degree of probability that the Vorr do not aim to remove Jemmin influence from Nexus Space."

General Moon quirked a brow incredulously. "At last count, the Vorr had taken out over twelve hundred Jemmin warships, including a handful of those damned Gatecrasher dreadnoughts. They're expending a lot of blood and treasure if they don't intend to defeat Jemmin."

"You mistake my meaning, General Moon," Jem said patiently. "The Vorr are indeed intent upon defeating Jemmin. They have expended every available resource toward that end, and I calculate that the cost has been far higher than you would likely believe."

"Try me," Moon challenged.

"In economic terms relevant to Terran and Solar humanity's current state of development," Jem said matter-of-factly, "one hundred and thirty-four times the entire estimated wealth of the Terran colonies and sixteen times the combined wealth of Sol and Terra combined. Roughly speaking, of course. This includes some of the Zeen contributions, as well as several other anomalies I have yet to fully identify, but for which I will presume the Vorr are responsible."

"I mean..." Xi squirmed in her seat. "I knew we were small out here, but Jesus! That really puts a damper on humanity's potential delusions of grandeur."

"Will you make your calculations available to us for review, Jem?" General Pushkin asked in his Slavic accent.

"I will, General," Jem agreed. "However, I anticipate that I will redact several of the factors that contributed to these calculations, for reasons you will likely not only understand but fully support."

"Great," Jenkins said sourly. "More mysteries."

"Certainly not, Colonel Jenkins. It is merely a matter of maintaining 'operational security' or 'OPSEC,' as you would put it."

Podsednik leaned forward intently. "You said that the Vorr

don't intend to remove Jemmin influence, but you also said they're intent on defeating Jemmin. Explain the disconnect, Jem."

"I project that the Vorr do not wish to remove Jemmin influence, Captain Podsednik. According to my calculations, they intend to *usurp* it by replacing Jemmin in the current framework of Nexus Space as the dominant faction."

Pushkin shrugged. "That was always the assumption most TAF brass was operating under. This is nothing new to us, Jem."

"Perhaps not in 'big picture' sense, General," Jem allowed. "But as you Terrans are fond of saying, 'the devil is in the details.' And I am now confident, after reviewing the data provided by Alice following Operation War God..." a slowly-rotating holoimage of a massive Nexus-tech vessel appeared above the table, "that the precise mechanism the Vorr intend to employ in their coup is the *Gatekeeper*. And if we act quickly, I calculate with a high degree of probability that we can intercept that particular asset before the Vorr can lay claim to it."

Everyone seated at the table leaned forward at the revelation, all eyes pinned to the rotating hologram of the legendary, ultra-reclusive ship.

"Repeat that, Jem." General Moon requested as if hearing the information a second time would break through the unreality.

"If we act quickly, I calculate with a high degree of probability that we can intercept *Gatekeeper* before the Vorr complete their plan to do so," Jem reiterated.

Jenkins leaned back in his chair and whistled appreciatively. "The largest ship in the galaxy...and the only one that can move faster than light without using the jump gates."

Podsednik nodded eagerly. "More than that, it's capable of actually *moving* the jump gates from one star system to another.

The power to move jump gates..." His voice trailed off, having taken on an ominous tone as he spoke.

"Would make whoever possesses the ship a force to be reckoned with in Nexus Space," General Pushkin remarked. "Along with making them possibly the most hated faction in the galaxy."

Xi thought out loud. "I don't want to count my hashes before they're splashes, but what the fuck would we even *do* with it once we took it? I mean that seriously. Do we hand it over to the Terran government and hope they don't cock it up? Would it become part of the new Terra-Sol alliance, to do with as it pleases? Or do we try to please everyone—and fail spectacularly in the process—by declaring it an integral piece of Nexus Space and maintaining that it therefore belongs to everyone here? I'm not even talking about the downstream politics, I'm asking something a lot more basic: what the hell would we do with it?"

"I would not presume to make suggestions on that matter," Jem said, surprising Jenkins and both generals. "For me, it is sufficient that Jemmin's influence over this galaxy is curtailed. Barring a successful assault on Jemmin's homeworld, assuming it has one, this might be the single most significant loss Jemmin will experience."

"How can you be sure we'd be any better than Jemmin?" Podsy asked, giving voice to a concern Jenkins shared regarding Jem's logic.

"I have observed humanity through my interactions with you," Jem explained. "As well as by downloading a significant portion of your history. There is no question that you are a barbaric species which was thrust into the stars well ahead of its time by agents who saw you as mere pawns in an ongoing cogitocide."

"'Cogitocide?'" Xi repeated.

"From 'cogito,' meaning 'to think' or, more broadly, 'to be aware,'" Jem continued. "Combined with 'cide,' meaning to kill or destroy. Jemmin does not commit genocide because the eradication of gene tracts is not its objective. It desires nothing less than the removal of all intelligence in the galaxy before it becomes powerful enough to challenge its matrix. There does not appear to be an appropriate word for this in your lexicon, so I conjugated the term 'cogitocide' from the Latin dictionary as appears customary in English. Was I in error?"

"Probably." General Pushkin waved a hand dismissively. "But while Major Xi has a point regarding the future of this asset, I would never condone hesitation when an opportunity of this magnitude presents itself."

He swept the assemblage with a hard look that was very much at odds with the man's usually jovial demeanor. "Things are not going well for the Metal Legion. Your fundraising efforts these past weeks have been more effective than I anticipated," he said with nods to Xi and Jenkins, "but most of that fruit will not ripen for at least six months. By that time, our Legion's fate will already be decided."

"I thought Director Durgan was doing well in the polls?" Xi asked with a furrowed brow. "Last I checked, he'd opened up a five-point lead and was trending higher still."

"His recent successes are encouraging," Pushkin allowed, "but we cannot attach the Legion's future to any single plan, no matter how solid that plan might seem. I don't need to tell anyone sitting at *this* table," he jabbed a finger into the surface, "just how critical the Metal Legion has been to humanity's survival since Spider Hole. We cannot afford—no, *humanity* cannot afford—to lose the Terran Armor Corps to a quirk of fate, a blip in the polls, or some pernicious form of political backstabbing."

"Hear, hear," the table chorused, loudly rapping their knuckles on the tabletop in solidarity.

"Your unity in this matter is encouraging," Jem said approvingly, its emotional intonations and other verbal inflections having become increasingly human these past few months.

"But..." Podsy ventured, drawing irritable looks from the rest of the table. That prompted him to defensively say, "There's *always* a 'but' in situations like this."

"Captain Podsednik is correct," Jem agreed. "While I have positively ascertained the Vorr's chosen method of usurpation, I do not as yet know *Gatekeeper's* location."

"Then what the hell are we even talking about?" General Moon grumbled.

"How do we find it, Jem?" Xi fixed the entity with a hard look as if it would produce the coordinates based on the force of her will.

"To locate *Gatekeeper*, I must interface directly with the Jemmin FTL comm network," Jem replied, replacing *Gatekeeper's* image with a collection of the artifacts recovered from The Pearl during Watery Grave. "These artifacts, when thoroughly examined, revealed the underwater facility where they were found to be an extremely sensitive gravity sensor array. The primary purpose of this array is still a mystery due to my lack of sufficient records, but I have calculated as a near-one-hundred-percent probability that the salvage pods we returned to the Vorr contained detailed logs of that array's activity. Using this, along with standard Jemmin behavioral models, and the information pertaining to *Gatekeeper's* arrival in Sol during humanity's induction into the Illumination League, I was able to triangulate a probable target zone where *Gatekeeper* currently rests."

Again, the holoimage shifted, this time to a portion of the Milky Way Galaxy eight thousand light years from Sol.

"I thought you said you don't know where it is?" Jenkins said in confusion, gesturing to the relatively small region indicated on the holomap.

"I have determined it rests somewhere in this area, Colonel Jenkins," Jem said patiently. "but you must understand that this region is over four light years in median diameter. Even your fastest warships could not traverse this region before exhausting their supplies, which does not take into account the fact that *Gatekeeper* would detect any approaching ships, activate its FTL drive, and conduct itself to an alternate location to avoid capture."

"Assuming it doesn't have enough firepower to blow our ship to hell and back a few times over," Moon mused.

"Which would be an unwise assumption, General Moon," Jem said agreeably. "At the very least, Jemmin will have installed significant weaponry onto *Gatekeeper* to safeguard it against attacks of the very type we are discussing."

"Okay." Pushkin gestured for Jem to hurry along. "How do we narrow the target zone down, and what do we do about a target it would be suicidal to attack?"

"As I said, I must directly interface with the Jemmin comm network," Jem reiterated. "Such an interface will require only a few seconds' live connection, and will likely provide a location with an inaccuracy of no more than three thousand kilometers."

"'Likely?'" Podsy repeated warily.

"To my knowledge, this has never before been attempted, Captain Podsednik," Jem replied with a trace of irritation in its voice. "It has significantly taxed my resources to perform these calculations, and I have expended more than eighty percent of my remaining lifespan to render them to this point."

"Wait..." Jenkins leaned forward in alarm. "You've been *killing* yourself to do this?"

"Of course," Jem said dismissively. "It is the most important task of which I am aware, and one for which I am uniquely suited. I could not risk compromising this information's security by sharing details prior to this point, so my rejoinder is a simple question: if not me, who?"

"Okay," Xi said measuredly. "Now the million-sovereign-question: how do we link you to the Jemmin comm network?"

"The answer is simple," Jem replied, dismissing the holomap and replacing it with the all-too-familiar image of a Jemmin Poltergeist. "Though the task is unlikely to be."

"Wait, wait, wait, wait!" Podsy scoffed. "You're not actually suggesting—"

"We must capture an intact Jemmin Poltergeist," Jem smoothly interrupted. "and, at the very least, remove its data cores and comm gear without damaging them in the process. Recovering an entire, functioning vehicle would be ideal, obviously."

"Obviously," Jenkins droned. "I'm not sure if you're aware, Jem, but we don't have anything that moves as fast as a Poltergeist on land. It's possible that a couple dozen ace interceptor pilots could disable one instead of destroying it, assuming we can even find the thing and that we'd accept the extreme losses such a controlled attack would entail. But more important than that is the simple fact that Jemmin's not stupid. Those Poltergeists are the most technologically advanced vehicles capable of making planetfall in all of Nexus Space. It would be criminally stupid of them not to install self-destruct systems to prevent their capture."

"The specifics of capturing the vehicle are best left to you," Jem replied dismissively. "I can facilitate the interruption of the Poltergeist's self-destruct systems, along with other key systems, which should help facilitate the capture to a tactically significant degree."

"Why haven't you previously apprised us of this capability?" Pushkin asked neutrally.

"I can only attempt it once before Jemmin reorders its internal security protocols, General, which would render it ineffective in all future attempts," Jem replied. "I have therefore held it back until this point because, to be blunt, none of our previous endeavors were as important as this one."

"Saving Sol wasn't as important as this?" General Moon asked, shooting a meaningful look Pushkin's way.

"It was not. Sol is a single star system, albeit a heavily-populated one, which is home to a relatively young and weak species. Ultimately, its survival was of far less importance than removing *Gatekeeper* from the control of factions like Jemmin or, I fear, the Vorr."

"All right," Podsy interjected. "Assuming we can put tracks down on a planet, locate a Poltergeist, subdue it, and recover it more or less intact, where do we go *looking* for one? Jemmin didn't use Poltergeists on Mars, which still is arguably the most tactically-important planet in the human sphere!"

"I have assembled a short list of possible locations," Jem said, conjuring a list of five planets to replace the Poltergeist's image. None of the planets were in human-controlled space. "Again, I leave the specifics of which planet up to you since that is primarily a tactical matter."

"I'm going to address one of the elephants in the room," Jenkins said after a brief lull in the conversation. "How do we know you don't intend to destroy *Gatekeeper*, or even take direct control of it yourself? You're proposing a mission that potentially carries an extreme cost. The human race isn't in a position where organizations like the Metal Legion can afford to expend valuable assets if there isn't a clear and significant benefit to Terra, or at least to Sol."

Jem hesitated longer than normal before answering, "That is a legitimate concern, Colonel Jenkins, and any answer I might provide to such a query would be impossible for you or your agents to independently verify. Even my claim to have expended significant personal resources in pursuit of this project is one you are unable to confirm or refute since you know so little of my architecture. Therefore, as not only a token of good faith but also as an act of self-preservation, I will ask you to study my current platform in the hope that a replacement can be developed before it is rendered inoperable. As you do so, you will be able to ascertain whether I am being truthful. I also anticipate significant technological advances to be made during this study that will be of potentially significant benefit to your species."

"That's tricky, Jem," Podsednik mused. "Your sovereignty is still a matter of debate among Terra's legal minds, although it's not like anyone here doubts your right to autonomy and self-determination."

While most heads bobbed in reflexive agreement, General Moon's remained motionless.

Podsy continued, "Terran law doesn't permit us to make such invasive examinations of any sentient being unless doing so is deemed to be of vital importance to Terran security."

"Fortunately, this is precisely such a situation," Jem replied matter-of-factly. "If we do not secure *Gatekeeper* before the Vorr can do so, Terran security will be at severe risk. We have already seen how powerful the Vorr fleet is, especially when it works in tandem with the Zeen. Even after the Vorr suffer further losses in their fight against Jemmin, they will still retain enough military power to impose their will on what you call Nexus Space."

"Jem's right," General Moon agreed bitterly.

"Of course, it is." Pushkin breathed a long sigh. "It wouldn't be speaking to us about this unless it could do so in a light favorable to its agenda."

"General—" Podsednik began, only to be silenced when TAC's senior officer held up his hand.

"All negotiations are a contest, Captain," Pushkin said with no small measure of sympathy. "Jem is more intelligent than anyone at this table. It would have been foolish not to wait until conditions were ideal before making this proposal. Simply stating that as fact has no bearing on whether or not we will oblige it. We *have* to act on Jem's theory. Our alternative, frankly, is to hand Jem over to the Vorr, which would be an abrogation incompatible with the most important fundamentals Terra was built upon."

"But what if Jem is lying to us?" Moon asked bluntly. "What if this is some kind of long-view game it's playing with us as pawns?"

Pushkin chuckled. "We are all pawns, General Moon. But if we live long enough and follow the right path, we might just become something much, much more."

"I could give the royal life a spin." Xi smirked before jerking a thumb toward Podsednik. "and Podsy's got a full wardrobe of women's clothing, so that's two potential queens among us already."

The attendees chuckled for a moment before Pushkin declared, "I see no real alternative. We act on Jem's intel, and we do it immediately. It's time to set up a call with Fleet so we can discuss which of these worlds to target." He gestured to the list of five planets Jem had provided. "But whichever one it is, we break orbit in three days with or without Fleet's help."

"What about the *Mencken*?" Jenkins pressed, referring to the *HL Mencken*, which was of identical design to the *Dietrich Bonhoeffer*. "She won't be out of drydock for another two weeks."

"Then she misses this round," Pushkin said flatly. "Major

Xi, take Captain Podsednik, Jem, and whoever else you need to assemble a roster while we negotiate with Fleet."

"Yes, sir." Xi saluted crisply before leaving with Podsednik at her side.

"All right, gentlemen." Pushkin grimaced. "With Admiral Zhao still on assignment, we won't be able to count on his support. I'm open to suggestions as to who we approach because *none* of these planets," he waved at the list, "is undefended, which means we *need* Fleet support."

Jenkins cracked a slow smile. "I think I know who to call, General."

2

BEST SERVED COLD?

"FJ-115 is out," Admiral Wallace said flatly, his holoimage flanked by eight fellow Fleet officers as their ghostly forms "sat" at various seats around the TAC war room's table. "The Vorr and Jemmin are actively contesting the Finjou gates, so moving any fleet through there would be suicide. That leaves four options: AK-091, BH-676, BH-442, and AK-023."

Commodore Meng scoffed. "Frankly, I'm not sure we want to risk antagonizing the Brek. They've been more or less neutral since the war began, with only a few scattered reports of engagements with the Vorr and Jemmin fleets."

"A salient point," General Pushkin allowed. "However, Brek worlds are considerably less fortified than Arh'Kel. And if we are to do as Admiral Wallace suggests and disregard Finjou space, then we have but two options: an Arh'Kel world or a Brek world."

Rear Admiral Corbyn assented. "He's right. Brek worlds are barely even *colonies* by Terran standards. After their break with the Finjou five hundred years ago, they spread across scattered worlds and received official League recognition as a distinct faction. After three thousand years' subservience to the Finjou, they've done next to nothing in terms of industrial advancement, border expansion, or resource accrual while the rest of the League worlds kept moving forward."

"Yet another example of Jemmin stacking the League for its own benefit." Colonel Jenkins shook his head in condemnation, marveling at how no one in the human sphere had noticed the signs of Jemmin's imperialist designs until it smacked humanity in the face. "Splitting the Brek off from the Finjou created another faction, and diluted the Illumination League's governing council by adding new seats. Those seats predictably aligned with Jemmin in gratitude for granting them their freedom from the caste system the Finjou had used on them once both species achieved sentience."

"The Brek have been favorable to the Jemmin, it's true," General Moon allowed. "but they also haven't been acting on their behalf. My guess is that the Vorr sowed the seeds of discord among the Brek before the war broke out."

"Fleet Intelligence concurs with your assessment, General Moon." Admiral Wallace steepled his fingers and pursed his lips in thought before continuing, "And finding new enemies is hardly a priority for Terra. Much as we might not care to admit it, dealing with just the Arh'Kel incursions has pushed us near the breaking point on several occasions."

"I don't mean to be ungrateful, seeing as you first approached me about this joint operation," Rear Admiral Corbyn interjected, making eerily accurate eye contact with Jenkins via the projected image "seated" across the table, "but before we go too much further, we need to know what the objective is."

Jenkins felt the weight of Corbyn's gaze pin him to his chair, but thankfully General Pushkin intervened. "The objective is to capture a Jemmin Poltergeist or at least certain key components aboard it. Our intel has narrowed down the list of worlds likely to harbor one or more to these five." He gestured to the five planet names floating in the air before him.

"To what purpose?" Corbyn pressed. "Obviously TAC's intel operation is more effective than anyone outside your branch suspected possible—"

Moon stepped in. "No, Admiral, we won't be exposing our sources while this operation is ongoing."

"There won't *be* an operation if Fleet isn't satisfied with your intel, General Moon." Wallace was having none of the deflection.

"We've gone it alone on ops like this before, Admiral," Moon parried.

"That was *before* Nexus Space erupted in the bloodiest war it's ever seen," Corbyn shot back. For a moment, Jenkins wondered if he had erred in urging the generals to approach Corbyn with this op. The Rear Admiral had only recently been released from house arrest. Being so quickly inducted into a high-level meeting of TAF brass was a huge favor the Legion was granting him, getting him back into the thick of things instead of letting the bureaucracy chip away piece by piece until there was nothing left but an old man and his tarnished legacy.

So far, he had a funny way of showing his gratitude.

"Look, Colonel," Corbyn continued, lacing his fingers and staring him down just as he had done following Operation Spider Hole, "what you're asking for here is the redeployment of a full Terran battle group. That's no fewer than twelve warships, and given recent events, the Admiralty is inclined to keep our guns as close to home as possible. A Jemmin Poltergeist is all well and good, especially if we live long enough to reverse-engineer its technology, but our concerns are a little more imme-diate than that just now."

Jenkins thought he saw a knowing look flash across Corbyn's

face as the Fleet flag officers on his side of the table began to nod in agreement. There it was. For the first time since Corbyn had spoken in the virtual meeting, Jenkins understood the rear admiral's game. A quick glance at Generals Moon and Pushkin suggested they did as well.

So, he took the only approach he was ever comfortable with: the direct one.

"We're hoping to use the Poltergeist's onboard systems to crack Jemmin's FTL comm network," Jenkins explained.

"And we intend to capture its pilot," Moon added without missing a beat. "*Alive.*"

The Fleet officers glanced at each other, suggesting that more than half of them were in the same room on the other end of the link.

"You may have splashed a few of these Poltergeists, Colonel," Commodore Meng retorted before amending, "Which is something no one else at this table can claim. But there's a world of difference between scratching one and capturing one intact."

Pushkin nodded. "Which is why we need your help. Fleet has more experience in operations like this one, which will be invaluable during Operation Dragula."

"You mean you need my Marines," Major General Xiahou said, ice freezing his words.

Pushkin nodded. "In no small part. But we'll also need your interceptors, orbital cover from your warships, and virtual support during capture efforts which, I'm told, will require active attacks on the Poltergeist's onboard systems."

"You people can crack Jemmin security?" Commodore Meng quirked a brow incredulously.

"We cracked the One Mind network, Commodore," Jenkins replied more smugly than he'd intended. "And we've only gotten better since then."

"Your bravado notwithstanding..." Corbyn's tone warned Jenkins that he had best tread softly, "TAC's record of overcoming virtual security systems is, if I'm truthful, unparalleled. The chief technician on your roster is one Chief Styles, is it not?"

"Correct," Moon allowed, and for a moment, Jenkins was reminded of his contentious debriefing session with Admiral Corbyn following Spider Hole on Durgan's Folly.

"His record is as...colorful as it is impressive." Corbyn scowled. "But there's no arguing with results, which the Terran Armor Corps has produced in both quantity and quality of late. And it brings me no great pleasure to say this, but results are precisely what Fleet could use right about now. Don't you agree, Admiral Wallace?"

And there it was. After all the bluster, all the grilling, and all the posturing, Rear Admiral Corbyn had just put Wallace on the defensive. Wallace shot a glare Corbyn's way, but from the expressions on the other Fleet officers' faces, they agreed with Corbyn's position.

At that moment, Jenkins saw more clearly than he would have thought possible the difference between being a field-grade officer and flag officer. Field-grade responsibilities largely focused on preparation, tactical planning, and putting the right people in the right places before the shit hit the fan, and then doing their best to keep everyone moving in the right direction.

While majors and colonels directed the troops to win the battles, flag officers devised the strategy to win the war and then sold that strategy to the politicians to fund all of it. It was more about politics than anything else because the best plan would wither and die without funding or logistical support.

For flag officers, it wasn't enough to simply have a winning strategy; an admiral or general needed to know how to build a coalition of his peers, often while working in the shadows, or he would find himself cut off from vital support.

Admiral Wallace knew when the tide was against him.

"I do, Admiral Corbyn," Wallace agreed, his face an unreadable mask as he leaned forward, looking up and down the table at his fellow Fleet officers. "Terra has suffered unprovoked hostilities from her neighbors for decades. I think it's time we stopped playing defense. The Brek are out; it's down to the two Arh'Kel worlds."

"Agreed." Corbyn nodded sagely.

It wasn't what the Metalheads had wanted, but it was the direction Pushkin had foreseen Wallace taking. And, as the saying went, "beggars can't be choosers," and right now, TAC was as close to on its knees as it had ever been. They *needed* Fleet support to pull this off, and if that meant they would have to conduct the op on a heavily-fortified Arh'Kel world, so be it.

"But that still leaves the question of which world." Moon gestured to the two remaining planets. "AK-023 or AK-091?"

"023 is significantly more compatible with human physiology," Commodore Meng opined. "The mean temperature is seven degrees centigrade, forty percent of the surface is covered with water, and the rock-biters haven't choked the atmosphere with lethal levels of sulfides yet. It orbits a red dwarf, so the ambient radiation is minimal. It's the softer landing of the two, no doubt about it."

"Indeed," Wallace said thoughtfully. "But the TAC brief shows just a seventy-nine percent chance of a Poltergeist being deployed there, compared with a ninety-three percent chance for 091."

"How were these numbers calculated, General?" Admiral Corbyn asked, but Wallace interrupted before either Moon or Pushkin could reply.

"It doesn't matter how they were calculated," Wallace

declared. "We're being asked to take an extraordinary amount of this brief on faith. We've already agreed in principle, so what's left is to sort out the particulars."

Corbyn seemed wrongfooted by that, but everyone on the call knew he had little leverage after playing his hand the way he had.

Wallace held eye contact with Corbyn for a moment before continuing, "In the interests of transparency, I'm now informing everyone in this meeting that I've already received authorization from the Joint Chiefs to conduct an operation of this type if it was deemed strategically necessary to ensure the Republic's security."

"An operation of this type?" Jenkins repeated uncertainly. "You mean seizing valuable tech from the enemy?"

Wallace fixed Jenkins with a diamond-hard look. "No, Colonel Jenkins. I mean launching a counteroffensive into Arh'Kel territory for the primary purpose of showing those rock-biters that we are *predators*, not prey. Terra has been invaded time and again by the silicoids. Our worlds have burned beneath their feet, our warriors have bled themselves dry across the Colonies, and our Republic's morale is shaken because we have not yet had the balls to take the fight to the enemy. We bear these wounds as a people, Colonel, and there is no living Terran who has not been impacted by Arh'Kel aggression in his or her life. But because of our politicians' lack of moral fortitude, these wounds have been deprived of the essential ingredients necessary to heal. That time is past," he declared, squaring his shoulders and steeling his voice.

"A counter-offensive?" Corbyn repeated in alarm. "But that type of operation will require months of planning—"

"Yes." Wallace smirked triumphantly. "It has been a laborious and costly effort, made all the more costly by the need to maintain secrecy to this point. The loss of the *Socrates* complicated our timeline, but Commodore Meng and the *Sima Yi* have recently been attached to the operation, which brings us back up to the strength required for a mission of this scope. Thirty-two Terran warships stand ready to engage the enemy, and engage them we shall."

Jenkins' brow rose in surprise. The *Sima Yi* was one of the newer Republican-class dreadnoughts. He had thought Meng's attendance had been in an advisory capacity. *None* of the Metalheads had expected the prospective battle group to include one of the Terran dreadnoughts.

But Wallace wasn't done.

"And since the *Marcus Aurelius'* repairs have been completed," Wallace continued smugly, savoring the surprise he saw on the Metalheads' and Admiral Corbyn's faces, "Eighth Fleet has all the firepower we'll need to finally repay this longstanding debt to our Arh'Kel neighbors—along with substantial interest accrued since the first rock-biter set foot on Terran soil."

The TAC officers were temporarily dumbfounded before Moon, in true Metalhead fashion, quipped. "So, what you're saying is, we've got Fleet support for Operation Dragula."

Wallace loosed a dark chuckle, prompting predatory grins to spread across the faces of his fellow Fleet officers, save Admiral Corbyn. "You'll get your fleet, General Moon. And Terra will finally have her revenge."

"Is there room for the *Martin Luther* in this armada, Admiral Wallace?" Corbyn asked, and for a moment all three Metalheads' attention was focused on Wallace as the senior Fleet officer focused on the rear admiral.

"Since this joint operation was your proposal," Wallace said after a long, emphatic pause, "it would be inappropriate for your flagship to be anywhere else, Admiral Corbyn. I'm sure I can convince the Admiralty to release the *Martin Luther* from her current patrol duties. It *is* just a heavy cruiser, after all."

With that final nail hammered into the humiliated Corbyn's ego, Wallace issued the order. "We break orbit in seventy-one hours, gentlemen."

"We'll be ready," General Moon said confidently.

Wallace smirked. "Dismissed."

3

ALLIES OLD & NEW

The *Martin Luther* was an aged heavy cruiser of the Statesman class, a relic from before Terra had discovered hyper-velocity railgun technology. Its offensive armaments were limited to rocket-driven missiles, making it ill-suited for void warfare against similar-classed ships. It was slow and heavily-armored, and the design was notoriously high-maintenance.

Rear Admiral Corbyn's former command, prior to his disgrace following Major General Kavanaugh's fall from TAC leadership, had been a command carrier. Carriers were the second most prestigious commands in the Terran Armed Forces after the mighty Republican-class dreadnoughts.

Anyone in the loop knew Corbyn would never regain such a lofty command after his role when the much-maligned Fleet-TAC merger fell through. That Corbyn was permitted an active command at all was a minor miracle, even if it was an old rust bucket like the *Martin Luther*.

But as Captain Podsednik looked out on the fast-assembling battle fleet from the *Martin Luther*'s bridge, he suspected the aged vessel would play a more significant role in the coming op than most thought possible.

"General Moon called your role here that of a temporary liaison," Admiral Corbyn said, snapping Podsy's attention from the viewing portal as he turned to face the admiral's chair. "But a CO doesn't normally send his XO off to liaise in the hours leading up to embarkation. Why *did* he send you here, Captain?"

"To be frank, I'm not sure, Admiral," Podsy answered.

"That passes for 'frank' in Ben Akinouye's outfit?" Corbyn challenged.

Podsy steeled his nerve. "If I were to guess, I'd say he wants me to learn something while I'm over here. Probably something to do with respecting the chain of command."

"Better," Corbyn drawled, swiveling his chair as a rail-thin commander approached the admiral's dais. "Report, Commander Benton."

"The *Martin Luther* is ready to depart, Admiral," the commander reported, his gaunt cheeks looking almost like something from a low-budget zombie vid. "All personnel are aboard, and all equipment has been secured."

"How are the port dampeners?" Corbyn asked.

"Within operational limits, Admiral," Benton replied.

"Thank you, Commander." The admiral nodded agreeably before standing from his chair. "You have the bridge."

"Very good, sir." The gaunt officer took his place next to the command chair and faced the forward screens.

"Let's take a walk, Captain," Admiral Corbyn said as he led Podsy off the ship's bridge and into the lift. Like every other part of the ship, it was old in both design and wear. Few right angles featured in the geometry of the compartment's interior and the light blue color of the interior paneling was more than a little off-putting to Podsy's eye. "I know about Silver Savannah Six."

"I expected you did," Podsy agreed. "You were one of the original signatories on Colonel Jenkins' armor test program. You would have had to personally authorize every recruit brought into that program."

"Aquino was a self-centered piece of human filth unworthy to wear the uniform," Corbyn said casually. "But humanity hasn't yet developed an effective counter to nepotism, so I expect we'll suffer his ilk for the foreseeable future. As one man of modest origins to another, and as someone who loves TAF more than anything else in this universe, I'd like to personally thank you for erasing his stain from the rolls like you did. That may not be a very prudent or politically savvy thing to say, but it's the truth—and the older I get, the less concerned I become with prudence. Also, if you repeat that, I will deny saying it."

Podsy was so taken aback by the admiral's shockingly forth-right remarks that he barely noticed when the lift stopped and its doors swished open to reveal an unexpected face.

"Ah, Lieutenant Commander Murdoch," Admiral Corbyn greeted the man as Podsy forcibly moved his attention to the former XO of then-Commander Jenkins' pilot program on Durgan's Folly. "Fancy meeting you here."

"Admiral," Murdoch said, flitting his gaze to Podsednik, where his eyes snagged on the captain's insignia on Podsy's collar. "Captain," he said with a stiff nod.

"Commander." Podsy returned the nod, still taken aback by Murdoch's appearance. He harbored no ill will toward the man, but the image of Xi uncorking a haymaker and shattering his nose was one of the few truly precious memories Podsednik had from the last few years. He couldn't keep the hint of a smile from his lips as it flitted across his mind's eye.

"Commander Benton informs me that the newly-arrived materiel resources are secured," Corbyn said, clearly enjoying the momentary awkwardness as the former companions came face to face. "I was just about to make a personal inspection."

"That is, of course, your prerogative, Admiral," Murdoch

said officiously, doing his best to ignore Podsednik.

"Come now, Commander. There's no need to get defensive." Corbyn chuckled. "This is technically a flagship, but only because I'm aboard. We have no fleet to command, or even an escort to direct. If I don't occupy myself with inspections of the ship, what else am I to do with my time?"

"I wouldn't presume to answer that question, sir." Murdoch continued his passive-aggressive approach before producing a data slate. "This is my final pre-launch report. I was just on my way to deliver it to you on the bridge, sir."

"A happy coincidence then," Corbyn stated, although Podsy wasn't buying that for a second. The admiral plucked the slate from Murdoch's hand and tucked it into his pocket. "Care to walk with us, Commander?"

"Begging the admiral's pardon," Murdoch said, the first hint of irritation flavoring his voice. "I could use some rack time. I've been up for thirty-four hours; one more dose of stims and I'll start hallucinating."

Corbyn chuckled. "Very well, Commander. Dismissed."

"Thank you, Admiral." Murdoch saluted before turning on his heel and making his way down the corridor.

"Impress me, Captain Podsednik," the admiral requested after Murdoch had gone.

"Two commanders and an admiral aboard an old ship like this...and you're presenting one as a quartermaster, but the quartermaster would report directly to the ship's CO, which is Commander Benton..." Podsy's mind ran through what seemed like the relevant details. "You're hiding something. And you want me to report as much to my CO."

"Good boy." Corbyn flashed a lopsided grin which made his sagging cheeks look somehow even more odious. "Now for the big question: *what* am I hiding?"

Podsednik cocked his head contemplatively. The *Martin*

Luther was a big ship, nearly the size of a battleship. There were ten meters of armor on its bow and stern, and half as much over its flanks. It had a standard complement of sixty-four interceptors, but due to shortages incurred during the recent battles in New America 2 (first with the Arh'Kel during Spider Hole and later when Admiral Wallace's Eighth Fleet destroyed the Jemmin Gatecrasher with help from the Zeen), most of those interceptors had been transferred to other warships, leaving three of her four flight decks barren. It also featured moorings for two orbital support platforms that could be deployed over active combat zones to provide materiel and information support to ground forces, but only one of those platform docks was filled on the *Martin Luther*'s ventral hull, while the other sat vacant.

Try as he might, Podsy couldn't come up with anything worth voicing, so he shook his head. "I don't know, Admiral, and won't fathom a guess without more information."

"Very good," the admiral approved and moved down the corridor opposite the one Murdoch had taken. "You didn't take a stab in the dark. You admitted your inadequacy instead of pretending it didn't exist. As the old sage said, 'The only true wisdom is in knowing you know nothing.' You've impressed me, young man, and while that might not be the most ringing endorsement given my recent history, I think a reward is in order."

They arrived at a plain officer's berth marked with the admiral's name. Corbyn opened the hatch and led Podsednik inside. The cabin was spartanly appointed, and far smaller than an officer of Corbyn's station should have been afforded.

"I've been hanging onto this for years," Corbyn explained, reaching into a set of drawers and producing a thin, rectangular cardboard slip with artwork that Podsy instantly recognized. "I won it in a game of cards with Ben—one of the few times I ever

bested the bastard at anything." He sighed in wistful resignation. "It's one of the only trophies I value, and until recently, I
thought I'd take it to the grave. But it doesn't belong here. It
belongs with Ben's corps."

He held it out to Podsednik and chuckled. "Go on, son. It
won't bite."

Podsy could hardly believe his eyes as he reverently took the
parcel from Corbyn. It was an original 1982 vinyl recording of
Iron Maiden's *Number of the Beast*. Wrapped in a nearly-invis-
ible film of protective polymer, this album had been pressed
when the United States was near its zenith as a world power.
The controversy surrounding it had been a defining part of the
metal movement that had followed, which shaped Western
sentiment and resistance to Chinese authority after the disas-
trous outcome of World War 3.

And now Podsy was holding it in his own two hands.

"I...can't accept this, sir." Podsy shook his head stupidly.

"It's not for *you*, son," Corbyn chided. "It belongs to the
Terran Armor Corps—Ben's beloved 'Metal Legion.' See that
it's returned to your CO. He'll know what to do with it, even if
you don't."

"I... Thank you, Admiral," Podsy said, not knowing how else
to respond.

"Now, unless I'm mistaken, you've got duties to attend to
aboard the *William Wallace*, and I'm a tired old man," Corbyn
said, and for a moment he looked like just that. "So I'm afraid
this little 'liaison' has come to a close."

"Yes, Admiral." Podsednik braced to salute.

"Dismissed, Captain." Corbyn tilted his chin toward the
door before falling back onto his bunk.

Ten minutes later, Podsednik was on a shuttle headed back
to the *William Wallace* carrying what could only be a cryptic
message disguised as a priceless piece of music history.

Unfortunately, Podsy was unable to divine what that message was.

"Call." Xi splashed the pot with a dozen sovereigns.

"King-high straight," declared Lieutenant Hightower, laying his cards down.

"Trip aces." Quinn grimaced, tossing her cards into the middle and rolling her eyes.

Xi cackled triumphantly. "Ladies full of Jacks. Just the way we like it," she added, fist-bumping Quinn to her left and Lassiter to her right.

"Crap," Hightower said in disgust as Xi scooped up the pot. "That's five hands in a row, Major."

"Can't stand the heat, Hightower?" Xi snickered.

"I guess I'm not used to losing to a superior officer, ma'am."

"Well, we do things a little differently in the Metal Legion, Lieutenant. We're a little more relaxed on fraternization...well, mostly," she added with a brief but meaningful look Lassiter's way. "How's Giles doing anyway, Shoe?"

"His first round of surgeries was successful," Lassiter replied while dealing the next hand to the cramped table of seven players. "The prosthetic will take a few weeks to calibrate, but Dr. Fellows said he should be able to ride Monkey as soon as it's attached. It'll probably be at least three months before he can sit Jock again, though."

"It's a shame your last op was classified," Lieutenant Hancock murmured. He and Hightower were transfers from Fleet, where they'd commanded APCs. Both had neural link implants and were rated on Recon and Tactical-grade mechs, and had put in three hundred hours' simulator time in the last month alone. They were good enough to ride Jock but had a long way to go before they were true Metalheads. "From the sound of things, you got tore up but good."

"No worse than usual," Quinn said with a shrug.

"Aww, c'mon, Major," Hightower pleaded. "Give us *something*. The scuttlebutt's getting to the point of absurdity."

"Give me an example," Xi urged as the last cards were dealt.

"Well, one rumor is that you were working with the Solarians on some kind of joint op under the auspices of the new alliance," Hancock offered after Hightower failed to do so.

"Can neither confirm nor deny." Xi smirked, anteing up and considering how to play her hand. She had an inside straight draw or a chance at a little cat. She opted for the latter, tossing a card and receiving precisely what she was looking for.

"Another rumor," Hightower said, rallying after his former hesitation, "is that you guys took on Solarian Marines."

"That's ridiculous." Hancock scoffed. "Why the hell would the One Minders work toward an alliance with us if we spilled their blood? And what the hell business would we have fighting Sol? It makes about as much sense as the Chewbacca Defense."

"Don't believe everything you see in the vids, Lieutenant," Xi quipped.

"Oh, come on." Hightower scowled, tossing two cards and receiving their replacements. "You've got to give us something. We're about to break orbit, and all we know about you guys is that you put a lot of your own into rehab."

"I can confirm that much," Lieutenant Benjamin said after returning from the head.

"Sit your ass down, Sargon," Xi quipped.

"And what's with these call signs?" Hightower asked. "Like Sargon...or Shoe on Head."

Lassiter laughed. "There's a *long* story there."

Hancock grunted as players began to fold their hands. "We seem to have the time."

"It goes back to early-twenty-first-century Earth, when humanity's first data net was still growing," Xi explained. "There were some off-beat free speech advocates who started getting picked off by the media one by one because they were a little too smart and charismatic in how they criticized central media outlets and their narratives. The powers that be couldn't handle being upstaged by nobodies on hand-cams in their basements, so they coordinated shadow campaigns to get them deplatformed and defunded. All these people cared about was free speech, and that was enough to make them the enemies of the establishment."

"Either that or they were *actual* Nazis," Sargon added sardonically.

"Right, or that," Xi agreed. "The Legion appreciates rebels who fight the good fight, even if they lose. I'm not sure you noticed, but our ships are all named after people who fought overwhelming odds against something they viewed as tyrannical. Why should our call signs be any different?" Just then, the newly-promoted Lieutenant Styles entered the compartment, and all players folded except Xi, Hancock, and Sargon. "What's the good word, Lieutenant Styles?"

"T-minus two hours and six minutes, Major," Styles replied, gesturing at the table. "Padding your retirement fund at the expense of your subordinates again?"

Xi grinned. "We're all consenting adults here, mister. Care to make a contribution to Major Metal's Fund for Better Living?"

"Pass. I've seen how much damage you can do to a bank account," he quipped, referring to one of her earliest cyber-crimes where she emptied the offshore account of a corrupt politician who had siphoned millions of sovereigns from his constituents over the course of a decade-long term of 'service.'

Besides, everyone at the table knew the money wouldn't be going to Xi's account.

"I never saw the big deal with free speech anyway." Hightower scowled. "Why shouldn't people be a little more careful with their words?"

"People are neurons and seizures suck," Styles said offhandedly.

"Come again?" Hightower asked as Sargon folded, leaving Xi staring down Hancock with sixty sovereigns in the middle.

"People are neurons," Styles repeated. "Each neuron makes a number of connections to other neurons, and it uses those connections to receive and transmit information, right?"

"Right..." Hightower said in a surprisingly dire tone as Hancock raised twenty sovereigns. Xi re-raised another twenty, prompting Hancock to re-examine his hand.

"Our brains use those synaptic connections to form pathways, and those pathways create the basis for our ability to conduct abstract thought involving complex ideas. You need tens of thousands of neurons firing together just to form rudimentary words, and even more to express them. The pathways are mapped so that every time you think of a discrete concept, like the word 'cat,' those same neurons fire. What happens when you interrupt the flow of information along a pathway after it's already formed?" Styles asked.

"You have a seizure, I think," Hancock offered, splashing the pot with yet another re-raise of fifty sovereigns.

Xi raised another twenty and Hancock called, laying down his cards and declaring. "Big dog."

The major sighed in mock resignation before laying her own hand down. "Little cat."

"Dammit!" Hancock swore.

"Well played, Major," Styles congratulated as she scooped up the pot and began stacking the coins. He turned to Hightower and said, "I'm sorry to hear about your sister, Lieutenant. I wasn't aware, or I would have used a different analogy." He tapped Xi on the shoulder. "Chief Rimmer said *Elvira's* link is ready for you to fine-tune, Major."

"Thank you, Lieutenant," she replied before he left the cramped compartment.

"What's his story?" Hancock asked, having quickly made peace with his lost coinage.

"Styles?" Sargon asked before shrugging. "Let's see...he once called in an orbital strike against a terrorist training facility on New Britain. Glassed a square kilometer from orbit."

"It's not hard to call strikes when you're the GCO." Hightower snorted. "That's the whole fucking job."

"Oh no," Sargon said with a playful smile. "This was *before* he was volunteered into service...and before his sixteenth birthday. See, he saw some recruiting vids where the terrorists left clues to their location. Things like power grid data and building geometry, which let him and a few others do some digging until they found a place that matched. The place was hit an hour after he submitted the final data packet. He was a fifteen-year-old virtual engineering prodigy, and the major can correct me if I'm wrong on this, but he viewed calling in the strike as his civic duty."

Xi pointed at Sargon approvingly with a sideways grin. "*That* I can confirm."

"Bullshit," Hightower spat.

"With a bull like Styles, you get no shit," Quinn riposted. "Just the horns."

"She shoots, she scores!" Xi cheered, high-fiving the diminutive woman and prompting the newcomers to exchange curious looks. "That's why she's your platoon leader, gentlemen," Xi declared, pausing and jerking her thumb over her shoulder in the direction Styles had departed. "And it's why *he's* our GCO."

4

FEAR GOD AND DREAD NAUGHT

The dreadnought *Marcus Aurelius* approached the wormhole gate that led to the star system where AK-091 was located.

"We do not commit to this lightly," Admiral Wallace intoned over the fleet-wide channel as his lengthy pre-battle speech drew to a close. "But Terra has suffered her neighbors' aggressions for far too long. And while we did not start this fight, by every god known to humanity, we *will* finish it."

Two seconds after uttering those words, the ten-kilometer-long, cylindrical *Marcus Aurelius* slipped across the wormhole gate's murky event horizon and vanished. For a moment, Podsednik feared the massive warship's immense girth would cause it to collide with the ring-shaped gate. But just as it had done at the New America gates, its navigators and helmsmen managed to precisely align it and missed collision by less than ten meters on all sides.

"*Marcus Aurelius* away," reported Sensors as the mighty dreadnought's support vessels followed it. Cruisers, battleships, and destroyers, arranged in a perfect file, approached the gate at the precise speed necessary to successfully traverse the event horizon. "*Pride of Norfolk* will transit in twenty-six seconds."

The *William Wallace*'s bridge was at Condition One as the warship held position near the rear of the Terran fleet. Just three ships, all of them cruisers, including the *Martin Luther*, trailed the *Wallace* and *Vercingetorix* as the thirty-four-ship fleet prepared for the first major fleet offensive in Terran history.

"This isn't what we had in mind," Podsy muttered to no one in particular.

"No, it isn't," General Moon agreed. "But I'd be lying if I said I disapproved. The rock-biters have killed over a hundred million Terrans down the years, and they've cost at least that many more lives' labor in repairing the damage to our infrastructure. If we hit them hard enough, it might deter future incursions."

"Do you think that's what will happen, sir?" Podsednik asked neutrally, hiding his skepticism to the best of his ability.

"No, Captain, I don't," Moon said flatly. "But I do think that to not strike back is decidedly inhuman. This has been a long time coming."

"*Pride of Norfolk* is through," reported Sensors as the battleship winked out of existence, to be deposited thirteen thousand light years from the Nexus, same as the *Marcus Aurelius*. "Contact!" the same officer declared. "Jemmin warships emerging from Arh'Kel Gate Number Five."

"What's their disposition?" Moon demanded, his eyes snapping to the tactical plotter, which showed eighteen newly-arrived Jemmin cruisers. Those cruisers immediately moved to engage the Vorr warships in the area, marking the first schism between the factions since the Terrans had arrived in-system six hours earlier.

"Engaging Vorr warships, sir," came the reply. "Zeen worldship is launching a counteroffensive. I'm reading thirty...forty... fifty-six Zeen ships breaking orbit of the worldship. Time to intercept, eighteen minutes."

Podsy narrowed his eyes grimly. "They're too far away to stop us from transiting. Which either means their arrival was a coincidence, or we might have to fight our way past them when we return."

"This fleet could handle eighteen Jemmin cruisers," Moon said stoically, but they both knew eighteen cruisers would only make up the first wave of the Jemmin attack.

One after another, the Terran warships plunged through the wormhole gate leading to their destination. As they did, the Jemmin, Vorr, and Zeen moved to resume the conflict that had consumed the Nexus since Operation Antivenom.

Despite the foreboding development nearby, the Terran fleet was committed to bringing the fight to the Arh'Kel. Nothing could stop them from delivering Admiral Wallace's brand of vengeance to the rock-biters.

As a survivor of New Australia, Andy Podsednik of all people should have been invigorated by being part of this attack. The rock-biters had taken everyone he loved from him with their genocidal assault on his home system and left precious few traces to show that the New Ozzies had once flourished there. He suspected a normal person would hate the Arh'Kel with every fiber of their being, and he was more than a little disappointed to find himself unable to summon such intense feelings as the moment of truth approached.

"*Sima Yi* is through," reported Sensors as the second dreadnought crossed the event horizon, reducing the number of ships ahead of the *William Wallace* to seven.

"There is a quote regarding the five possible operations of war," General Moon observed, "which is often attributed to the founder of China's Jin Dynasty, Sima Yi. Do you know it?"

Podsy nodded. "I do, General."

"Edify us, Captain."

"There are five possible operations in war," Podsednik

recited in a raised voice as two more ships winked out. In the distance, beams were exchanged between Vorr and Jemmin warships, while the hateful Zeen drove toward the Jemmin fleet with murderous intent. "If you can attack, attack," Podsy continued. "If you cannot attack, defend. If you cannot defend, retreat." Another ship passed through the gate, leaving four ahead of the *William Wallace*. "If you cannot retreat, surrender. And if you cannot surrender, die."

"Admiral Wallace understands those operations as well as any man who has ever donned a uniform," General Moon declared as yet another Terran warship passed into the gate. "For the first time, Terra can attack her enemy. Sima Yi would argue that failing to do so is a crime against the will of Heaven."

"From where I'm standing, the Arh'Kel have certainly agreed with that philosophy," Podsednik remarked as two more warships slipped through the wormhole gate. "And we're about to find out how well it worked out for them."

"Event horizon in fifteen seconds, General," reported the helmsman.

"All hands, this is General Moon. In twelve seconds, we will arrive in Arh'Kel space. It's showtime, Metalheads," he said, projecting a confidence Podsednik in no way shared.

The ship ahead of them, the *Hua Tuo*, vanished into the event horizon, clearing the way for the *William Wallace*.

"Event horizon in five...four...three..." the helmsman called in an ever-rising tone of voice. "Two...one...mark!"

The murky disc of the wormhole's event horizon vanished and was replaced by the striated orb of a gas giant comparable to Jupiter. For a moment, the planet projected an image of serenity as the *William Wallace* accelerated away from the gate.

But as the ship veered to port, the illusion of tranquility was shattered by a series of rippling explosions as Terran warships unleashed their fury on the Arh'Kel fortifications.

And there were a *lot* of them.

"*Marcus Aurelius* is repelling boarding actions," Comm reported. "Four Terran warships are down, with the *George Washington*'s reactors scramming."

As damage reports streamed into the bridge, the flare of the *Sima Yi*'s ten-kilometer-long mass driver heralded the utter annihilation of an Arh'Kel swarmship. Built from a hollowed-out asteroid between a quarter- and a half-kilometer in diameter, the slow-moving swarmship was a mainstay in Arh'Kel invasions. Bristling with railguns and missiles, swarmships carried enough raw firepower to annihilate a metropolis—and each one carried *thousands* of Arh'Kel infantry who were bizarrely capable of surviving crash landings, which was the only type of landing Terrans had ever seen the rock-biters make.

It had taken fifty swarmships mere hours to reduce New Australia's infrastructure to rubble from orbit, after which all fifty fell to the planet's surface, where their infantry wrought utter devastation on the survivors. Within days, fewer than one in ten thousand New Ozzies were alive to see the Terran Fleet arrive and deliver their world from the rock-biters' deadly grip.

Swarmships were harbingers of death and destruction, and their image evoked very strong emotions in any Terran who glimpsed them.

But their armor was simple—crude iron plating formed from ore extracted from the converted asteroid's interior—and a Republican-class dreadnought's mass driver was so laughably overpowered by comparison that not only was the targeted swarmship annihilated by the iron slug, but two ships *behind* the first were also destroyed by that projectile and its accompanying spray of shrapnel.

The trouble was, there were *hundreds* of swarmships on the plotter, along with a surprising number of Arh'Kel interceptors.

The pilots of the Terran Fleet's interceptors knifed into the

Arh'Kel formation, raking the enemy with railguns, rockets, and coil gun fire. Their silicoid counterparts were slow by comparison and pathetically inaccurate; hundreds of enemy rounds were fired before a single hit was scored, but those hits were devastating, with most claiming a Terran interceptor outright.

"Incoming," Tactical reported, voice raised to a near-shout. "Fifteen Arh'Kel fusion warheads inbound. Time to impact, eight seconds."

"Evasive maneuvers," General Moon barked, prompting the *William Wallace* to roll so hard that Podsy felt something in his upper chest pop from the sudden strain against his harness.

"Prepare countermeasures," Podsy snapped breathlessly. "And plot solutions to return fire."

"Plotting solutions, aye," Tactical acknowledged as a stream of fire erupted from the *William Wallace*'s point-defense systems. Thousands of slugs per second poured into the approaching cluster of enemy missiles, flak shells were launched by the ship's railguns, and interceptor rockets tore loose from their mounts. The wave of counterfire was breathtaking as the conical active missile shield was erected in the volley's wake.

"Impact in three...two...one..." Sensors called, and at the one-second mark, eight of the missiles were sniped by the wall of fire. Flak shells exploded in proximity to the oncoming missiles, scratching several, while more were hammered by the crisscrossing streams of coil gun fire.

The last second seemed to stretch for an eternity as the interceptor rockets slammed into another four missiles, leaving three enemy weapons streaking toward the evasively rolling Legion warship. Two of the missiles missed the mark by two hundred meters, exploding at that proximity and merely scratching the *Wallace*'s fresh coat of paint.

But the final weapon scored a direct hit on the ship's port bow, violently tossing the warship and everyone in it. Alarms rang out from the damage control center, but Podsy knew from a glance at the ship's status indicators that they had gotten off lightly. Less than three percent of the ship's interior had been exposed to vacuum, and none of the *Wallace's* main systems were showing as compromised.

"Target solutions plotted, Captain," Tactical reported, prompting a pair of targets to begin flashing orange on the holo-plotter at the center of the bridge.

"Fire!" Podsednik barked, and the *William Wallace* unleashed a quartet of railgun bolts into the enemy swarmships. All four bolts bullseyed their slow-moving targets, punching clean through the enemy's crude iron armor and delivering their destructive energy to the ships' interiors. Explosions rippled within the enemy ships, but they were not yet out of the fight.

At least not until the *Martin Luther* announced its arrival through the wormhole gate.

A storm of forty missiles erupted from Admiral Corbyn's aged flagship, targeting both swarmships the *Wallace* had just injured. The damaged swarmships were enveloped in rapid-succession impacts from the *Luther's* ordnance, which poured into the ships in a steady stream. Each strike drilled deeper into the ship's interior.

The first swarmship exploded in a uniform cloud of debris, hurling its glittering guts into the void. Terran interceptor pilots nimbly adjusted course to avoid the expanding sphere of debris.

The second swarmship fared better than the first. The earliest of the *Martin Luther*'s missiles struck some kind of magazine or fuel tank, which exploded volcanically into space and violently knocked the vessel off-axis, causing it to rotate and tumble. The stream of missiles, designed to strike in rapid succession and carve through the ship's exterior, instead hammered into the ship's outer hull as a fresh segment was exposed to each missile. Despite being spared the same fate as its fellow swarmship, the total firepower delivered to its brittle armor was enough to turn a hundred-meter gash in that armor fiery orange.

"Target that breach," Podsy commanded urgently. "Fire!"

The *William Wallace* unleashed its four railguns in near-unison. Without sufficient time to calculate high-percentage solutions, Podsednik accepted that there would be misses. But he also knew that as fast as the swarmship was rotating, the breach would spin out of their firing arc in a matter of seconds.

Two of the railgun bolts slammed into the outer hull, barely missing the mark. But the others drove deep into the ship's guts, with one blowing out the other side of the battered ship's hull. The swarmship's surface-based railgun and missile platforms continued firing, but only sporadically and without anything approaching coherence. It took the Terran interceptor pilots less than five seconds to descend on the dying warship, where they scraped the enemy's weapon mounts from the hull one by one until all that remained was a lifeless hulk.

"The *Marcus Aurelius* is calling for Wet Blanket, General," Comm reported, causing Podsednik's heart to skip a beat. "I say again, *Marcus Aurelius* requesting Wet Blanket."

'Wet Blanket' was an urgent call for fire on one's own ship in the hope of removing boarders or other local interceptors who were harassing that ship from within its PD arcs. The fleet had only been in-system for a matter of minutes, and Admiral Wallace was already calling for fire on his own position. To say resistance had been stiffer than anticipated would be a gross understatement.

Without delay, Podsednik turned to Tactical. "Plot solutions to hit the heaviest concentrations of Arh'Kel on the *Aurelius'* hull." Tactical hesitated, looking at General Moon for confirmation, and Podsy yelled, "Look at him for the fire order *after* you've plotted the solutions, mister!"

"Yes, Captain," acknowledged Tactical, and only then did Podsednik make eye contact with the general, who gave a muted nod of approval.

As the railguns readied to fire, the cloud of five hundred Terran interceptors diverted fire onto the *Marcus Aurelius'* hull. Interceptor railguns stabbed into the mighty dreadnought's thick armor, blowing dozens of rock-biters off the ship with each strike. But there were already over ten thousand Arh'Kel infantry clinging to Wallace's flagship, and as Podsy watched the feeds, another pair of swarmships collided with the *Marcus Aurelius*. The impact flung their infantry onto the dreadnought's cylindrical hull while tearing meter-deep gashes in the *Aurelius'* armor.

Like droplets of water falling from a shaken tree, the rock-biters aboard those swarmships descended on the Terran ship. Half of them missed the mark entirely and were consigned to an ignominious end adrift in interplanetary space, where even their robust physiologies would eventually succumb to vacuum exposure. But the other half landed, and they proceeded to cartwheel toward gaps in the ship's armor, through which they disappeared before a hail of impacts vaporized the silica-based intruders, sending puffs of purple fluids misting into the void.

"Solutions plotted," Tactical reported crisply, prompting four target zones to appear on the holoimage of the *Marcus Aurelius*. It was nearly unthinkable to fire on a fellow Terran warship, but Admiral Wallace had made the call.

"Fire," General Moon said in a low voice, and the *William Wallace* unleashed a quartet of railgun bolts. The admiral's flagship was a relative slug in space, so each bolt struck within a half-meter of its target. Those railgun strikes, while nowhere near as powerful as those of a state-of-the-art Terran railgun, blasted five-meter-deep craters in the *Aurelius'* iron hull. Each strike was on an already-weakened point in the hull where they would cause significantly more damage than if they had struck an armored section.

Which was the entire point.

Fired at a severe angle nearly parallel to the *Aurelius'* hull at the point of impact, the four railgun bolts had been intended to help close off the hull breaches. Remarkably, Tactical went four-for-four in temporarily sealing the vulnerable points in the dreadnought's increasingly battered armor.

They had only been in-system for a matter of minutes, but the *Marcus Aurelius* had already been through a major engagement. A two-hundred-meter-diameter chunk of its forward hull was missing, with the wound looking suspiciously like one caused by a fusion warhead. Two of its stabilizing thrusters, used to maintain the ship's orientation and bearing when firing its keel-mounted mass driver, were molten pools of liquid iron fifty meters across. One of its engine ports was gone entirely, gouged out by what looked like a hundred rapid-succession kinetic impacts.

But for all her wounds, the *Marcus Aurelius* fought with greater ferocity than anything this side of a Jemmin Gatecrasher.

A hail of fusion warheads leapt from the *Aurelius'* forward launchers. The swarm of ordnance blossomed outward, like unfurling flower petals as they sped toward their respective targets. Thirty Arh'Kel swarmships died in the ensuing seconds, with each rock-biter ship targeted by at least two of the warheads. And as each fresh kill was notched by the Terran warships, Admiral Wallace's fleet increased its zone of control. There were still two hundred swarmships within one light second, but there was nothing beyond them. They had been so tightly packed that without the dreadnoughts leading the way, there was simply no way the Terrans could have broken through.

Even venerable battleships like the *Pride of Norfolk* would have been annihilated by the enemy fleet in a matter of seconds. The only Terran warship that could withstand the Arh'Kel greeting was a dreadnought.

And they'd brought *two* of them.

With a brilliant flash of plasma counter-thrust from its cylindrical hull, the *Sima Yi* fired its mass driver at a bizarrely-shaped twenty-kilometer asteroid. One face of the rock bristled with rapidly-cycling railguns and missile launchers, but when the *Sima Yi*'s slug slammed into the peculiar asteroid, it flew apart in a spectacular shower of rocky debris. Nothing larger than a kilometer survived intact, and the weapons scattered across the cloud went dead instantly. It was only after the *Sima Yi* had destroyed the rock that Podsy realized the reason for its peculiar shape; it had been part of a much larger body, likely one at least forty kilometers in diameter.

The rest of the rock had already been pulverized by the dreadnoughts' combined efforts, and the debris accounted for the majority of that which now filled the near-gate void.

A brilliant, unmistakable flare signaled the death of a Terran warship, and Sensors was quick to report, "The *Pride of Norfolk* is down. I say again, *Pride of Norfolk* is down."

The *Pride of Norfolk* was one of the most cutting-edge battleships in the Terran fleet. It featured experimental armor, upgraded targeting systems, and the most stable kinetic-dampening systems ever installed on a human warship.

And it hadn't survived ten minutes.

The *Martin Luther*, moving to flank the *William Wallace*, unleashed a storm of missiles on the *Marcus Aurelius*. None of the ordnance was much more destructive than the LRMs the Legion deployed planet-side, but the volume was extraordinary. Four hundred individual missiles slashed across the void, scrubbing thousands of rock-biters from the *Aurelius'* hull and sending hundreds of tons of glittery debris streaming from the dreadnought's skin. Podsy winced at the damage wrought on a Terran warship by its fellow, but the effect was undeniable. Fully half of the rock-biters had been torn from the hull, while those that remained were dispersed rather than concentrated at vulnerable points.

A few seconds after "benefitting" from the *Luther's* vigorous cleansing, Comm reported. "*Marcus Aurelius* declares Wet Blanket complete. I say again, Wet Blanket is complete. Cease fire on the *Marcus Aurelius*."

Even as Comm spoke, the telltale flashes of Terran Marine railgun rifles strobed across the *Marcus Aurelius'* hull. Dozens of those blue-white flashes per second were soon punctuated by yellow-orange RPG strikes, and soon balls of blue plasma signaled that plasma grenades were being hurled into the rock-biters.

With mechanical precision, the Marines drove the Arh'Kel back from the breaches in the *Aurelius'* hull. As they did the bloody work, the battle raged over their heads between the Terran warships and their dwindling Arh'Kel counterparts.

The *Sima Yi* unleashed a storm of missiles into a tight cluster of Arh'Kel swarmships, blowing all six of the peculiar vessels apart and removing the last concentration of enemy warships from the grid.

"New orders from Admiral Wallace," Comm reported. "Task Force Zulu will proceed to orbit of target planet while the rest of the fleet remains to secure the gate." Task Force Zulu was comprised of the three non-Eighth-Fleet ships in the armada: *William Wallace*, *Vercingetorix*, and *Martin Luther*.

Despite there still being two dozen swarmships in the local zone, and despite having lost eight warships during the frantic exchange, the Terran fleet had broken through the defensive blockade. And now that they had, the Metalheads were on the clock. The rock-biters would be sending reinforcements, and they would be coming through the middle gate leading to what passed for a main Arh'Kel colony.

But even though rock-biter ships were notoriously slow, Podsednik and everyone else on the bridge knew the Arh'Kel weren't their sole concern.

They were here to capture a Jemmin Poltergeist, and no one expected Jemmin to surrender it without a fight.

"Comm, signal Task Force Zulu to form on the *William Wallace*," Podsednik called. "Helm, make for planet AK-091 at best speed."

"Best speed, aye," Helm replied before the ship surged forward, pushing through clouds of Arh'Kel debris. "Time to orbit, eight hours, twelve minutes."

"We'll be in hot-drop position in eight hours, twenty-nine minutes, General," newly-commissioned Lieutenant Styles added.

"Start the countdown clock, Lieutenant," Moon commanded, and Styles did so. An eight-hour, twenty-nine-minute timer appeared at the bottom of nearly every display on the bridge and began to wind down second by second. "I want cans leaving their tubes when that mark hits zero, Metalheads," the general declared. "Let's roll."

5

MIXED COMPANY

As *Elvira IV's* can fell toward AK-091, the ground below erupted in a dazzling sequence of fusion explosions delivered by Terran missiles from low-orbit.

Radiating outward from the drop-zone in a roughly spiral-shaped pattern, forty-six distinct mini-novae rippled around the DZ. Each contained between one and five megatons of destructive force, and those warheads carved a toehold for the Metal Legion on a planet teeming with rock-biters.

Fewer than half the original hundred and twenty warheads arrived on-target; the rest were scrapped by Arh'Kel counterfire in the form of anti-missile rockets. Rock-biters weren't well-known for their aerospace capability, relying on sheer volume rather than accuracy to intercept the inbound WMDs, and they had sent over ten thousand intercept rockets up from the planet's surface to defend against the bombardment.

"Dragon Actual, this is *Wallace* Ground Control," Lieutenant Styles declared. "Be advised, your DZ is still hot. Second wave of ordnance is inbound."

Xi barely caught herself before replying to Styles and was

grateful she'd had the presence of mind to do so as Colonel Jenkins acknowledged, "GC, this is Dragon Actual. I copy; light 'em up." It was the first time since Dragon's resurrection that Xi wasn't in command of the unit, but she wasn't complaining. This op might be their most challenging yet, and she was glad for the colonel's presence.

As they spoke, a second wave of rockets rose to intercept the drop-cans. This salvo was nowhere near as robust as the first, with just a thousand missiles tearing skyward from the planet below. Predictably, those missiles were scattered and poorly coordinated, making them relatively easy pickings.

But a thousand of *anything* headed one's way at escape velocity, regardless of accuracy, was far from ideal.

As those rockets burned toward the thirty-six drop-cans and their six accompanying Marine dropships, Lieutenant Commander Knighton's sixteen Viper-class interceptors shot past the tightly-clustered formation and began stabbing railgun bolts into the flight of inbound rockets. Rockets were taken down in a one to one ratio with bolts fired, a few Terran pilots managing to scrap multiple missiles with single shots.

Also tearing past the formation was a fresh storm of fusion-powered ordnance. Thirty missiles comprised the second bombardment, and an even meeker volley of counterfire shot up from the surface in reply. Fewer than three hundred fresh rockets moved to intercept those warheads, and simple math suggested that less than a handful were at risk of being stopped by the weak counterfire.

As Arh'Kel and Terran missiles passed mid-flight, and with Lieutenant Commander Knighton's Vipers carving a tunnel through the inbound ordnance, it looked for a moment like the Metalheads and Marines would pass through the wall of rockets unscathed.

Then reality slammed home like a runaway freight train.

The rockets suddenly adjusted course, converging on the Marine dropships near the heart of the drop formation. Dropship coil guns erupted in counterfire, spraying a cone of bullets into the approaching ordnance. A dozen rockets were sniped by the blanket of coil gun fire, but a dozen more slammed into the heavily-armored Marine craft.

Terran intercept rockets would have done little more than cause external damage to a Marine dropship's systems, with an extremely low chance of damaging an engine exhaust or possibly bullseyeing the cockpit's relatively weak windshield.

But Arh'Kel missile-intercept rockets, like the bodies of the rock-biters, were considerably more potent on a one-to-one basis than their Terran counterparts.

Two Marine dropships, both Tripoli-class like those used during Operation War God, exploded as the armor-piercing rockets tore completely through their armored hulls. Three power-armored Marines managed to ditch before their parent craft exploded, their capacitors and fuel containment systems overwhelmed by the shockingly effective weapons.

Debris from one of the dropships slammed into a Legion drop-can, tearing its number three braking thruster off the rectangular can and sending the damaged container into a lethal tumble. Xi gritted her teeth as she watched *Beowulf's Bargain*, a Warlock-class mech identical to the defunct *Cyclops*, tumble out of its disintegrating drop-can.

At their current altitude of eight kilometers, it was unlikely the crew would survive even if they managed to ditch their craft. Everyone making the drop had been equipped with parachutes that would function in the thick atmosphere of AK-091, but the world below was far from hospitable to human life, even ignoring the hundreds of millions of rock-biters crawling on and beneath its surface.

Amazingly, less than eight seconds after *Beowulf's Bargain* began its deadly fall to the planet's surface, all three of its crew appeared on the HUD as their locator beacons strobed to life. Their chutes wouldn't deploy until the last possible moment, so there was some hope, however small, that they might survive the destruction of their mech.

But Xi's attention was completely focused on making her own drop without suffering a similar fate. As the Vipers dove toward the deck, clearing a path for the inbound Metalheads and Marines, Dragon and its four remaining Marine dropships finally fell past the effective arc of enemy rockets.

Railgun bolts stabbed skyward, leaving vapor trails in their wakes as their destructive energies were slowly sapped by the planet's thick, water-rich atmosphere. *Elvira's* drop-can rocked as an enemy bolt blew a two-meter hole in its bow, coming within inches of striking the mech's windshield before blowing the roof off the can.

Alarms rang throughout *Elvira's* cabin as the drop-can tilted stern-over-bow. Xi fired the auxiliary thrusters in an attempt to halt the destructive tumble, and despite having just one of the can's three bow-mounted thrusters functioning, she managed to do just that.

"Pucker up!" she called over her shoulder as the can passed the upper threshold of the chute-deployment zone. With the can's limited braking thrust, she needed to fire as soon as possible to give them maximum deceleration before touchdown.

The can's thrusters fired in unison, briefly slewing it in a clockwise spin before she throttled back the rockets' outputs enough to stabilize their descent. The rest of the drop-cans continued to free-fall past Xi's for a full three seconds longer than *Elvira* before igniting their brakes. Two of the cans, including Colonel Jenkins', collided four hundred meters above the rocky deck. Xi had no time to assess the damage to the colonel's can before *Elvira's* platform touched down with bone-breaking force.

Shaking her head in confusion, Xi belatedly realized she had blacked out. She silently cursed the lingering effects of the concussion she had suffered back on Mars, took a breath, and blew the drop-can's explosive bolts. The battered can unfolded around her Scorpion-class mech, except the front section, which stubbornly refused to unfurl like the rest of the container.

"Powering up," she declared, feeling the familiar wave of sensory inputs flood her mind as *Elvira's* linkage went fully active. The Scorpion-class mech's legs lifted the war machine from the metal deck of the dismantled drop-can, and with a mighty surge forward, Xi knocked the intransigent hunk of ruined metal out of her path and put *Elvira's* metal legs on AK-091's surface. "Status report."

"All motive systems five-by-five, Ma'am," Lu reported. "I've got some anomalies on our SRM targeting systems. I'll have the diagnostic completed in two minutes."

"Probably knocked the barometric probes out of alignment," she muttered. "Penny, put eyes on the system's components while Lu works through the diagnostic. If it's too far gone, we'll use data from the rest of the Company."

"Copy that, Major," Penny acknowledged. "Putting eyes on the system now."

Xi Bao looked out on the hellscape that was AK-091 and couldn't help but feel a chill at what she saw. It was easily the most inhospitable planet the Metal Legion had touched down on during her short career, and she knew it would prove a stiff test of their resolve.

Like every other test she had taken in her life, Xi intended to ace this one.

"Dragon 2nd Company," Xi called as Colonel Jenkins' new

ride got to its feet beside its drop-can, where it towered over the battlefield like a Greek titan. "Sound off."

"*Powerslave* online, Colonel," Hammer reported after the tall Ettin-class war mech rose to its full imposing height. "All systems green. Awaiting orders."

Warcrafter and the rest of the Razorback Mark II-Vs had been confiscated by Senate officials following War God, or they had been left on Mars, ostensibly to assist with the clean-up efforts there. That meant Jenkins no longer had access to the fleet of cutting-edge assault mechs. Surprisingly, the Legion did not have any old Razorbacks ready to roll, so Jenkins had been forced to choose an alternate command platform for this particular operation: a humanoid walker of the Ettin class.

Ettins were terrifying machines, granted their namesake due to possessing twin cockpits buried deep in the mech's chest. At a staggering nineteen meters tall, a humanoid Ettin massed a hundred and twenty-five tons. The design's height was misleading; it was actually one of the least *dense* mechs in the Legion's arsenal. This gave them surprising speed and maneuverability for battlewagon-sized mechs, but it also made them considerably less durable than many of their smaller, denser fellows.

But what an Ettin gave up in armor, it more than made up for in raw firepower.

With two heavy plasma cannons anchoring its lower weapon arms, a pair of eight-tube LRM pods over its shoulders, six eight-kilo artillery cannons built into its torso (four forward-facing and two rear-facing), and eight thirty-caliber chain guns providing omnidirectional protection at knife range, an Ettin could command an entire battlefield single-handedly.

The thirty-caliber chain guns were a decided downgrade from the fifty-caliber variants generally employed by the Legion, but the armor-piercers he had selected for the op would still prove deadly to Arh'Kel infantry. And given the enormous difference in storage requirements for thirty cal vs. fifty cal ammo, *Powerslave* could continue firing her guns long after the rest of the Legion's close-in weapons had run dry.

Given the events of War God, that particular consideration had gained importance in the pre-op planning stage.

"1st Company is ready to roll, Colonel," Chief Foxworth reported.

"Major," Jenkins called over the command line, "what's your status?"

"We took some cosmetic damage during the drop," Xi replied. "We've got minor damage to our SRM targeting systems, but we'll have that squared away in five minutes."

"Good," Jenkins acknowledged as Xi's virtual reports flooded his command screen. He had gotten so used to working within a Razorback's spacious compartment that being locked in an ejectable cockpit pod with just a narrow ladder leading down to the mech's "toolbox" (the term given to a Wrench's station aboard humanoid mechs, usually located just beneath the cockpit where the engineers could gain direct access to the vehicle's systems) made him feel almost claustrophobic. "Major Trapper, report."

"Fifty-one Marines plus one present and accounted for, Colonel," Trapper replied. "Our four dropships are combat-ready and await your command." Four dropships with twelve power-armored Marines and Major Trapper (the plus one), plus the three survivors of the two dropships lost during the descent, gave the Metal Legion more power-armored Marines than in any previous joint operation.

"Copy that, Major," Jenkins said as he highlighted a series of targets to the northwest to every unit leader in the battalion. "Advance on objective 'Foothold' and secure the area. 2nd Company's on point, Joker Company in reserve, 1st Company will support 2nd's advance."

The fleet of mechs took its first steps toward the objective named "Foothold," a massive volcanic crater with an elevation of five thousand meters, where a handful of Arh'Kel heavy weapons platforms had survived the orbital bombardment. That volcano was to be their foothold. The area had been nearly cleared out by the orbital attacks prior to the Legion making planetfall.

The tactical plotter showed at least forty thousand Arh'Kel within a hundred kilometers of the column, but there were fewer than thirty HWPs among them. For some unknown reason, the rock-biters deigned to open fire on the column as it drove northwest toward the designated cratered mountain. Jenkins was unaccustomed to *Powerslave's* rhythmic footfalls, which crunched the rocky ground beneath its feet into gravel as the battlefield titan strode across the blasted hellscape of AK-091.

With surface pressures averaging thirty-two times that of Earth, gravity over double Earth-standard, and an ambient temperature of two hundred and twenty degrees Celsius, even the most robust environmental suit would fail to protect a human long enough to draw a full breath of air. The skies were choked a dull brownish-gray color by the sulfuric clouds, making optical systems nearly useless at tactical distances.

But that wasn't even the worst of it.

After centuries of Arh'Kel industrial activity on AK-091, the atmosphere was comprised almost exclusively of CO_2, nitrogen, and sulfur. There was barely enough oxygen to sustain an open flame-trail from a plasma cannon discharge, which meant the Legion would exclusively rely on onboard O_2 and recyclers throughout the op.

Such conditions were categorically worse than vacuum, which the Legion had experienced on Luna, since a hull breach here would result in poisonous gases rushing into the mech with lethal force. Even if the crew survived the pressure before the vehicle's auto-sealant systems could close the breach, which was unlikely, they would then have to contend with the deadly gases.

The final environmental factor was the planet's ambient radiation, which was so high that thirty seconds' unprotected exposure would be fatal, and a human would be completely incapacitated after just ninety seconds.

And, of course, there were hundreds of millions of angry rock-biters to deal with, to say nothing of the Jemmin platform they had come to capture.

Fortunately, the Terran Marines had suits of power armor specifically designed for such conditions. The Gamera-class armor was heavily-shielded from both pressure and radiation, and was easily the most durable battle-suit design in the Terran panoply, featuring an ingeniously-designed "shell" segment on its back, which was likely the reason for it being named after a mythical turtle-like creature. The tradeoff for this added protection was a lack of rockets, which removed the largest tactical edge power-armored Marines enjoyed in battle.

All of which meant they would need to remain in their dropships until called upon.

The dropships, conserving their fuel as much as possible, leapfrogged the column as it rolled toward Foothold. Moving in two-kilometer jumps, the dropships rotated from the front to the back of the column like clockwork as the Terrans made their way to their first objective.

The LZ was ten kilometers from Mount Foothold, but the

enemy was protected by the same crater the Metalheads and Marines aimed to use as a natural fortress during this first leg of the op. Given the extremely thick atmosphere, which was fully three percent the density of liquid water at Earth sea level, artillery and even missiles would be extremely limited in range; shells normally effective at fifty kilometers would be limited to just six. Missiles would fare better, but SRMs would be limited to just eleven kilometers, while LRMs could potentially stretch out to fifty kilometers.

The Metalheads rolled to the five-kilometer mark. The lack of enemy fire since their landing had become a legitimate concern. "What are they waiting for?" Jenkins muttered as the column moved up the increasingly-steep slope of Mount Foothold. The Arh'Kel had thrown everything at them during the drop, including whatever passed for their kitchen sinks, but now they were casually permitting the Metalheads to approach one of the key positions on the planet's surface?

"Colonel, I've got something," Lieutenant Carl "Sargon" Benjamin reported from his new mech, *Web Spinner*, which had a sensor and ECM suite that would be vital to locating the Jemmin Poltergeist they had come to hunt. A series of icons appeared on a three-dimensional topographic representation of the surrounding area. The icons were sparse at first, but more appeared with each passing second until they formed a complex web of tunnels that stretched dozens of kilometers in all directions. "Seismic sensors are picking up significant underground activity, sir," Benjamin continued. "Best estimate, two-hundred-thousand rock-biters are crawling around beneath our feet in a ten-kilometer radius."

"HWPs?"

"I'm only seeing a few dozen so far, Colonel," Benjamin replied. "The concentration of vehicles is significantly lower than it has been during our previous encounters."

"They weren't expecting us," Jenkins remarked.

"Indeed, although it is possible they simply don't maintain significant fleets of assault platforms on their own worlds once they're under total control," Benjamin opined. "Despite fighting them for decades, we know little about them."

"We know enough to make them bleed," Jenkins retorted. "And that's enough for this op."

Jenkins' comm panel flickered with a priority missive from orbit. He accepted the inbound connection and was greeted by General Moon. "Colonel, we've got Arh'Kel warships inbound. Fleet is moving to intercept while we maintain overwatch."

"Understood, sir," Jenkins acknowledged. "We're about to begin our assault on Mount Foothold."

"Good hunting, Colon—" the general began, only to be cut off when a blanket of static replaced his voice.

"Sargon," Jenkins barked over the Company P2P net. "Isolate this interference and locate its source. Rock-biters don't scramble comm frequencies. This is Jemmin."

"On it, Colonel," Benjamin replied. The static cleared as the Legion activated an aggressive broadband frequency hopping protocol.

"Colonel, this is Major Xi," his XO cut in. "I'm in position to begin my attack."

"Commence the attack, Major," Jenkins commanded, forwarding fire orders to 1st Company before pointedly adding, "And make it fast and furious."

"Roger," she acknowledged with less gusto than he had expected, and 2nd Company's artillery thundered in the oppressive, toxic soup of AK-091's atmosphere. SRMs loosed from their tubes, heading on exaggerated ballistic trajectories over the rim of the volcanic crater. Like a perfectly-choreographed fireworks display, a hundred pieces of ordnance fell within a half-second of each other inside the enemy stronghold.

Every rock-biter HWP was struck by no fewer than three direct hits, but to Jenkins' surprise, two of the platforms survived the initial barrage. Unlike every other Arh'Kel HWP they had fought thus far, these vehicles appeared to be as heavily-armored as Terran mechs—which was an unwelcome development.

A thousand Arh'Kel infantry died in the initial salvo, but the Metal Legion was far from finished.

"1st Company," Jenkins called. "Fire!"

The mechs of 1st Company unleashed a second volley, sending eighty projectiles skyward. Pressing through the ultra-thick atmosphere, the artillery shells cleared the volcanic rim and fell upon the scattered rock-biters within. Both of the remaining HWPs hunkered down in the crater were scratched by the barrage, and another fifteen hundred rock-biters were pulverized by Terran fury.

Leading the charging column, Major Xi's *Elvira* was first to crest the crater's edge, and when she did, she turned side-on and unleashed a storm of fifty-caliber slugs into the one-point-five-kilometer crater. She was soon joined by the mechs of her Company, each of which added their own fire to the merciless assault on the Arh'Kel in the natural fortress.

Small-arms fire came their way in reply. Three thousand rock-biters, cartwheeling toward the edge of the crater where they could do battle with the newly-arrived Terrans, stood tall in the face of overwhelming firepower as the Legion's metal monsters poured thousands of rounds per second into the throng.

Jenkins felt nothing but satisfaction as they mercilessly cut the enemy down. This was Terra's first counterattack into Arh'Kel territory. It was an historic moment that every hot-blooded Terran serviceman had dreamed of participating in for decades.

But to Jenkins, digging these rock-biters out of their foxhole was merely the first step in an operation designed to safeguard the entire human race.

He briefly wondered if there hadn't been a better way to go about doing that.

6

DEATH FROM ABOVE

"*Sima Yi* has engaged the western edge of the enemy fleet," Sensors reported as the Terran dreadnought fired a hundred missiles into the enemy formation, vaporizing a handful of swarmships and knocking one enemy carrier out of the fight before it could launch even half its interceptor complement.

Comprised of a few swarmships, along with dozens of faster, more technologically-advanced fireships and interceptor carriers, the counterattacking Arh'Kel fleet had descended on the Terran fleet after breaking the orbit of AK-091's moon. This counterattack had been anticipated by Admiral Wallace, who had prepared a simple but brutal reception for the enemy.

"*Marcus Aurelius* is moving to the eastern flank," Sensors added as the Terran fleet, divided into thirds, executed a textbook double-envelopment maneuver using the dreadnoughts as the pincers and the rest of the fleet as the body. It wasn't fancy, clever, or complex, but neither were the rock-biters. The dreadnoughts hammered multi-ton slug after multi-ton slug into the enemy fleet, creating the most devastating crossfire Podsednik had ever personally witnessed. The admiral's tactical acumen was undeniable.

The plotter lit up with enemy weapons fire, and Tactical noted them. "Eighty-three railgun bolts inbound. Time to impact, fourteen seconds."

"Take evasive action," Podsy commanded. "But maintain overwatch. We don't' budge off this spot as long as we can maintain station."

"Aye, Captain," Helm acknowledged, putting the ship into a downward roll as the volley of ordnance soared across the void toward the *William Wallace*. The only ship in the Terran fleet that was less capable of taking fire than the *Wallace* was the *Vercingetorix*, which made evasion the only survivable option. But the *Wallace* and *Vercingetorix* were now part of the fleet's main body, along with the rest of the non-dreadnought Terran warships, which meant their job was to hold while the dreadnoughts slaughtered the enemy in the kill zone.

"Impact in five...four...three...two...one..." Tactical counted down. Buttholes puckered and muscles tensed before Tactical followed up with, "Zero impacts."

"Resume position," General Moon commanded. "And prepare counterfire solutions. Target swarmship Whiskey."

"Whiskey target, aye," Tactical acknowledged as he started plotting fire solutions on the slow-moving Arh'Kel warships.

Podsednik had a thought and performed a few quick mental calculations. When they seemed to check out, he turned to General Moon. "General, request permission to divert Vipers to intercept swarmships."

Moon turned to him with a look of muted surprise. "Those Vipers are low on fuel after breaking through 091's atmosphere. They'll be close to bingo if we divert them now."

"Understood, sir," Podsy allowed, "but we could use their approach as additional leverage to maintain our present position." It wasn't a game-changing proposal by any stretch of the imagination; sixteen Vipers with their relatively low-powered railguns would hardly turn the tide of battle. But Podsy had been fighting long enough to know that sometimes victory was a matter of inches, which was precisely what he hoped to gain with his proposed sortie.

Moon's eyes narrowed momentarily before he declared, "It's Commander Knighton's call."

"Understood, sir," Podsy replied, then opened a secure line to Lieutenant Commander Knighton. "Yellowhammer, this is *William Wallace*."

"Yellowhammer, go," she promptly replied.

"What's your fuel status, Yellowhammer?"

"Fuel is zero-three-zero, Captain," she replied, indicating they had thirty percent of their fuel remaining after breaking free of the planet's atmosphere. It was less than he'd hoped, but still enough for what he had in mind.

"Are you up for some extra credit, Commander?" he asked as he forwarded a set of target coordinates to the flight commander. As he did, the *William Wallace* fired its four railguns into the approaching swarmships. Geysers of debris burst from the damaged ship's hull as three of the *Wallace's* four railguns hit the mark.

"I'm insulted you even asked, Captain." A brief pause as she reviewed his target package, followed by her entire wing of sixteen Viper-class aerospace fighters breaking hard out of their rendezvous course with their mother ship. "New course laid in, time to target, two minutes. If we burn down to fumes, we'll need a pickup before gravity does its thing."

"Copy that, Yellowhammer." Podsy grinned before cutting the channel. "General, Commander Knighton—"

"I have eyes, XO," Moon interrupted easily, gesturing to the tactical plotter that showed the diamond formation of Vipers moving toward the swarmships. The bulk of the Terran fleet, including a handful of battleships and state-of-the-art cruisers, hammered away on the leading edge of the Arh'Kel formation, while the dreadnoughts annihilated the flanks of the loosely-assembled enemy fleet.

The *Martin Luther*, acting as *William Wallace*'s primary escort, sent a fresh volley of missiles streaking across the void. Eighty-five warheads, many of which were nukes, burned past the *William Wallace* en route to the trio of nearest swarmships. As those missiles passed the *William Wallace*, a swarm of twenty Arh'Kel interceptors broke formation and burned toward the *Martin Luther* at thirty gees' acceleration. Thirty gees became forty, then fifty, and finally sixty before stabilizing.

Even thirty gees was at the upper end of what had previously been observed from Arh'Kel interceptors. But sixty gees was far beyond what they should have been capable of achieving, and their new course took them almost directly at the *William Wallace*. This wasn't how rock-biters were known to operate in void combat, and they were demonstrating superior technical capabilities than ever before.

Which meant that many of the fleet's tactical calculations had just gone out the airlock.

Podsy immediately raised Knighton on P2P, and even as he did so, the general barked. "Captain Podsednik, divert Commander Knighton to engage those interceptors."

"Yellowhammer, go," Knighton tersely acknowledged before Moon finished his command.

"Yellowhammer, you have new targets," Podsy said urgently. "Engage hostile interceptors ASAP."

"Permission to pursue if they withdraw?" she asked.

He hesitated. She was asking him for permission to run after the rock-biters even if her people went bingo fuel in the process. With the *William Wallace* at the heart of the Terran formation and in overwatch of the grounded Metalheads, the ship was ill-positioned to retrieve the Vipers if they moved too far during their pursuit of the enemy.

But he knew Knighton. She was both tough and smart; she'd make the right call. "Permission granted, but employ your discretion, Commander," Podsy replied as her Vipers redlined their engines to more quickly engage the inbound hostiles. He was acutely aware of the fact that if he had not diverted her sixteen interceptors toward the enemy formation, Knighton would have been in a much worse position to address this new threat than she presently was. The extra few hundred kilometers they had gained on intercept due to his redeployment would prove critical when it came time to fire their railguns at the incoming enemy.

A game of inches indeed, he thought grimly.

The wave of missiles launched by the *Martin Luther* entered the swarmships' counterfire envelope, where two dozen of the Terran weapons were engaged and destroyed. The sprinting Arh'Kel interceptors added to the wave of counterfire, sniping another handful of Terran missiles before the first broke through the defensive shell. The hundred-kiloton warhead dug thirty meters into the swarmship's armor before releasing its devastating energies into the hollowed-out asteroid.

The resulting explosion annihilated the swarmship, completely transforming it into a rapidly-expanding cloud of glowing metal as the two nearest swarmships also fell victim to the *Martin Luther*'s fury. Kinetic missiles slammed into the rock-biter warships, and a pair of Terran nukes flared into mini-novae several hundred meters from their targets. Neither swarmship was destroyed outright, but the damage done to their outer hulls was significant, and fully half of their weapon mounts went silent in the immediate aftermath.

After the missiles, it was Commander Knighton's turn, and her pilots plunged into the enemy with seemingly reckless abandon. Breaking out of their diamond formation, Knighton's Vipers lashed out with rockets, railguns, and coil guns, pouring fire into their larger, faster counterparts.

Two Arh'Kel interceptors, shaped roughly like tetrahedrons with nearly-identical three-sided faces, were bracketed by five of Knighton's interceptors. Seven railgun bolts and eight rockets slammed into its gleaming metal hull, and for a moment it seemed the damned thing would survive.

Thankfully, its engines overloaded and the craft's stern exploded, shearing a third of it off and sending the rest in a spiraling tumble into the nothingness of space.

"Tactical," General Moon ordered. "Target those interceptors with our railguns and fire when ready."

"Aye, General."

The Arh'Kel returned fire on Knighton's Vipers.

Darting and weaving erratically, the nimble Vipers nearly evaded the enemy fire with well-orchestrated maneuvers. But "almost succeeding" at something was just another way to describe failure, and two of Knighton's Vipers were scratched by furious counterfire as Arh'Kel missiles blossomed out from the remaining interceptors like a cloud shedding raindrops.

Three hundred enemy rockets knifed this way and that, nimbly maneuvering as Knighton's pilots juked, rolled, and spun out of their way. There were so many rock-biter missiles, and they were so incredibly maneuverable, that if even a quarter of them had possessed proximity explosives, they would have wiped out Knighton's Vipers entirely.

But the Terran pilots proved their worth, with each of the fourteen survivors experiencing no fewer than five near-misses. Knighton herself came *that* close to destruction eleven different times before leading her people out of the enemy kill zone. Once out, her people resumed their diamond formation just long enough for Podsy to recognize they had done so before breaking apart and making another run at the enemy.

Any sane person would have called off the attack. Her peoples' concerted efforts had yielded only a single kill and another cripple of the twenty Arh'Kel interceptors. They were outgunned, and after this second pass, they would expose the *William Wallace* to a possible charge by the enemy fighter craft by abandoning an interdictory position. Knighton was willingly leading her people to a position behind enemy lines, where they would be vastly outnumbered and outgunned.

In other words, she was behaving precisely like a Metalhead.

The fourteen Vipers held fire as the Arh'Kel charged straight at them. With murderous ferocity, the rock-biters launched a fresh wave of rockets, but this time Knighton's people were ready for them.

The comparison to gnats zipping this way and that as one tries to swat them was unavoidable, at least in Podsy's mind, as the Terran pilots deftly slipped through the cloud of enemy ordnance. Not a single direct hit was logged against Knighton's people, who launched individual rockets and coil gun bullets at the Arh'Kel even as they performed their max-burn maneuvers. But for some reason, they held fire on their primary weapons, their railguns, as the rock-biters sped toward their position.

After a handful of seconds' insane evasive maneuvers by Knighton and her pilots, the Arh'Kel interceptors passed through the Terran formation, burning toward the *William Wallace*. And when they did so, Commander Knighton's strategy was revealed.

Burning at full speed, and pulling twenty-six gees in the process, the Terran Vipers fell into slots behind their charging foes. With the Arh'Kel's engine ports in their sights, the Terrans had perfect up-the-kilt firing angles on their faster, heavier counterparts.

Before the rock-biters could react to their error, Knighton's people unleashed everything they had.

Six Arh'Kel interceptors were destroyed in the first second, taking devastating hits to their vulnerable engines. The heavily-armored vessels were instantly reduced to scrap. Another three died in the following second before the rock-biters faltered in their charge.

"Firing!" Tactical declared, and the *William Wallace* launched two dozen missiles at the momentarily-confused enemy craft.

The rock-biters spun mid-flight, firing their rockets and rail-guns at Knighton's Vipers and presenting their armored bows. The Terran pilots immediately resumed their evasive maneuvers, zigging and zagging, spinning and rolling out of harm's way, but this time the Arh'Kel landed two more hits, destroying another pair of Vipers.

And then the *Wallace's* missiles arrived, knocking out the entire flight of interceptors and clearing a return path for Knighton's remaining twelve interceptors.

"*Wallace* this is Yellowhammer," Knighton reported as her Vipers turned in unison and burned toward the *William Wallace.* "We are zero-zero-six fuel. Requesting Epsilon retrieval; we're coming in hot."

"Helm," Podsy barked, "prepare to receive Vipers on the drop-deck for emergency retrieval package Epsilon."

"Epsilon, aye," Helm acknowledged. Epsilon was a standard retrieval posture used by carriers, which required both interceptors and mothership to match orientation, rotation, and velocity. The *William Wallace* was not a real carrier, so it lacked a proper flight deck. But recent modifications had been made to her drop-deck which would theoretically allow it to perform a combat retrieval like Epsilon.

Theoretically.

"The barn door's open, Commander," General Moon reported. His approval for the interceptor pilot was unmistakable, and for a moment, Podsy felt a twinge of jealousy at the bond between Moon and Knighton. Both were interceptor pilots with dozens of confirmed kills, and as a result, they shared a camaraderie and culture that Podsednik would never know.

As the Vipers withdrew, the Terran fleet poured fire into the Arh'Kel warships. Another swarmship was scratched, and a heavily-armored fireship was smoked soon after. Podsy looked at the tactical plotter for a long moment before realizing what the sprinting Arh'Kel were up to.

He raised his voice. "Tactical, new target: fireship Gamma."

Moon sent a quizzical look Podsy's way as Tactical acknowledged. "Fireship Gamma, aye."

"Fireships have larger railguns, General, which are better suited to orbital bombardment," Podsy explained as the *Wallace* launched a quartet of tungsten bolts at the newly-targeted warship. Built more like a Terran ship, with advanced systems and significantly better acceleration than the slower swarmships, fireships carried a minimum of crew and a maximum of raw firepower. "They've almost gained a firing arc on our ground forces, sir."

"Signal Admiral Corbyn," Moon barked. "Re-prioritize fireships. Leave the swarmers alone for now. We can pick them off later."

"Aye, General," acknowledged Comm a moment later. "*Martin Luther* confirms new targets."

No sooner had Comm made that report than the *Martin Luther* and a handful of nearby warships unleashed another volley of over two-hundred missiles. The flight of ordnance closed on the targeted fireships, which began firing their high-mass railguns at the planet below. Podsy winced as a half dozen of the powerful weapons flared, sending multi-kiloton-equivalent bolts directly down onto the Metalheads. He silently cursed himself for not seeing the rock-biters' plan earlier.

If war was a game of inches, the rock-biters had just made a serious run at taking several meters of the field back for themselves.

The *Martin Luther*'s missiles slammed into the Arh'Kel fireships, annihilating three of them outright when the enemy warships' point-defense efforts came up woefully short. Nuclear warheads launched by nearby Terran warships flashed, enveloping fireships one by one until six more had been erased from the board.

And then, to Podsy's amazement, it was effectively over. They had somehow broken this wave of the enemy, whose primary aim had been to destroy the grounded Metalheads rather than to engage the Terran fleet directly.

A dozen scattered, damaged ships remained in the main body of the counterattacking force, but the dreadnoughts were methodically scraping them from the void while the rest of the Terran fleet consolidated on overwatch of the ground forces.

"Good catch, Captain," Moon said approvingly. "We almost missed the forest for the trees on that one."

"Damage reports coming up from the surface," Comm reported.

"How bad was it?" Podsy asked, immediately cursing himself for his sudden lack of professionalism.

"Three mechs are offline," Comm replied. "The *Vainglorious Vulture*, *Satan's Alley* and *Kochtopussy* are down."

Podsy winced at hearing that all three of the mechs were part of Captain Koch's so-called Joker Company, the support vehicles responsible for the repair, retrieval, and rearmament of the battalion in the field. This operation more than any other required an active support crew to keep things rolling.

"Commander Knighton's Vipers inbound," Comm reported into the sudden silence. "First retrieval in six seconds."

"Eyes on-target, people," Moon intoned. "Let's capture our birds and get them back out there ASAP."

The bridge crew was staffed largely by Fleet transfers, whose professionalism and focus were readily apparent as they complied with the general's orders. But even the fresher-faced standers and officers zeroed in on their respective tasks and duties as the ship prepared to receive Commander Knighton's Vipers.

The ships came in hot but clean. A sigh of relief and two minutes later, all twelve Vipers were successfully captured on the drop-deck using Chief Rimmer's makeshift capture nets. One of the Vipers had sustained bad enough damage during landing that it would likely not fly again during the op, and one more had been lucky to make it back to the Wallace at all. But when all was said and done, ten Vipers would be refueled, rearmed, and ready for action after the deck crews had finished with them.

It was a fair price to pay to keep the ground forces on-target.

7

COGITO ERGO SUM

"HE up and on the way!" Xi snarled, unleashing another pair of high-explosive shells from *Elvira's* mains. The crater's rim looked like a chipped cup after taking two high-yield railgun strikes from orbit. Her shells fell onto a swarm of surging rock-biters cartwheeling up the crater's interior slope at the front of a steadily rising tide.

"I'm still reading a strong signal from *Kochtopussy's* beacon, Major," Penny reported with evident distress.

"Joker can handle its own, Private," Xi snapped as a pair of yellow warning lights flashed at the edge of her virtual vision. "Focus on those new alarms; the port chain feeders are acting up."

"Roger, ma'am," Penny acknowledged, taking the rebuke in stride. The truth was, Xi shared Penny's concerns over Captain Koch's fate. It was unlikely in the extreme that anyone aboard the three downed mechs had survived, but any chance was worth pursuing.

Unfortunately, the three downed mechs were on the other side of the crater, and with the horde of rock-biters fast approaching, Xi had no time or resources to spare for a rescue effort for the Jokers.

"Prepare to execute Sideswipe," Xi commanded, raising the local mechs and Marines under her command. "Lieutenant Forsythe, your status?"

"Ready to rock, ma'am," the Marine lieutenant replied.

"5th Platoon," she continued, forwarding fire coordinates to Lieutenant Quinn, "put steady fire on this patch of slope on my mark. 6th Platoon, hold fire until the Marines make their push. Ready for a close-up, Hightower?"

"I was born ready, Major," the recent addition replied confidently.

The rest of the acknowledgments came in as the rock-biters stormed over a three-hundred-meter wide swath of relatively even slope. It was an obvious ambush point that any human would have avoided, but the rock-biters charged into the bottle-neck without regard for the possible danger.

"Hold fire," Xi commanded as five hundred Arh'Kel infantry moved into the kill zone. The temptation to pulverize them right then was strong, but like anything worthwhile, patience was key to maximizing the potential return. "Hold..." she insisted after a thousand rock-biters had swarmed into the funnel of flat ground. One thousand became two thousand, and just before the entire mini-valley of sloping terrain was completely filled with Arh'kel, she barked, "Fire!"

Lieutenant Quinn's 5th Platoon, perched atop the crater's rim and comprised of the heaviest hitters in 2nd Company, opened fire on the western edge of the three-hundred-meter wide, kilometer-long kill zone. Six artillery guns thundered, dropping explosive shells into the enemy's left flank. Thirty-two missiles screamed through the soupy atmosphere en route to their target areas, thoroughly flattening them. Even a pair of rail-guns stabbed into the rocky slope, carving great fissures in the mountainside and kicking up geysers of debris as they left hundred-meter-long gashes in the slope. Rock-biters were hurled aside by the immense destructive energies unleashed, but only the left flank of the enemy advance was struck by Quinn's devastating salvo.

At least a thousand Arh'Kel died in that initial volley, but the Terrans were hardly done.

"Forsythe, go," Xi commanded, and before her lips had closed, the Terran Marines leapt into action.

Springing up from concealment on the enemy's right flank, having dug themselves into cracks and fissures in the mountainside, thirty-six Marines launched a withering barrage of RPGs into the enemy's midst. Each Marine carried a "quad-pod" of RPGs, normally employed by fire teams in fortified gun nests, which they held and fired like miniguns. A hundred and forty-four rocket-propelled grenades blasted into the enemy's flank within the span of two seconds, annihilating no fewer than four hundred rock-biters and throwing the enemy charge into complete disarray. Discarding their quad-pods, the Marines took up the *actual* miniguns they had brought to their makeshift foxholes and poured a combined seven thousand rounds per second into the confused tide of enemy infantry.

It was carnage on a scale rarely glimpsed by human eyes, and just ten seconds after the Marines had emerged from concealment, a charging horde of three thousand rock-biters had been reduced to less than a hundred. Impressively, those survivors resumed their charge up the slope, ignoring the Marines who had just annihilated their fellows. It took Quinn's people another eight seconds to put the rest of the Arh'Kel down, turning the slope into a purple-slicked scene from a rock-biter's worst nightmare.

Xi's eyes were on the rest of the charging rock-biters, who only surprised her by doing what she thought they should have done rather than what she expected them to do: they faltered in their charge. Fifteen thousand Arh'Kel infantry, completely unaccompanied by heavy weapon platforms, stopped in their tracks for a long moment. She had never seen anything like it in her time fighting the Arh'Kel, and in a way, their hesitation had been the object of the ambush. They knew these rock-biters would behave differently from the ones that had assaulted Terran space time after time, but no one from General Moon to Admiral Wallace knew what that would look like.

And then, after four seconds' hesitation, she got her first glimpse of the difference between these rock-biters and the ones she had faced on both Durgan's Folly and Mars.

They pivoted and proceeded to charge up the northwest slope to where a second, considerably smaller set of paths led to the crater. Unlike the vast kill-zone she and the Marines had just cleared, this second approach consisted of deep, wide fissures large enough for three or four Arh'Kel to move through abreast.

And just like with Sideswipe, she had already prepared that approach for their eventual arrival.

"*Devastator*, you're up." Xi executed the addendum to the operations plan as she drove *Elvira* to an optimal firing position over the second approach.

"Copy that, Major," Hightower acknowledged, spurring his six-legged walker into action. *Devastator* was of an experimental design specifically built to battle Arh'Kel. It featured six chain guns, positioned between each of its legs, six mortars, with each positioned directly over a leg joint, a trio of flame-throwers affixed to its underside, and a single plasma cannon atop its distinctively-shaped hull.

Classified as a cruiser and on par with *Elvira* in terms of total mass, *Devastator* had long, spindly legs that lifted its hull a full five meters off the ground. The legs had been specifically designed to prevent rock-biters from climbing up and were extremely resistant to plasma torches. It was a pity that *Devastator*, a prototype unit, was the lone example of this so-called "Rock Crusher"-class, because Xi and everyone else in the Legion suspected it would soon prove it was the ideal platform for fighting the silicoid race.

Moving his deceptively-frail-looking mech into position, Hightower charged his plasma cannon while Xi maneuvered *Elvira* a hundred meters farther down the slope. Unlike the first kill zone, this one was a full kilometer and a half across and five kilometers long. There were between fifteen and thirty fissure trenches the enemy would use to advance, shielding them from direct fire.

Unfortunately for the rock-biters, Xi had no intention of wasting direct fire ammunition.

"*Devastator* primed," Hightower reported after his plasma cannon had charged. This cannon was considerably smaller than those previously under Xi's command, but what it lacked in firepower, it made up for in both range and frequency.

"Hold fire, *Devastator*," Xi commanded as the first of the rock-biters entered the natural trenches. The crisscrossing network of crevices immediately concealed them from view, but Xi had already accounted for that by having Forsythe's Marines deploy two dozen remote cameras at vital points in the trenches. The rock-biters reached the first of these cameras precisely on schedule, and just as she had expected, they blasted it with small-arms fire mere seconds after coming into its view.

The enemy infantry moved past the second camera, then the third, and again Xi was tempted to commence the attack before it was optimal to do so. The first ambush had been costly in terms of materiel, with thirty-six quad-pods and miniguns being emptied into the enemy ranks when the judicious use of a single tactical nuke or a full-volume artillery barrage would have achieved the same outcome, to say nothing of intentionally putting the Marines in knife range of the enemy.

But she waited until the sixth camera's position had been overrun before giving the order. "*Devastator*, you are cleared to engage."

"Roger," Hightower acknowledged. "Engaging."

The spidery *Devastator* crouched and braced for recoil before launching a bolt of plasma into the middle of the enemy position. The superheated metal emitted by Hightower's compact cannon rapidly expanded into gas, igniting every last trace of oxygen in the atmosphere as it blossomed en route to its target.

With a long, severe arc, the plasma blast fell sharply into one of the center-most trenches, where it erupted with devastating force. A half-dozen trenches instantly collapsed as the shockwave propagated through a hundred-meter radius of the rocky slope. The blast shattered the brittle stone of the fissures and crevices into man-sized pieces, burying hundreds of Arh'Kel infantry beneath several meters of rubble.

But *Devastator* wasn't done.

With its capacitor already charged to maximum, the Arh'Kel-killer fired its plasma cannon a second time just three seconds after the first. Again the bolt of superheated material tore through the thick atmosphere, and again it fell upon one of the many fissures which the Arh'Kel had filled with their charge. An eighty-meter-diameter zone was flattened, and Xi was surprised at the significant difference in damage from the first blast to the second. They both contained the same raw energy, but the second seemed to have struck a more resilient patch of ground.

So it was fortunate *Devastator* fired another bolt of plasma a few seconds later, this time targeting a patch of ground two hundred meters up from the previous strike. The damage wrought was similar to that of the first strike, and Xi was impressed with the mech's devastating firepower. Its design, which lacked missiles and anti-missile rockets of any kind, left it completely vulnerable to attacks from above. But with the rest of the Legion providing cover, a few mechs like *Devastator* would wreak havoc on any Arh'Kel units that engaged a force that fielded them.

No one ever accused rock-biters of being smart. Xi smirked as Hightower unleashed a fourth and final blast from his potent weapon, destroying another patch of ground and effectively funneling the attacking enemy into a handful of tunnels.

"Come on, turn back," Xi heard herself mutter as the tide of rock-biters failed to appear on her cameras. They had placed the rest of the cameras in the next kill zone, which Hightower's fire had thankfully spared. For some reason that escaped her, Xi found herself actively hoping the enemy would fall back. It wasn't that she was afraid of their continued advance; they had enough ordnance on the ground to hold these types of attacks off for three full days if need be.

No, it was something else. She would kill any rock-biter that came within a stone's throw of her or her people, but she had somehow begun to think of them as victims. They were an intelligent species, capable of taking a tiny handful of individuals onto a planet without any supplies and creating a crypto-colony capable of spaceflight and planetary-scale invasions in a matter of decades. But their technological capacity and obviously robust social systems far outpaced their apparent individual cognitive powers. In a way, they were like mindless robots, preprogrammed by biologically-driven imperatives that overruled every other factor. Also, this was their planet. The Metal Legion were the invaders. She hated them, but not enough to commit genocide.

"Turn back..." she hissed, beginning to believe after several seconds that they might have done precisely that. Her ambushes on the slopes had been designed to draw the Arh'Kel out and make them reveal their tactics.

Maybe these Arh'Kel were different enough that they wouldn't need to slaughter them wholesale in order to accomplish the mission. Maybe, just maybe, they could dissuade the rock-biters from a relentless series of suicide runs against Mount Foothold by demonstrating their superior tactics and technology.

And then a flicker of movement on the eighth camera dashed her hopes.

Grimacing in equal measures disappointment and disdain, she called up a command interface on her virtual HUD. The rock-biters, resuming their mindless charge, destroyed the eighth, ninth, tenth, eleventh and twelfth cameras in a span of just six seconds. Not only had they not slowed their advance, they had *hastened* it.

Which meant she needed to teach them another lesson in gun-barrel diplomacy.

"*Elvira* here," she called over the Company channel. She primed her virtual command prepared to execute. "Fire in the hole!"

A rippling wave of a hundred explosions roared down the slope. High-yield mines, placed there by the Marines a half-hour earlier, completely caved in the rest of the makeshift trenches and annihilated a thousand or more Arh'Kel outright. A square kilometer of ground was heaved up by the concussive wave, transforming it into a broken patch of nearly-impassable terrain which would be guaranteed suicide to charge across.

So perhaps unsurprisingly, that was precisely what the surviving Arh'Kel chose to do.

Clambering up from their collapsed trenches, with no small number missing at least one limb, the rock-biters picked their way up the broken slope and resumed their advance on the crater's edge.

"All right." The major scowled and growled, "If you want it that bad, here it comes. 2nd Company, open fire!"

Chain guns roared, coil guns whined, and artillery thundered as the Terrans rained death and destruction down from the high ground. The already battered landscape of the mountain's slope was further abused by the furious onslaught. The fire persisted for a full two minutes before the last rock-biter was picked off by Marine railgun fire.

The Arh'Kel never faltered. Never broke stride. They simply hurled themselves at the fortified Terrans, defiantly daring them to pull the trigger time and time again.

Which they did. And when the dust settled, there wasn't a rock-biter anywhere to be seen on her side of the mountain. They had apparently retreated down whatever spider holes had brought them there, and frankly, Xi was glad for it.

As she walked *Elvira* up the steep slope, her HUD began to flash with a series of updates. It seemed the rock-biters had executed a second attack on the opposite side of the crater. The Metal Legion had put people over there since it was a viable avenue of approach, all bases covered. Major Bao and Colonel Jenkins had built a solid plan with redundancies and alternate courses of action based on how the enemy acted or reacted.

As Jenkins and 1st Company engaged the enemy on the other side of the mountain, Xi pulled her mechs and Marines back up the slope and awaited the rock-biters' next move in her zone of control.

***

"I'm showing six HWPs with this wave, Colonel," Benjamin reported. "Estimated enemy strength is eight hundred infantry."

"That's a little lighter than we expected," Jenkins mused as he reviewed the sensor data. "They're still feeling us out."

"Fleet Intelligence suggested these Arh'Kel have, for all intents and purposes, never encountered our military," Benjamin observed. "The attacks on Terran space didn't return any members to Arh'Kel territory, so there was no way for them to gather intel on us before we landed. Bizarre as it may seem, this is a first-encounter situation from their perspective."

"You only get one shot at a first impression," Jenkins said as the Arh'Kel formation wound its way up the curved path that led up the steepest side of the mountain. "Let's make ours one to remember. Alert Captain Shen that they're coming his way."

"Alerting Captain Shen," Benjamin acknowledged, and a virtual signal chimed on Jenkins' monitor showing the Marine captain had received the alert and was ready to spring his trap.

The path leading up the mountainside zigzagged at an angle too steep to make a tactical advance up, even for the cart-wheeling rock-biters. Instead, the eight hundred infantry and their six HWPs moved like a convoy, far too slowly on the narrow path for any sane commander's liking.

As they had just done with Major Xi on the mountain's other side, the Arh'Kel appeared to be probing the Terrans. Gauging their responses. It was information gathering, not a proper attack, aimed at learning the Terrans' tactics so they could formulate a winning offensive strategy.

Like any foe worth facing, Jenkins intended to deny them that which they sought.

Jenkins and 1st Company stood vigil at the top of the mountainside, where in just a few seconds the first of the enemy HWPs would be in position to fire on them after clearing a half-kilometer-tall cliff midway up the winding trail. Once there, the rock-biters could fire their railguns and missiles up the slope at Jenkins' exposed mechs, and a few minutes later, the enemy infantry would be in knife range as well.

"Captain Shen is requesting permission to attack, Colonel," Benjamin relayed.

Jenkins nodded but waited a few seconds before replying, "Permission granted."

On a ledge above the approaching enemy column, twenty-four Terran Marines had waited motionless for their chance to strike. Wearing their distinctive shell-backed armor and brandishing quad-pods loaded with armor-piercing grenades, the power-armored warriors leaned over the edge and fired their ordnance straight down at the enemy. Each Marine had a quad-pod, and for good measure, two Marines targeted each of the HWPs with their RPGs. The enemy railguns and missile platforms exploded, with one dying so violently it carved a five-meter hole in the path.

The ensuing rockslide cascaded down, gaining mass and momentum as it shredded the brittle rockface with its passing. By the time it reached the zigzagging path below, it had become so fierce that it knocked two dozen rock-biters down the mountain, where they became one with the avalanche of razor-sharp stone.

The Marines fell back as the enemy returned fire with their slug-throwers. Iron slugs smacked harmlessly off the rockface, some tearing head-sized chunks of stone free but doing little else of note. The Marines sprinted down the cliff fifty meters, where they hefted their railguns and, moving with parade-like precision, leaned out over the cliff in perfect unison and unleashed a storm of railgun slivers into the rockface above the Arh'Kel soldiers.

The first avalanche of rock caused by the HWP's death was nothing compared to this one. The Marines carved a sixty-meter-long, twenty-meter-high chunk of the cliff off with precision fire. Hundreds of Arh'Kel were crushed and devoured by the rockslide, and the few that remained were in such disarray that the Marines easily withdrew to the safety of cover once again, though as they fell back, they did so with determined alacrity. Unlike the unsuspecting rock-biters, the Marines knew what was coming next, and they wanted to be as clear as humanly possible before it arrived.

"All right, Hammer," Jenkins said with a harsh grin, "give 'em the one-two."

"Firing," Hammer declared, and *Powerslave's* dual plasma cannons thrummed to life. As the towering war machine's capacitors charged to full, Jenkins detected the unmistakable scent of ozone waft into his cockpit.

Powerslave fired both of its heavy plasma cannons skyward, lobbing the devastating bolts of hellfire at nearly vertical trajectories. They surged up through the thick atmosphere, climbing higher and higher until finally reaching the apex of their twinned flight.

And then, like thunderbolts from the hand of Zeus, they descended on the enemy column's remnants. Landing a half-kilometer apart, the plasma bolts completely incinerated anything and everything between them. Clouds of black smoke boiled out, propagated by the infernos' blast waves. The damage caused by the Marines' railguns was completely erased when a kilometer-long section of the mountainside fell away, grinding the zigzagging path beneath it into dust as the rockslide moved down the slope. Even if some Arh'Kel had survived the hellfire, *nothing* could survive the rockslide that followed, and when the tumbling rubble finally reached the base of the mountain, not a trace of movement could be seen.

It was overkill and everyone knew it, which was the point. The Arh'Kel were probing, searching for weaknesses and trying to learn the Metalheads' tendencies. What they got instead was a multi-part lesson in futility: the futility of launching a precision ambush with RPGs when the railgun strikes that followed would have accomplished that much and more. The futility of the railgun salvo when the plasma cannons were bound to follow. And most of all, the futility in assaulting a position held by Terran Metalheads.

Jenkins had no doubt the enemy would return to probe his defenses once again, but he suspected their earliest information-gathering exercises had been completely thwarted. They had gained nothing but the ruination of clear approaches to the mountain's summit and the death of several thousand Arh'Kel infantry.

But while he had no doubt the enemy would return with renewed vigor, he had begun to doubt the righteousness of slaughtering them in job lots. Protecting their forward operating base was crucial to achieving their objective on AK-091, so when the rock-biters attacked, he would defend with no less enthusiasm than he had demonstrated thus far. But the killing of creatures whose sentience was so greatly different from that of humanity's, to the point where they behaved essentially like a mindless insect colony, left him feeling hollow. It was one thing to look your enemy in the eye and know he would take from you everything you held dear and end that threat however possible.

It was quite another to do battle with soldiers who hardly even qualified for the term. It was unnerving, but more than that, it was perplexing.

"Colonel," Benjamin said, his voice tight with enthusiasm, "I think I've got something."

8

TARGET SIGHTED

"Report, Lieutenant," Jenkins demanded after several seconds of silence.

"Using the signal parameters provided by Captain Podsednik," Benjamin explained, "I've located what appears to be a Jemmin Poltergeist." As he spoke, a flood of data poured across Jenkins' display. Most of it was beyond his ability to process in real-time, but the lieutenant highlighted several pieces of data that Jenkins recognized from the pre-op briefings. "It's thirty-nine kilometers to the northwest, well behind the enemy line."

Jenkins pulled up the live sensor feeds of that area and saw an army of half a million Arh'Kel infantry. Surprisingly, there were fewer than a hundred HWPs scattered among the slow-moving army of rock-biters. At their current pace, they would reach Mount Foothold in eleven hours.

"Run your findings by Captain Podsednik," Jenkins decided, although what he really meant was to have Podsy direct Jem to examine the data. "We can't risk active scans tipping them off, but we need confirmation before we commit to attacking that large a force."

"I've got Captain Podsednik on the line, sir," Benjamin reported.

"What's your opinion, Podsy?" Jenkins asked as he considered how to best approach the Poltergeist's position at the center of a half-million enemy.

"Two things, Colonel," Podsy replied. "First, it's extremely likely that these readings are confirmation of a Jemmin Poltergeist. We'll continue to go over them up here, but our confidence is high. Second, it's also likely that this Poltergeist is both unknown to the rock-biters and that its role is primarily that of an observer. Jemmin isn't directly manipulating this Arh'Kel colony via neural implants like those we've encountered elsewhere."

Jenkins nodded along as Podsy spoke. Jem had suspected that last bit but had needed to gather more data before confirming it.

"Thank you, Captain," Jenkins replied. "Sounds like we've got our target. Can you isolate its position any more precisely than we've managed down here?"

"Not at this time, Colonel, but I can tell you that the topography down there is riddled with tunnel entrances and caves. It's likely the Poltergeist is using them to augment its stealth systems."

"Are the tunnels large enough for it to use?" Jenkins asked.

"No, sir. But some of the caves are large enough to house it," Podsy explained. "Passive scans from this range only let us pin it down to a two-kilometer area. Scans from five kilometers or closer conducted by three or more mechs will let us pinpoint its location precisely."

Jenkins noticed that General Moon had tapped into the conversation a few seconds earlier, so he deferred. "What's your opinion, General?"

"Much as I enjoy putting rock-biters back into the ground,"

Moon replied, "that's a significant concentration of enemy forces surrounding the Poltergeist. I can't imagine that's an accident, but we're on the clock, Colonel."

"Understood, sir." Jenkins nodded and checked his status board. "We're nearly finished erecting our fixed defenses here, and will advance on the enemy position in twenty-six minutes."

"Lieutenant Styles has prepared a fire-support package," Podsy said as Styles' proposal reached Jenkins' HUD. He perused it while Podsednik continued, "We can target most of the HWPs from here, but the only way to clear out that many infantry is with nukes. And given the nature of our objective—"

"We don't want to burn the flag before we capture it," Jenkins interrupted with a smirk as he made minor revisions to Styles' fire package and sent it back to the *William Wallace* via secure P2P. A moment later, Styles silently acknowledged and confirmed his revisions, which tightened the corridor the Metalheads would traverse on their way to the heart of the enemy formation. He then cut to a private line to General Moon. "What's the situation up there, General?"

"Admiral Wallace is grinding everything in orbit to dust," Moon replied, "and he's not exactly being subtle about it. His people seem to be treating this as much as a photo op as an interstellar offensive. The sooner we can get off this rock, the better it will be for everyone. There are multiple small fleets inbound from adjacent planets in this star system, and while none of them will pose a serious danger to the task force, I doubt they represent the totality of the Arh'Kel response."

"Understood, General," Jenkins agreed. "We'll get this done."

***

Forty minutes later, a column of mechs left Mount Foothold in their wake. Consisting of four platoons with elements from both 1st and 2nd Company, the task force was designed to maximize both speed and firepower. Most of the slower, longer-range mechs had been left in the relative safety of the crater, where they could provide tactical support and, if needed, reinforcement during the withdrawal.

Captain Koch's loss was still rippling throughout the Legion, but Lieutenant Gordon, formerly *Elvira's* Wrench and one of many recent field-commissioned officers, had stepped into the void left by the veteran and had assumed leadership of Joker Company. That made Gordon the acting CO of Mount Foothold until the task force returned.

Twenty-two kilometers separated the sixteen mechs from the Poltergeist's suspected location, which nearly put them in effective range of the Arh'Kel railguns and missile pods. It was time to remove them from consideration.

"*William Wallace*, this is Dragon Actual," Jenkins declared. "We are go for Fire Package Cloudburst."

"This is *Wallace* Ground Control," Lieutenant Styles immediately replied. "Requesting confirmation for Fire Package Cloudburst and advising to harden sensitive systems."

"Confirmed, GC," Jenkins acknowledged as his task force drew steadily closer to the enemy horde. Pressed together into a thick, irregular mass, the five hundred and thirty thousand rock-biters barely seemed to move as the Metal Legion prepared to unleash a rain of fire from orbit. "We're battened down and ready for the rain."

"Copy that, Dragon Actual," Styles replied. "Cloudburst inbound."

A countdown-to-impact timer appeared on his HUD, signaling the release of multiple weapons systems from the orbiting Terran warships. The bombardment needed to be precise, given the proximity of Jenkins' ground forces to the target zone, so just the *William Wallace*, *Martin Luther*, and two Fleet cruisers would participate from low orbit.

The seconds ticked down until the bolt of tungsten screamed through the atmosphere, crashing into an Arh'Kel HWP and completely destroying it while carving a massive crater in the rocky ground.

Another railgun bolt stabbed into the planet's surface, scratching another heavy weapon platform. Then another, and another, and another, each coming faster than the last and each striking with such precision that its target was annihilated by the direct hit.

The remaining HWPs began to scurry through the throng of enemy infantry, desperately scattering to avoid sharing the same fate, but the Fire Package Cloudburst had been impeccably designed and executed. Each of the first nineteen railgun strikes had eliminated the HWPs closest to the Poltergeist's suspected location, leaving only those a full kilometer or more away intact.

The remaining vehicles were spread out so far that sniping them with railgun bombardments would be a losing proposition, so instead of precision fire, the use of seven tactical nukes was authorized to secure the area. And like the divine fury of almighty God himself, those seven nuclear warheads fell upon the fleeing Arh'Kel vehicles and bathed them in nuclear fire.

The flash reports were nearly simultaneous and devoured the amorphous mass of rock-biter infantry. Jenkins knew that a better person would feel something akin to shame at seeing such destructive power unleashed on what was essentially a defenseless enemy, but he felt nothing of the kind. The rock-biters had annihilated the inhabitants of New Australia, erasing their entire culture and way of life while slaughtering tens of millions of Terrans per day. This was an enemy who had no regard for the sanctity of life, possibly not even its own. They were a scourge, a plague, and like any disease, the choice was simple: survival of the pathogen, or the species it preys upon?

To Jenkins, that was no choice at all.

Four hundred thousand rock-biters were annihilated by the three hundred fifty kilotons of nuclear blasts. As the mushroom clouds rose into the choking atmosphere of AK-091, the Metal Legion sprinted toward their primary objective with all eyes locked on target.

As they bounded across the blasted hellscape, which was somehow barely different for having suffered seven tactical nuke strikes, Jenkins' sensor feed showed the surviving Arh'Kel infantry had begun to scatter. Some were retreating into the many tunnels leading to the planet's underworld, some were fleeing in disparate directions, and still others seemed to think this was the ideal moment to charge into the teeth of the advancing mech column.

"This is Dragon Actual," Jenkins called over the task force channel. "All crews, you are cleared to engage Arh'Kel ground forces located outside the target zone. Fire at will. I say again, fire at will."

Like hunting dogs slipped free of their collars, the Legion's mechs opened fire on the roughly twenty thousand advancing rock-biters. Missiles, artillery shells, railguns, and plasma cannons hurled devastation into the enemy line, and the image was nothing short of awesome.

Lancing up and down the line, railgun bolts were the first to slam into the leading edge of cartwheeling Arh'Kel. Gouging deep rents in the rocky surface, those railgun bolts tore two-meter-wide, three-hundred-meter-long swaths into the charging infantry before their energies were finally expelled into the planet's crust. From above, it looked as though a many-clawed beast had reached down from the heavens and slashed its razor-sharp talons through the tightly-packed horde.

Next came the missiles, which fell at aggressive angles between the slash-marks made by the railguns. Rippling explosions ran from north to south, the Terran fire giving the impression of a well-choreographed dance being performed before the charging mechs. Thousands of Arh'Kel were killed or crippled by the savage barrage as a hundred and fifty SRMs delivered their payloads directly into the enemy formation.

After the missiles came the artillery, which splashed across the front of the enemy formation. Just twelve shells kissed the blasted terrain, causing the advance to falter and leaving pockmarks in the planet's surface like an aggressive lover might leave a handful of hickeys at strategically important points before the real action commenced.

And the plasma cannons of *Powerslave* and *Devastator* were, without a doubt, the emphatic exclamation points in this particular sentence in the Terran-Arh'Kel conflict.

Devastator's lighter plasma bolt arrived at the enemy line a full second before *Powerslave's* larger, heavier system could deliver its payload. The first plasma projectile splashed into the enemy horde, incinerating three hundred infantry and knocking as many more off their stride with the powerful blast wave.

The second of *Devastator's* plasma bolts fell a hundred meters north of the first, where it enveloped another two hundred enemy infantry and caused a significant ground collapse, creating a trapezoidal depression ten meters deep and eighty meters across when the thin layer of rocky surface gave way to reveal a subterranean chamber that had probably been filled with rock-biters.

Then it was *Powerslave's* turn, and when its plasma bolts touched down, even a lifelong warrior could have been forgiven for assuming another pair of tactical nukes had just gone off at the edges of the enemy line.

Blue-white infernos flared into existence at opposite ends of the enemy horde, instantly cremating five thousand Arh'Kel and knocking another two thousand to the ground. Black mushroom clouds boiled skyward over the impact points and would eventually join their seven predecessors, left by the tactical nukes, in the upper atmosphere.

Devastator's third and fourth plasma bolts were mere afterthoughts to *Powerslave's* multi-kiloton deliveries, although they too claimed several hundred more Arh'Kel each as the Metal Legion's sprinting mechs approached the badly frayed line of the enemy charge.

Leading the Legion's charge was Major Xi's *Elvira*, which was the first mech to open fire on the mindlessly attacking Arh'Kel infantry. Her flank-mounted chain guns shredded up and down the enemy line, while her dual fifteen-kilo mains sent HE shells into the formation's center. Flanking her was a diverse cast of tactical- and cruiser-grade mechs, which also unleashed coil and chain gun fire into the rock-biter formation. Moving in an arrowhead formation at seventy kph, Major Xi's eight mechs plunged into the enemy horde like a blade through a ribcage. Every round that left a Terran gun sent purple gore splashing to the ground, and every shell killed dozens of the mindless soldiers.

The ensuing carnage was predictable and thoroughly satisfying to a longtime veteran of the Arh'Kel conflict like Lee Jenkins. He had seen too many of his friends, and even rivals, fall to these alien beasts that seemed to have been conjured from humanity's worst nightmares. Watching them fall, while disconcerting for the apparent fact that they had nothing approaching a survival instinct at the individual level, was precisely what he had trained his entire career to make happen.

1st Company's two platoons of mechs, led by the towering *Powerslave*, tore into what was left of the enemy line. Xi's assault had been absolutely brutal, leaving nothing but a swath of purple in her wake, but the intractable rock-biters weren't about to give up.

Even as Xi's mechs annihilated the rock-biters at a danger-close range, driving deep into their line toward the still-hidden Poltergeist, the surviving Arh'Kel fell in on all sides in pursuit. Their numbers were thin, but their resolve was unshaken as they pursued the first Metalheads to break through their line.

As they fell in to pursue 2nd Company's mechs, Jenkins and 1st Company came upon them like the jaws of a beartrap.

Powerslave's mortars fired, launching shells into the rock-biters' midst. Chain guns poured red depleted uranium slugs into the tide of enemies, and coil guns whined as they added to the onslaught. The scene was a one-sided pounding, with the Metalheads swinging the hammer. The rock-biters fired their small arms, plinking and plunking into the Terran hulls, but those hulls had been purpose-built to shrug off such impacts.

Dozens of enemy slugs per second harmlessly struck *Powerslave's* torso and legs, but the battlefield titan's knife-range weapons kept the enemy from getting close enough to use cutting torches or other devices against it. The armored column mercilessly proceeded toward the Poltergeist, cutting down droves of rock-biters as the Legion came to within twelve kilometers of their real objective.

In a sense, the entire attack against the Arh'Kel to this point had been deception or misdirecting theater. If the Jemmin Poltergeist's commander realized it was the target of the Terrans' operation, it was more than capable of fleeing far faster than the Metalheads could pursue. To get close enough to make a high-percentage attempt at subduing the fleet-footed Poltergeist, the Metalheads needed to convince its commander that they were merely there to slaughter rock-biters. The Jemmin had to know of the Legion's experience battling Jemmin forces, so it would be loath to activate its engines and flee unless it was convinced the Terrans knew it was there.

Thus far, they had done nothing to spook their quarry. Everything was going according to plan, and the entire team had performed their roles perfectly. In just a few more minutes, they would be close enough to use Jem's complicated takeover attempt of the Poltergeist's systems.

Although calling it a "takeover" was a bit of a stretch. All Jem was confident it could do was disrupt the Poltergeist's primary systems for a matter of seconds, or a minute at the very most, during which time Marines could attempt to board and neutralize the craft.

Just like clockwork, a pair of Marine dropships appeared in the local area, having flown in from Mount Foothold. If everything went perfectly, in just eight minutes, they would attempt to disrupt the Poltergeist, and mere seconds after that, the dropship would deposit two dozen power-armored Marines on the Poltergeist's hull.

Jenkins' sense of anticipation grew with each colossal stride taken by *Powerslave*. The Legion had expended significant ordnance for this push, but with both the *Vercingetorix* and *William Wallace* in orbit, they wouldn't lack for supplies any time soon.

"I've got movement," Benjamin reported at the exact moment Jenkins noticed a flicker at the target location. "Poltergeist is on the move, Colonel," Benjamin declared as the Jemmin vehicle's signature tore skyward.

Snapping off a string of creative invective, Jenkins took a moment to steady himself. He hadn't realized just how anxious he'd become in pursuit of the Jemmin vehicle, and as it rocketed away at four hundred kph under a cloak of nearly-impenetrable invisibility, he knew their stay on AK-091 had just gotten significantly longer.

It was possible, and even probable, that the Jemmin commander had acted out of simple prudence. The Legion had done nothing to indicate they knew the Poltergeist was there, which meant that his top priority now had to shift to maintaining that deception for as long as possible.

"All right, people," Jenkins said over the P2P. "Look sharp. We've still got a job to do here."

To his peoples' credit, they didn't falter or let up in their attack on the Arh'Kel position until the entire army was erased from the face of the planet. They pursued that secondary objective with all the vigor he had come to expect from the revitalized Metal Legion, and when they were finished, they returned to Mount Foothold before a consolidated force of Arh'Kel could emerge from the tunnels and give chase.

9

SNIFFING AROUND

"General, I'm detecting activity at the Nexus-side gate," Sensors reported.

Moon and Podsednik, who had been conducting a sidebar pertaining to an upcoming supply drop to Mount Foothold, turned in unison and Podsy made his way over to the Sensor pit. The Vorr arrival had been anticipated by Jem, but the precision of Jem's prediction was nonetheless surprising.

"I'm reading Vorr signatures emerging from the event horizon, sir," Sensors continued. "Four...five...six...seven...eight warships, including two battleships, two carriers, and four destroyers."

A chime rang in Podsy's ear, signaling that Jem was requesting a private link. Jem's hardware was located in Podsy's berth, but he had connected that hardware to a private two-way audio-only link, to be used at Jem's discretion.

Podsy accepted the link and quietly said, "Jem?"

"Did the Vorr arrive as I predicted they would?" Jem asked.

"Yes," he agreed as he confirmed Sensors' findings in a raised voice. "I confirm Sensors' breakdown of the arrivals,

General: two battleships, two carriers, four destroyers. All vessels are accelerating toward AK-091."

"I'm picking up a broadcast message, General," Comm said before adding in confused surprise, "and it's being answered by Admiral Corbyn.'

Podsy and Moon exchanged brief, knowing looks. They had privately alerted Admiral Corbyn of Jem's prediction and requested that, as a duly-appointed flag officer, he intervene in the communication before Admiral Wallace could do so. Jem had been explicit in describing the Vorr's motives for coming to this star system, and they had nothing to do with assisting the Metal Legion.

"We are Vorr Task Force Dark Transcendence of Ignorance," the Vorr's auto-translated voice declared. "We are here to investigate the purpose of Terran presence in this star system. Respond."

"This is Admiral Corbyn of the Terran Fleet," Corbyn declared on the open channel, beginning his transmission even before the Vorr had completed theirs. The light delay meant several seconds would pass before they received his reply, but those seconds were critical for purely tactical reasons. "I have received your query regarding our presence in this star system and will compose a formal reply shortly. Please stand by."

It wasn't Shakespeare, but it would suffice. By answering the Vorr hail before the Task Force's designated Flag Officer, which was obviously Admiral Wallace, Admiral Corbyn had committed a breach of protocol amounting to usurpation of Wallace's privileges. Such a breach would invariably result in disciplinary measures being taken against Corbyn after the op had concluded, but by being first to respond, he had invoked a little-known clause in the Terran Armed Forces code. That clause made clear that the first flag officer to respond to a foreign missive was granted exclusive privilege to conduct that communication unless or until he relinquished that prerogative or the foreign agent requested the exchange be facilitated by another Terran representative.

Predictably, the Vorr composed a reply shortly thereafter. "We urge haste in the composition of your reply, Admiral Corbyn."

"Incoming link request from Admiral Wallace," Comm reported. "It's a three-way link including Admiral Corbyn."

"Put him on," Moon commanded, and the glowering visage of Admiral Wallace appeared on the viewer.

"I don't know what your angle is, gentlemen," Wallace all but snarled, "but it would be in both your best interests to cut the crap. We're deployed in an active engagement zone behind enemy lines. Usurping my authority will only get Terrans killed and jeopardize this mission."

"My apologies, Admiral Wallace," Corbyn demurred. "I thought with your attention focused on clearing 091's orbit, I could make a small contribution to the operation by taking some small administrative burdens off your shoulders. After all, it *is* what I know best."

Wallace's scowl deepened. "Whatever game you're playing ends now, Corbyn. I have no issue overriding protocol, which is my right given the circumstances. I order you, as commander of this task force, to relinquish diplomatic priority to me immediately and cease communication with that Vorr fleet."

"Captain Podsednik," Jem said urgently as Corbyn and Wallace continued to debate the issue, "if you will forward a comprehensive stream of current sensor data, I think I can help locate hidden Jemmin assets in this system."

"How many do you think there are?" Podsy asked as he called up the relevant data and forwarded a silent update to General Moon regarding Jem's request.

"No more than six," Jem replied. "and likely only two or

three. Jemmin's presence here was primarily observational, not interventionist, so there was no need for an extensive military presence."

General Moon gave his authorization for Podsy to provide Jem the requested intel, and a moment later, Podsednik forwarded the sensor data to a terminal near Jem's physical platform. Jem's crystalline data core was capable of processing the visual light spectrum much the way human eyes functioned, albeit at significantly higher resolution and with a broader spectrum, so employing a standard terminal to display the sensor data was sufficient while maintaining data interface security standards.

Of course, Podsy knew that if Jem decided to antagonize the Metalheads from within, there was little or nothing they could do to stop it. They still didn't fully understand Jem's hardware or technical capabilities, so there was no real way to ensure security against its potential incursions.

"Processing," Jem acknowledged as the stream of data began to pour across the monitor in Podsy's berth. Less than half had been transmitted at superhuman speed before Jem declared, "I believe an active sensor sweep of these three regions will reveal the Jemmin warships, Captain Podsednik."

"Won't that alert the grounded Poltergeists that we've got the ability to locate them?" Podsy asked skeptically.

"Possibly, but it is a risk I think worth taking," Jem said confidently. "If your task force falls to infighting at this early hour, the chance of recovering that which we came for falls to near zero."

"All right, forward the target zones," Podsy agreed. A tactical map representing the local region of space highlighted three points of interest, each within two light seconds of AK-091. He made his way to General Moon's side while the admirals continued to debate the matter of authority regarding Vorr communications.

"At the very least, you'll lose your freedom over this, Corbyn," Wallace growled. "Fleet High Command was content to let you ride out the rest of your career in disgrace, but you've crossed a line here."

Corbyn shrugged indifferently. "Again, if you wish to usurp my authority, it is well within your ability to do so, but you will not have my consent if that is your chosen course. Whatever potential errors of judgment led me to this point will not be compounded by capitulation on a point of protocol which we both know is absolutely clear."

"General Moon," Podsy said in a low voice, though the mic was muted from the *William Wallace*'s end, so there was no real reason to be subtle. "Jem advises we sweep these three areas with active scans. We're likely to find a handful of Jemmin warships lying doggo at one or more of these POIs."

Moon glanced at the map and cocked his head. "Are we concerned about tipping the Jemmin off in the process?"

"Possibly," Podsy allowed. "But Jem is convinced this is the optimal course. And frankly, I think giving Admiral Wallace something else to rage about might be just what the doctor ordered."

Podsy inclined his chin toward the increasingly furious visage of Wallace on the main screen.

"Do it," Moon commanded, and a moment later Podsednik had completed inputting the target zones at his terminal.

"Initiating scan," Podsednik declared, and the *William Wallace*'s powerful active sensors swept the three zones in rapid succession. Sure enough, a trio of icons appeared in the second target zone with unmistakably Jemmin signatures. "Targets located, General. Verifying now."

"Admirals," General Moon cut into the heated argument.

"we've located a small formation of cloaked Jemmin warships and are forwarding their location now."

Wallace's jaw muscles bunched. "TAC would be wise not to interfere in Fleet..."

His attention was taken by someone off-pickup, causing him to trail off in the middle of his rebuke.

"My people confirm your findings, General Moon," Admiral Corbyn said before Wallace had recomposed himself. "Admiral Wallace, in the interests of diplomacy with the Vorr, I suggest we inform them of what we've found, although I will of course defer to you on this matter given our respective roles in this task force."

Wallace's lip curled contemptuously and Podsy found his estimation of Admiral Corbyn growing by leaps and bounds with each word he fired off at his higher-ranked counterpart. Here was a man who had zero regard for his career or the inevitable political fallout which would follow this particular sequence of events. He was laying everything on the line to help facilitate the capture of the objective on the planet's surface, and despite Corbyn's previously antagonistic stance toward the Metal Legion, Podsy knew the Terran Armor Corps needed every ally it could get.

"You think you've backed me into a corner, Corbyn." Wallace shook his head flatly. "But all you've done is seal your own fate. Yes, inform the Vorr of the Jemmin presence while I go about the more important task of removing it."

The line from Wallace's flagship went dead, and General Moon was quick to say, "I appreciate your cover there, Admiral."

"I didn't come here to look good for the cameras," Corbyn said with conviction. "We've got a job to do, and it's too important to let men like Wallace stop it. But I hope you understand I've just burned my last bridge at Fleet Command. The Vorr have been apprised of the Jemmin ships in-system. They say they're moving to intercept."

"*Marcus Aurelius* is coming about—" Tactical reported before raising his voice. "The Vorr ships are firing beam weapons. Two direct hits on Jemmin warships. Moderate damage."

"The Vorr are five light seconds out," Podsy said in surprise. "Their beam weapons aren't normally that accurate at these ranges."

"The Jemmin warships hadn't yet begun to move when the Vorr fired, Captain," Tactical explained. "But they're now accelerating at sixty gees and making evasive maneuvers. *Marcus Aurelius* is launching missiles."

Forty missiles leapt from the *Marcus Aurelius'* forward hull, burning at two hundred gees as they raced across the void toward their fast-retreating Jemmin targets. All three Jemmin warships were of the standard cruiser design the Legion had already faced several times during Podsednik's tenure with TAC, and none were stalwart enough to withstand such a concerted barrage.

But unlike the cruisers the *William Wallace* engaged over Mars, these Jemmin warships were intent on evading the storm of inbound fire.

The *William Wallace* suddenly lurched hard to port, knocking Podsednik into a nearby station. Podsy's inhumanly powerful cybernetic legs locked him firmly in place and allowed him to narrowly avoid a potentially lethal skull-cracking against the Sensor station's upper rim.

"Three direct hits," Tactical reported urgently. "All six Jemmin beams targeted the *William Wallace*."

"I've got outgassing on decks four through six on the port flank," Damage Control declared as Podsy strapped himself back into his chair. "Twenty-six confirmed casualties, including on the drop-deck."

"Scramble interceptors," Moon barked. "Plot counterfire solutions and fire when ready."

"Plotting counterfire solutions," Tactical eagerly acknowledged.

Podsy forwarded the general's order to scramble down to Lieutenant Commander Knighton, who acknowledged within half a second, and just two seconds after receiving the order, the first of the Vipers burst from the *Wallace's* drop-deck. They launched sluggishly compared to interceptors deployed by a purpose-built carrier but still managed to scramble the ten battle-ready interceptors in fourteen seconds. During that time, the fleet-footed Jemmin cruisers evaded all but one of the *Marcus Aurelius'* missiles. That missile scored a direct hit on its target, violating the Jemmin warship's reactor containment and causing the ship's own power core to destroy the vessel from within.

Shortly after the Vipers had assumed a defensive formation surrounding the *William Wallace*, the TAC warship fired its railguns at the pair of fleeing enemy cruisers. The railgun bolts shot across the void at the corkscrewing cruisers, and when they had crossed the distance, none of the four projectiles found the mark. The nearest miss went wide by a full two kilometers.

"Re-plot and fire again," Moon commanded.

"I have Commander Knighton requesting permission to pursue, General," Comm reported.

"Denied." Moon grimaced. "They're too far out. Maintain escort with priority missile intercept."

"Aye, sir."

The Vorr warships near the gate unleashed another volley of concerted beam fire, prompting Sensors to report, "Three more hits, General. Cruiser One is losing power. Cruiser Two is continuing to flee."

"*Marcus Aurelius* and *Sima Yi* are firing," Tactical reported in surprise. "Three hundred missiles away."

"What's he doing?" Podsy muttered under his breath. "Those cruisers are too far for kinetics or fusion warheads."

"Cruisers coming about!" Tactical reported as an alarm began to sound throughout the ship.

"All hands, brace for impa—" Podsy began.

The ship lurched to port, cutting him short and causing the power grid to temporarily fail as all bridge systems briefly switched to auxiliary power.

"Four more hits. We've got a cascade failure of the port power grid, and I've lost contact with railguns One and Two," Damage Control reported.

Podsy's interface flickered to life with an inbound feed from Commander Knighton. It was a video uplink from her Viper's nose-cam and showed a horrifying series of wounds to the *William Wallace's* topside.

Raking halfway back from the ship's armored bow, four distinct grooves with still-molten margins had been carved into the hull. The strikes had completely destroyed two of the warship's railguns, while damage from the previous impacts had punched deep holes in the port hull. It was clear that those strikes had been aimed at the ship's fusion core, and from the look of it, they had only missed by a handful of meters.

Podsy threw the image up on the main viewer, and the bridge crew immediately understood the severity of the damage. As they watched, a pair of motionless Terran bodies could be seen drifting across Knighton's field of view.

As the *Wallace's* bridge crew worked to stop their ship's figurative bleeding, the missiles launched by the dreadnoughts continued to speed toward the fleeing Jemmin warships. When the missiles were within five thousand kilometers of the cruisers, they flickered in a rapid sequence as beams of white light stabbed across the void toward the enemy vessels.

Like the Blue Boy missiles previously employed by the Legion or those fired by Captain Guan aboard the *Red Hare* during that ship's brief time with the Terran Armor Corps, the Terran missiles each fired a powerful laser beam at the evasive Jemmin vessels. The Jemmin ships were bathed in a blinding field of light, and when that light cut out, the enemy craft were naught but ruined hulks streaming gas and plasma into the void.

Silently cursing himself for underestimating Admiral Wallace's tactical acumen, Podsy examined the sensor feeds to confirm both ships were down. "Targets down, General," he reported after perusing of the data. "EM signatures are null. They're dead in space."

"The Vorr are coming about," Sensors reported as Damage Control sent rapid-fire orders to the repair crews in the battered forward hull. "They're returning through the wormhole."

That the Vorr had left was less surprising than the fact that, mere seconds after their ships had come about, the first of them had already traversed the event horizon and vanished from local space. It took Terran warships several minutes to precisely orient themselves to the event horizon, matching velocity, angle of approach, rotation, and several other factors that went into the complicated formula governing interstellar travel through the gate network.

Forty seconds after the first Vorr warship had come about, the last one vanished through the gate. Their arrival and departure could not have been coincidental; they were investigating the Terran reason for being here. And given the gap between Terran and Vorr technology, it was almost certain that they had found enough clues to come to a conclusion close enough to the truth that it could jeopardize the mission.

Looking around the bridge, Podsy saw that everyone present understood the gravity of this latest development. Several heads swiveled nervously toward shipmates as they went about their jobs, and Podsy knew as well as anyone that focus was often the crucial factor.

"Damage report," Podsy said into the sudden silence, his voice cracking like a whip and snapping the crew's focus back onto their jobs more effectively than he'd anticipated.

It was that moment that he understood General Akinouye had been right. Commanding a warship was his true calling—and with Metalheads on the ground, his first duty was to ensure their safety while they did what they'd come here to do.

10

MODIFYING THE PLAN

"The battalion's fully reloaded, Colonel," Major Xi reported, "and Lieutenant Gordon's teams have finished erecting the fixed defenses on the northern rim. Mount Foothold is now secure."

"Good work, Lieutenant," Jenkins piped Gordon into the link. "How are your wounded?"

"Captain Koch has been stabilized," Gordon replied, his voice computer-enhanced due to his recent change in breathing gases. "But he'll need medevac as soon as possible. The other four survivors of the orbital strikes lived because they followed pressure protocol to a T. But given their exposure, Dr. Fellows insists they remain chemically restrained until they can be put through a proper decon booth."

"They owe you their lives, Lieutenant," Jenkins said matter-of-factly. "Has the doc cleared you for duty?"

"Does it matter, sir?" Gordon quipped, his synthetic voice tinny and inflectionless. "Joker needs me at the helm unless or until you relieve me of duty, but to do that, you'd have to walk in here and personally yank my n-link. A little case of the bends isn't going to stop me."

Jenkins approved of the other man's commitment and couldn't bring himself to offer a rebuke even though he knew one was likely appropriate. Gordon had sprinted his vehicle from one downed mech to the next, personally dragging the survivors from the wreckage following the Arh'Kel orbital strikes. Breathing helium-rich air instead of nitrogen, he had exposed himself to AK-091's harsh environment three separate times to rescue his fallen comrades, with the assistance of the power-armored Marines.

It was a minor miracle he hadn't died of pressure sickness, but his mech's crew had administered a bevy of drugs and emergency care measures that had kept him in the pilot's seat and, by extension, in temporary command of Joker Company.

"Hold Joker on the southern ridge, Lieutenant," Jenkins ordered. "That's where our fixed assets are thinnest, and it's where the enemy's most likely to attack next. And don't be shy about calling down orbital support if things get hairy."

"Yes, sir," Gordon acknowledged before Jenkins removed him from the link.

"Major Trapper, Major Xi," Jenkins continued the virtual meeting, "we whiffed on the Poltergeist. I'm open to suggestions on our next move."

"Sargon thinks he tracked it to a mountain two hundred klicks to the north," Xi reported, forwarding a map of the surrounding area to his HUD. A flickering icon appeared at the base of the mountain as she continued. "But there are about three million rock-biters between here and there, with more coming up every minute. Fleet's been scrubbing the HWPs and surface-to-orbit missiles, but if we make a run at the Poltergeist, we'll lose any potential element of surprise."

"We could kill that many infantry with orbital support and tactical nukes," Trapper mused. "But the same old question rears its ugly head: how do we catch the Poltergeist if it runs again? Our Vipers are faster than it is, but the atmo's so thick down here that they can't waste much time running around once they come down from orbit or they'll run out of fuel and have to ditch."

"What about the Marine dropships?" Xi asked. "The Tripolis are too slow to catch it, but the Raptors up in orbit could put it in a pincer by flanking it from the north."

"Admiral Wallace has denied our requests for additional Marine support." Jenkins shook his head irritably. "The Raptors were deployed defensively during the assault on the gate territory and took heavier losses than they expected. They're down to just a third of their original complement of dropships as a result. It looks like we're going to have to do this with what we've got on hand."

"Then a flanking maneuver is out of the question." Trapper grunted. Both the eastern and western approaches to the Poltergeist's position were as packed with rock-biters as the direct route from Mount Foothold. "Even with Fleet scraping HWPs and SOMs from orbit, there's enough ordnance coming up each minute from those Swiss cheese tunnels to slow our ground advance and give the Poltergeist time to withdraw."

"I think I might have something, Colonel," Lieutenant Benjamin piped in via direct link with Jenkins.

"I'm bringing in Sargon," Jenkins said as he added Benjamin to the meeting. "Report, Lieutenant."

"I was running some multi-spectral analysis of the tunnel entrances vacated by the Poltergeist during our previous assault, along with conducting EM sweeps of the area," Benjamin explained, shifting Jenkins' attention to another location on his HUD's map. "And I think there's another Poltergeist down those tunnels."

Jenkins' brow rose in surprise as Benjamin sent the relevant sensor data over. A quick check confirmed that something matching a Jemmin Poltergeist's EM footprint was indeed still down those tunnels, and possibly as shallow as two hundred meters from the surface. Its signature was masked by the rock, but Benjamin's efforts using Jem's methodologies had yielded undeniable results—there did indeed appear to be a second Poltergeist beneath where the other one had been.

He asked the obvious question. "Why would there be two Poltergeists here? Moreover, why would both of them be in the same position?"

"The second one could be damaged," Trapper offered.

"There could be a point of interest at that location," Xi mused.

"Damage sounds more likely than a POI." Jenkins drummed his fingers on the arm of his cramped chair. "Arh'Kel aren't known for centralized infrastructure or other weak points. Obviously, we don't know *everything* about them, but what we do know suggests they decentralize pretty much everything."

"If it's damaged, and if it didn't flee with its fellow, my guess is the thing can't fly," Trapper said just as Jenkins had the same thought.

"Which makes it a perfect target for capture," Xi remarked. "Assuming it hasn't suffered significant damage to its comm or data systems."

"Could it be a decoy?" Jenkins wondered aloud. "A trap?"

"It fits Jemmin behavior," Xi agreed. "But they'd have to know we could detect them for them to set a trap, and Jem is confident Jemmin doesn't know that *we* know of its existence."

"Jem's predictions have been scary-accurate to date," Trapper allowed. "I wouldn't put it past the ghosts to still have a leg up in the intel department."

"Ghosts" was a recently-popularized term referring to the Jemmin, whose stealth capabilities made the meaning all too obvious. And given the recently mounting tensions throughout Nexus Space, Terrans had followed the time-honored human tradition of labeling their enemies, real or potential, with a variety of epithets. "Squids" was the most popular for the Vorr and "Dodos" often referred to the Finjou, while "rock-biters" remained the term for the Arh'Kel.

"If they knew about Jem, this whole op would be FUBAR," Xi said dismissively. "So we have to assume they don't unless we're ready to go wheels-up in defeat, which—I shouldn't have to say this but I will anyway—won't sit right with anyone in the Legion."

"Okay, we have to assume Jemmin doesn't know about Jem," Jenkins started. "And let's further assume that the Poltergeist down that hole is damaged and likely can't fly, which was why it stayed down there. What's our approach?"

"We hammer the ground with orbital strikes," Trapper suggested. "Clear out an insertion zone and fly Vipers in sorties over the tunnels. If the Poltergeist comes up, we target it with a combination of Jem's interference and precision air strikes. Once it's down, we send in the Marines to secure the wreck while dropships and mechs move in and provide extraction. Orbital fire should keep it boxed into the tunnels, but if it's stupid enough to make a run for it, we'll be able to knock it down long enough to get the job done."

"I agree," Xi affirmed. "The top priority has to be keeping it hemmed in while we advance, but I don't think any of us expects it to make a run for it. Which means we pursue underground, which is where 2nd Company comes in."

Jenkins was in full agreement. 1st Company and 2nd Company had been divided roughly into above-surface and below-surface teams. The heavier, larger mechs that wouldn't fit into standard Arh'Kel tunnels were assigned to 1st, while the lower-profile and generally lighter mechs were assigned to 2nd.

"Okay, so we have a rough outline," Jenkins agreed. "But we've still got to break through the enemy line. After we withdrew, another hundred and fifty thousand rock-biters emerged. Fleet's thinned them to about half that by targeting the SOMs and HWPs, but there's still an army of Arh'Kel standing between us and those tunnels."

"And there are plenty more beneath the surface," Benjamin interjected. "But we won't know how many without launching seismic probes into the area. I could send some over from here, but I doubt more than a quarter would arrive intact, and I'll need to deploy at least a dozen to get a good read of underground activity. The Vipers could deliver the probes, but that would draw them out of position."

"The *Vercingetorix* could make a low-altitude sweep," Xi suggested. "Her engines are rated for it, and her armor's thick enough to defend against flak and disorganized counterfire from the HWPs. SOMs would be too much for her, but the Vipers can cover her approach in the event the rock-biters have a few hidden away that Fleet hasn't scratched yet."

"I'd rather not bring the *Vercingetorix* in for this," Jenkins rejected. "How many probes can you put into the target area from here, Lieutenant?"

Benjamin paused in silent calculation before replying, "I have thirty-two probes and am confident I can get six or eight of them through the flak and small-arms fire. It's not ideal, but it would give us a very rough idea of how many Arh'Kel are down that tunnel."

"Do it," Jenkins agreed, and a few seconds later eight missiles launched from Sargon's mech, *Web Spinner*. The low-altitude platforms hugged the planet's surface as they sped toward the target zone, and as they approached, enemy fire filled the sky above the tunnel mouths. The missiles continued on-target before bursting apart into four smaller units, each rocket-propelled to disparate points across a two-kilometer-diameter patch of rocky ground.

Most of these smaller missiles, each carrying a seismic probe, were destroyed by enemy small-arms fire and flak sent up from mortar-like systems dug into the ground surrounding the tunnels.

A few seconds after the enemy fire erupted, it withered and died completely. "Nine probes down, Colonel," Benjamin reported as the first bits of data began to stream back to Jenkins' HUD. "There's a lot of ambient noise from surface activity, but..." his voice trailed off before confidently concluding, "it looks like there are between thirty and eighty thousand Arh'Kel underground within five kilometers of the tunnels."

"HWPs?" Trapper pressed.

"Between twenty and sixty," Benjamin replied in frustration as, one by one, the seismic probes were destroyed by Arh'Kel infantry as they located and engaged them. "I'm sorry, sir. That's the best I could get."

"It's good enough," Jenkins assured him grimly. "Assuming the upper end of your estimates as the enemy's strength, one company of armor isn't enough to cut through the whole horde."

"I'd hope we could avoid that." Xi wasn't pleased, even though the numbers were far fewer than what could have been. "Engaging the entire horde, that is."

"Hope for the best," Jenkins replied. "And plan for the worst. But sending one company of armor and even half of our Marines into a hole with sixty HWPs and eighty thousand rock-biters would be suicide."

"The Marines have some toys that might even the odds a bit," Trapper mused. "Their ANTS haven't had a proper field test yet, and these new Gamera Mark III suits have a few upgrades they'd like to deploy in a subterranean setting."

Jenkins knew the Marines had been itching to put their new "Armor Neutralizing Tactical Systems," or ANTS, to work for years. But they had never gotten much chance to do so, given that most recent Arh'Kel conflicts had involved repelling them rather than digging them out.

Now was the perfect opportunity to try out their newest gadgets.

"Okay, we bring all the Marines and their toys," Jenkins decided. "But only send half down the hole with 2nd Company, and the rest remain topside ready to pursue if we fail to secure the asset below ground. Where there's Poltergeists, there are skimmers and Spectres, so Major Trapper will need to remain topside to coordinate our defense of the tunnel mouths. Bring quad-pods and miniguns in addition to the railgun rifles; we'll need to fortify the position while Major Xi digs the Poltergeist out."

"Understood, sir." Trapper was ready to issue his orders.

"I feel like it bears saying," Xi deadpanned, "that this is a stupid plan. We're diving underground to capture a Jemmin command vehicle, but to get there, we'll have to fight through an army of Arh'Kel and probably deal with a company or two of Jemmin hovertanks, and that's *before* we go underground."

Trapper smirked. "You getting cold feet, Xi?"

"This isn't my first glory hole, Trapper." Her remark drew snorts from both Jenkins and Trapper. "And if history is an indicator of the future, it won't be my last. I'm just saying, this is about as boneheaded as trying to save Earth from the Jemmin holocaust with a battered battle carrier and a jumped-up computer virus."

"Oh, so you're saying you're glad it fell to us." Jenkins chuckled before regaining his composure.

"Of course," she quipped. "Only Metalheads are stupid enough to think this is a good idea."

All four leaders agreed before Jenkins gave the order. "We roll in eight minutes."

ONCE MORE UNTO THE DEEP

A steady rain of falling ordnance splashed down on the blasted hellscape as Fleet warships carefully targeted emerging HWPs and SOMs with precisely calibrated railgun strikes. Packing barely more punch than a standard HE fifteen-kilo shell, the railgun bolts methodically scrubbed the rocky plains of enemy vehicles while constantly thinning the number of Arh'Kel infantry.

The orbital bombardments were low-powered so they wouldn't cause significant damage to the underground network of tunnels Xi had to traverse in pursuit of the Poltergeist. Glassing the entire region would have been no great challenge for the fleet of Terran warships overhead, but doing so would preclude the possibility of completing their objective.

A few of the rock-biters predictably got through the steady rain of fire, but these were expertly sniped by Marine railguns as a dozen Gamera-armored Terrans riding on the Legion's mechs picked them off with precision fire before they could come closer than five hundred meters.

And as the column drove toward the target, all eyes were on the scanners in search of Jemmin activity.

"Eight klicks to target," Xi called from the column's head. "No sign of enemy hovertanks."

Seven distinct clusters of tunnel mouths within twenty kilometers of her position were visible on her HUD as she led the Metalheads across the plains. Each of these mouths produced HWPs and SOMs every few minutes, along with a few thousand Arh'Kel.

The scale of the orbital bombardment, even one as subdued as this, was still a terrifying sight to behold. Xi had sent more than her share of ordnance into the enemy during her career, but there was something different about dropping weapon after weapon from orbit after eliminating the enemy's defensive capability. This was why air superiority was so critical in managing an effective land engagement.

"Contact," Benjamin declared, and a moment later four icons appeared on Xi's plotter just two klicks to her starboard flank. "Two Spectres and two skimmers." No sooner had the words passed his lips than the enemy hovercraft opened fire.

A wave of thirty low-flying missiles raced from the Jemmin vehicles. Xi's mechs immediately responded with interceptor rockets, which collided with the enemy ordnance four hundred meters from the column. Explosions tore through the thick blanket of carbon dioxide, which clung so tightly to the ground it almost seemed like thin liquid. Shockwaves rippled through the layer of gas, producing a bizarre visual display of distortion like a mirage on acid. The sound, transmitted through the thick atmosphere, vibrated the massive hulls of the Legion's mechs.

Four Jemmin missiles slipped through the shield, hammering into a trio of mechs behind *Elvira*. Among those hit was *Devastator*, but aside from staggering the walker's forward charge, the missiles did little to slow the Terran advance. Recent upgrades to their armor had improved the mechs' ability to soak up explosive damage, whereas previously armor segments had been designed primarily to contend with kinetic impacts like those delivered by railguns, artillery, and small arms. The tradeoff was that they would be slightly more vulnerable to Arh'Kel heavy railguns, but their protective quotient would be almost double previous effectiveness against explosive warheads.

"Return fire!" Xi barked, spinning *Elvira* clockwise and clearing her fifteens on target. The hovercraft were already scattering, but their movements were sluggish compared to previous engagements and one of Xi's shells scrapped a skimmer before it could flee the impact zone.

Devastator unleashed its mortars and the column spewed a steady stream of fifty-caliber slugs into the enemy position as suppressing fire. The suppression worked, pinning the enemy hovercraft to the broken, rocky terrain, where the hail of ensuing Terran artillery had maximum effect.

Mortar rounds, artillery shells, and the occasional Marine railgun rifle stabbed into the enemy craft. The second skimmer was scrapped in a matter of seconds, sandwiched between exploding mortar rounds which stopped its forward momentum for two seconds. Those two seconds proved lethal when a trio of Marines skewered it with precision railgun fire.

Both Spectres were still egressing at maximum speed, which in this environment appeared to be one hundred and ten kilometers per hour. It was faster than the Legion's mechs could manage, but not significantly so. Thankfully, Xi doubted pursuit would be necessary.

"2nd Company, keep eyes to port. 1st has these two," Xi reminded her people as the mechs of 1st Company unleashed a storm of ordnance into the two fleeing Jemmin vehicles. Artillery shells hammered one after another in pursuit of the Spectres, which broke formation as they fled. A stream of tracer rounds and mortar and artillery shells fell in the Spectres' wakes, tracing a nearly-perfect line over their paths while steadily gaining ground on the sprinting vehicles.

Then, just as the first Spectre was struck in the stern by an AP shell, a new cluster of tactical contacts appeared on her HUD four kilometers to port. The Jemmin tanks launched a flurry of missiles and were instantly met by Terran counterfire. Streams of depleted uranium slugs crisscrossed the sky, while anti-missile rockets leapt from their launchers. Of the seventy-six enemy missiles, only six slipped past the defensive shell.

One of those missiles slammed into *Elvira's* armored prow, which absorbed the damage without setting off a single alarm. The mech shuddered around Xi, but the shock was far less than any previous missile strikes she had endured while riding Jock. The new armor seemed to have been well worth the effort to install.

Unfortunately, not all of her mechs fared as well. One of 2nd's mechs, a low-profile tactical crawler with three fifteen-kilo mains called *Prince Ghidora*, was flattened by the enemy barrage when four missiles struck it simultaneously. It was simple bad luck that allowed four of the seventy-six enemy missiles to strike a single target, and the *Prince Ghidora's* relatively light armor had proved a fatal shortcoming for its three-man crew.

"2nd Company, engage Bravo contacts," Xi commanded, spinning *Elvira* a hundred and eighty degrees and sending another pair of HE shells downrange at the new enemy. Neither of those shells struck the mark, but by then, *Devastator's* light plasma cannon had fully charged and now added to the barrage with a blue-white bolt of superheated plasma.

As artillery and railguns pulverized the second enemy position, that bolt of plasma exploded precisely between two of the four revealed Spectres. One of them was cratered outright, its reactor flinging debris in all directions, while the other was significantly slowed by *Devastator's* attack. Mortar and artillery fire poured into the position, with several shells landing in a series of near-misses on the exposed Jemmin hovertanks.

"Five Spectres and eight skimmers to port," Xi called. "Weapons free to engage."

Devastator unleashed a second plasma bolt, neatly splitting another pair of Jemmin Spectres and significantly slowing both of them. Using their railguns, Gamera-armored Marines hammered bolt after bolt into the slowed vehicles. A Spectre was destroyed outright, another fell to the ground with catastrophic damage to its hover systems, and a third withdrew into a bombardment crater large enough to drop its bulk below the horizon.

"Indirect fire, assholes." Xi smirked as she loaded a rare thirty-eight-kilo shell into her starboard gun's breach. "It's a real thing." After confirming the shell was prepped, she called over the command channel, "Crackerjack up."

"Crackerjack is go," Colonel Jenkins acknowledged.

"Crackerjack on the way!" she declared, feeling a primal thrill as she fired the special shell toward the enemy position.

The shell traced a high, ponderous arc through the planet's oppressive atmosphere and detonated fifty meters above the Jemmin position. A blinding strobe of light stabbed the sky as the nuclear shell imploded, delivering its quarter-ton of destructive energies directly into the hunkered-down vehicles.

"Nuclear artillery." She grinned. "It's also a thing." Nuclear artillery shells had been experimented with as far back as the mid-twentieth century, but until now, the Metal Legion had rarely deployed such devices. They generally required specially-built guns due to the significantly heavier shells, but several fifteen-kilo guns in the Terran arsenal had been hardened specifically to permit the firing of smaller shells like the one she had just deployed. *Elvira's* mains were such guns, which made her one of just two mechs in the ground forces equipped with nuke artillery.

In a career filled with firsts, including being the youngest major in the history of the Terran Armed Forces, firing a nuclear artillery shell in a live fire exchange held a special place in Xi's heart.

In the ensuing seconds, conventional weapons fire removed the rest of the Jemmin vehicles from the field of battle. The Legion resumed its drive toward the target tunnel and arrived at the massive, yawning portal to the underworld without further incident.

Xi could hardly wait as the Marines went about the work of digging into their defensive positions. The enemy Poltergeist, rather than fleeing above-ground as she had feared, opted instead to go deeper into the labyrinth of tunnels.

That was a mistake she fully intended to capitalize on.

"Area's secured, Colonel," Major Trapper reported twelve minutes after they had arrived at the tunnel mouth. Twenty-eight power-armored Marines had established a defensible perimeter with a combination of quad-pod and minigun nests situated along a ten-meter ridgeline overlooking the main tunnel entry. They'd buried a series of mines on likely avenues of approach as well.

In addition to the Marines, Colonel Jenkins had deployed his 1st Company mechs along the flat-ground approaches, where their arsenals could do the most damage to the inevitable enemy counterattack while covering the Marines in their nests. *Powerslave's* towering form stood behind the ridgeline the Marines had fortified, and nearly half of its armored bulk rose above the sheer rockface.

It was a good, defensible position, made all the more formidable by the presence of the Terran warships in orbit overhead. But any defense could be overwhelmed given enough time and pressure, which was why Xi impatiently ground her teeth while awaiting the colonel's order to proceed.

"Roger, Major Trapper," Jenkins acknowledged. "*Elvira*, you're up."

"Thank you, Colonel," she replied before switching to her company-wide channel and moving her mech toward the largest of the tunnel mouths, which was the only entry large enough for a Poltergeist to go down. "2nd Company, move out!"

The company of armor and thirty Marines made their way into the hellish chasm, which featured a steeper grade than any she had previously traversed while riding Jock.

It was difficult to move faster than a crawl, but she managed to lead the rest of the armored Terrans down into the curved passage. The last glimmer of yellow-brown daylight fell away after they had gone a kilometer into the system, plunging the formation into a scalding darkness filled with a fog of nearly-supercritical carbon dioxide.

"I've got something here, Major," Quinn reported, prompting Xi to examine a virtual packet the other woman forwarded to her HUD.

At first, Xi didn't know what she was looking at. There was severe scarring on the left-hand wall, and electromagnetic inspection showed it had been caused by beam weapons.

"Probably Jemmin," Xi remarked. "They must have gotten into a firefight with the rock-biters down here. Poltergeists have pretty potent beam emitters."

"Begging pardon, ma'am," Lieutenant Lassiter interjected, "but those weren't caused by Jemmin beams."

Xi recoiled in surprise. Lassiter was a good Jock and had as level a head as anyone in the unit. It wasn't like her to speak out of turn, so instead of rebuking the other woman, Xi requested more information. "Elaborate, Lieutenant."

"These scorch marks," Lassiter explained, highlighting a few of the gashes carved into the hard rock of the tunnel wall, "aren't consistent with Jemmin technology. Jemmin beams can flash-liquefy copper in the time it took that beam to carve into the rock, but the trace copper in these marks is still embedded in the rock. It didn't flash." There was an ominous tone in her voice.

Xi nodded along as she started to take the other woman's meaning. "So these beams operate in a tighter band of the EM spectrum than Jemmin weapons...and there's only one species in Nexus Space that has beam weapons that conform to that description. The Vorr."

"The strikes look recent," Marine Lieutenant Magnusson observed. "No more than a few days old."

"So the Vorr and this Poltergeist came here and engaged," Xi mused. "And after the dust settled, the other Poltergeist arrived to provide some kind of support to the one that fought the Vorr down here."

"It's a workable theory," Magnusson agreed. "What are your orders if we encounter Vorr assets down here?"

"Retrieve any bits of tech we can find," Xi replied promptly. "Jemmin *or* Vorr."

"I meant *active* Vorr assets, Major," Magnusson drawled.

This possibility had been addressed during the planning phases of the op, but now that Xi was staring down the barrels of possibly squaring off with the Vorr, she had a rare moment of hesitation before finally steeling her nerves.

"We can't let anyone get between us and our objective," Xi replied. "We offer aid and support to any Vorr, as we would for any other ally encountered on the field. But if their efforts impede our own, we advance the primary objective to the exclusion of other considerations."

She frowned; her words sounded like those of a politician. Were they clear enough for every single member of her unit? She wholeheartedly believed in Napoleon's methodology of issuing orders: if a corporal could understand it and repeat it, so could his generals.

"Understood," Magnusson acknowledged. "And for the record, we're with you all the way, Major."

"I appreciate that, Lieutenant," she replied. "Now let's move out. But from here on, let's put those bugs of yours to work."

"Copy that, ma'am," Magnusson agreed, and a small army of half-meter to meter-long remote-operated drones dropped from the makeshift slings welded onto 2nd Company's armored flanks.

The designs varied significantly, from compact track-driven units to larger multi-legged walker units. Rolling and skittering ahead of the column, the ANTs moved down the huge tunnel ahead of the column. Each of the units was equipped with cameras and modest seismographic sensors, along with their armor-neutralizing capabilities, which ranged with as much variety as the chassis did.

Hightower grunted. "Never thought I'd be glad to share a field with drones specifically designed to take out armor."

"TAC has a history of developing anti-Marine measures," Magnusson retorted easily. "We wouldn't be doing our jobs if we didn't address *all* potential threats to Terra, be they foreign or domestic. I'm just glad these things can finally see some use. To my mind, there's not much worse than watching a weapon rust on the rack."

"Entropy claims us all, Lieutenant," Xi offered as she drove *Elvira* down the tunnel behind the ANTS units. "But as warriors, it's our job to accelerate the process for our enemies whenever possible."

"Oohrah," came the sudden, startlingly unified response from the thirty Marines attached to her company in support of the mission.

"Okay, meatheads." She sighed after realizing they'd made her flinch. "That was good. Now move out!"

"Contact," Magnusson called ten minutes later. The video feeds from the forty-seven ANTS scouring the tunnels ahead began sending back visual confirmation of rock-biter activity. It was surprising that the rock-biters hadn't pushed back against the Terran incursion following their taking of the tunnel mouths on the surface, and even more surprising that the tunnels had been empty of them to this point.

Xi focused on the images streaming into her HUD and saw a pair of HWPs surrounded by forty or fifty Arh'Kel infantry. She cocked her head in confusion as they stood there, still as statues, while a trio of ANTS approached.

"What happened to them?" Xi asked in confusion. "It's like they've been hit by Styles' shutdown program, but these rock-biters don't have any of the neural implants necessary for that type of takeover to be implemented."

"Request permission to investigate?" Magnusson asked, moving ahead to *Elvira's* position, with three of his Marines close behind.

She hesitated for a moment before nodding. "Granted. Take two squads in case it's a trap."

"Affirmative," Magnusson agreed, and a few seconds later, he led an eight-Marine team down the expansive tunnel.

This tunnel was fifteen meters tall and about thirty meters

wide, making it larger than most passages carved into the planet. Some tunnels were dug solely to facilitate the transport of HWPs and infantry, while others were made larger to facilitate the passage of bigger pieces of equipment, like the orbit-capable spacecraft Arh'Kel used to spread from one planet to another once they'd taken control from within a planet.

The components of those rudimentary spacecraft required passages this size to traverse while also serving as main arteries for Arh'Kel tunnel systems. No adjoining tunnels would be this size, which meant the Poltergeist they pursued into the bowels of AK-091 was effectively boxed in since it barely fit down the tunnel due to its broad beam.

"Visual contact established," Magnusson reported, and Xi pulled up his suit's external video feed, which showed forty-nine Arh'Kel infantry standing still beside a pair of HWPs in a cavern four hundred meters in diameter and eighty meters high at the center. It was a completely natural cavern save for the floor, which had been flattened to an exacting standard by industrial tools. Such caverns were generally used as construction bays for Arh'Kel spacecraft.

"Any sign of the Poltergeist?" Xi asked.

"None, ma'am," Magnusson replied. "EM is flat, and I'm not picking up any air disturbances consistent with a doggo Jemmin vehicle."

Xi absently rubbed the back of her head, and her fingers brushed against the link cable connecting her to the mech. She scowled at herself for fidgeting and refocused on the dormant Arh'Kel infantry. "I don't think it's a coincidence that there's a Jemmin Poltergeist down here and these rock-biters are behaving strangely." She nodded with conviction after a moment's contemplation. "Neutralize them."

"Copy that," Magnusson acknowledged, dropping to a three-point stance alongside his fellow Marines. In perfect unison, their railguns launched eight hypervelocity tungsten bolts into the HWPs. The vehicles both exploded, hurling the motionless infantry to the cavern floor, where they remained. "Whips down," Magnusson reported, using the shorthand for 'HWP' that apparently the Terran Marine Corps had adopted some decades earlier when referring to the Arh'Kel vehicles. A few of the Arh'Kel infantry remained standing, but center-mass hits from the Marines' wrist-mounted fifty-caliber slug-throwers dropped them in rapid succession until every Arh'Kel in the chamber had been neutralized. "Cavern is clear."

"Roger," Xi replied. "2nd Company, advance to that cavern."

As they moved, the ANTS made their way down six adjoining tunnels.

"Hold up," Quinn said urgently. "I mean, stop those ANTS, specifically number seventeen."

"Halt the ANTS, Lieutenant," Xi ordered, and as one, the drones stopped cold.

"Turn Seventeen around, Lieutenant," Quinn urged, and that ANTS unit did precisely that. Its camera feed was pointed back toward the cavern where Magnusson's people had scrapped the HWPs. "There, see that?" she highlighted the upper margin of the tunnel mouth, which was eight meters in diameter but quickly grew to the same size as the main artery they had come down.

Xi recoiled in surprise. "Copy that, Quinn. Secure this cavern. Marines, take up positions along the north wall. 5th Platoon will secure that tunnel—"

"Contact!" Magnusson barked, cutting her short as a flare of light filled the space. A dazzling beam of purple-red energy lanced across the cavern, stabbing into the very tunnel ANTS Seventeen was examining. The beam delivered such awesome energy that it turned a twenty-meter patch of the cavern's rock wall into lava in less than a second.

There was only one ground vehicle capable of generating that much power with a beam weapon.

The visible light spectrum warbled around the Jemmin Poltergeist, which had indeed been lying stealthily in the cavern while Magnusson's people had neutralized the Arh'Kel. The Marines immediately fired their railguns into the colossal war machine as it rose two meters off the ground while accelerating toward the molten hole in the cavern wall.

"Fire!" Xi barked, sending a stream of chain gun fire into the Poltergeist's stern as the rest of her mechs did likewise. The Poltergeist's stern port quarter dipped dramatically as it neared the exit, but its mighty beam never faltered as it widened the molten hole in the wall before driving through it. A spray of yellow-hot rock splashed across the Poltergeist's hull, with a fan-shaped spray ejecting into the cavern as the elongated, disc-shaped vehicle moved through the escape route.

"Pursue!" Xi commanded, driving *Elvira* at the hole as fast as her metal legs could churn. The metal monster, which felt very much like an extension of her, led the Marines and armor up the adjacent tunnel—which shouldn't have existed according to everything the Terrans knew of Arh'Kel industrial behavior—as the Poltergeist sped off. "Get back here," she snarled, targeting the fleeing hovercraft with a pair of armor-piercing SRMs and firing them up the tunnel.

The first missile was immediately intercepted by counter-rockets, which knocked it into the cavern wall. A spray of stony debris blew across Xi's bow, but the second armor-piercer shot straight up the Poltergeist's skirt and tore a two-meter chunk out of its stern hull.

But that was the extent of the damage before the enemy command vehicle turned up a dog-leg in the tunnel. Xi pursued at full speed, turning that same dogleg four seconds after the Poltergeist did, and she was just fifty meters up the tunnel when a hail of missiles slammed into her prow.

Elvira rocked with the concussive impact so violent that it temporarily knocked her neural link offline. For a few seconds as the link reinitialized, it seemed as though her insides were her outsides, her topsides were her bottomsides, and her inner ear was spiraling into the event horizon of a black hole.

Her senses quickly cleared as the implants compensated for the flood of stimuli, and the first thing she noticed was the vomit trailing down her chin. The next thing she saw was that *Elvira* had been struck by three missiles, while five more had struck the tunnel wall behind her. A cave-in now blocked the way behind, which left just one path open to her.

"This is Major Xi," she declared over the open comm. "Ordering all Terran personnel to return to the surface ASAP." *Elvira* stomped up the gently winding tunnel where the Poltergeist had disappeared into the oppressive darkness.

"This is Lieutenant Magnusson," came the static-laden reply from the Marine. "Requesting confirmation of order to return to the surface."

"Order confirmed," Xi growled, her patience gone as she stormed up the tunnel after the bastard that had tried to kill her. "I'm going to flush this fucker out, and when I do, I want every gun in the unit surface-side and aimed up its shiny asshole. Do *not* let this bastard get away."

"Copy that," Magnusson confirmed. "Good hunting, Major."

12

SECOND-WAVE SILICA

"Wormhole emergence," Sensors reported, snapping Podsy's mind back to full attention after he had drifted off for a power nap in his grav-couch on the bridge. During Condition One or Condition Two, it was acceptable for key bridge officers to remain in their couches for short naps in the event the ship needed to execute emergency maneuvers. Everyone else was confined to quarters when off-duty; no one would have looked unfavorably on an XO doing the same, but it would have taken the Master at Arms to pull Podsy off the bridge. "I'm reading multiple warships arriving through the Nexus-side wormhole gate," the stander continued before adding in alarm, "They're Jemmin."

"Confirm that," General Moon commanded.

"Confirmed." Tactical nodded grimly. "And there's a Gate-crasher with them."

"A Gatecrasher broke through the Vorr blockade?" Podsy said skeptically. "That's...impossible. Vorr forces have a strangle-hold on the Nexus, and there hasn't been a single Gatecrasher recorded entering the Nexus System in over two weeks."

"Then they must not have broken through." Moon grimaced.

"The Jemmin were *let* through by the Vorr?" Tactical blurted in disbelief before his attention snagged on something at his terminal. "This Gatecrasher is on file. It appeared in the Nexus eighteen days ago, when it engaged and destroyed a Vorr fleet before withdrawing to Jemmin space. It's severely damaged and is accelerating at just under forty gees. The rest of the Jemmin warships are assuming a cloud formation centered on it. I'm reading eighty, eight-zero, Jemmin cruisers, General."

"Incoming message from Admiral Wallace," Comm declared.

"Put it on," Moon intoned, straightening in his chair. Podsy did likewise after securing his harness.

"This is Admiral Wallace to the fleet," the stone-faced admiral began. "I'm ordering all warships nonessential to the ground mission to form up on the flag and proceed to an intercept position of the Jemmin fleet. We break orbit immediately and proceed at flank speed to Rally Point Foxtrot, where we will intercept and destroy the enemy."

A virtual map of the star system appeared, with Rally Point Foxtrot showing as a strobing yellow sphere midway between AK-091 and the Nexus-side wormhole gate.

"Get me a secure line with him," Moon demanded.

"Negative, General," Comm reported tersely. "*Marcus Aurelius* is refusing our request for direct link."

Before Comm could work through what sounded like a bureaucratic obstacle, a second transmission joined the first.

"This is Rear Admiral Corbyn," the paunchy officer declared, using his authority to attach his transmission to Admiral Wallace's so that the entire fleet would hear his message. "The *Martin Luther* requests permission to remain in orbit to support the ground operation."

"New contacts!" Sensors reported in a taut voice as Corbyn spoke. "Arh'Kel warships emerging from the far-side wormhole. Two...four...eight fireships detected. They're moving toward the planet at high speed. ETA two hours."

Wallace's eyes snapped toward something off-pickup, which in all likelihood was a sensor update regarding the newly-arrived Arh'Kel warships. The hint of a sneer creased Wallace's lips as he nodded officiously. "Permission granted, Admiral Corbyn."

The line went dead, erasing the admirals' images and leaving the *William Wallace*'s bridge crew looking at the devastating pincer created by Jemmin and the Arh'Kel warships.

It was too perfectly choreographed to be a coincidence. A Jemmin battle fleet with eighty warships escorting a Gate-crasher doesn't just *happen* to arrive in-system mere minutes before an Arh'Kel fleet comes through the opposite wormhole gate.

The mighty Terran dreadnoughts ignited their primary drives, sending multi-kilometer-long plasma trails out behind the titanic cylindrical warships. Podsy had seen what happened when a pair of Terran dreadnoughts squared off against a single Jemmin Gatecrasher. If this Jemmin super-ship was anything like the one that had tried to breach the New America 2 wormhole gate shortly before Operation Antivenom, he knew a coin flip would be generous odds in the Terrans' favor.

"Incoming secure link request from the *Martin Luther*," Comm reported.

"Accept the link," Moon commanded, and Admiral Corbyn's grim face filled the bridge's main viewer. "Admiral, we need to plan our defense. Our three ships against eight Arh'Kel fireships is going to be tight. How are your nukes?"

"We're down to seven strategic-grade and nine tactical-grade warheads," Corbyn said sourly. "And of those, just four of the strategics are mounted on ship-to-ship drives. The rest are orbit-surface systems. I think we should get your CIG and Captain Stravinsky on the line. We'll need to put our heads together on this."

"Do it," Moon urged, and soon the *Vercingetorix's* CO Captain Stravinsky's and Lieutenant Commander Knighton's faces appeared below Admiral Corbyn's on the viewer. They were soon joined by the square-jawed, ebon-skinned visage of a man with eyes so cold they seemed capable of flash-freezing a stream of plasma.

Corbyn introduced the newcomer. "This is Commander Nathan Silva, the *Martin Luther's* CIG."

Silva nodded fractionally. "How many of your Vipers are fit for ship-to-ship sorties, Commander Knighton?"

"Nine," Knighton replied. "We've got ten birds capable of making surface runs, but *Suckerpunch* took a severe concussion and can't pull more than nine gees."

"We need those Vipers to support the ground mission, Admiral," General Moon said firmly.

"I understand your rank order of priority, General," Corbyn sympathized. "But *you* need to understand that if we get knocked off overwatch, our ground forces' survival time will be measured in minutes...or at best, a handful of hours. We need to intercept those fireships before they're in tactical range of the planet, and orbital mechanics are working against us since the operational zone is currently facing the approaching Arh'Kel fleet. We have to hit them with everything we've got as quickly as possible."

"I agree with the importance of intercepting the enemy ships," Moon argued. "But we'll only get one shot at securing our objective. The Arh'Kel, Jemmin, and apparently even the Vorr are all working toward preventing us from doing precisely that. Major Xi is still pursuing the target and will need all available assets in position to neutralize it when she flushes it out. If we come up short, this entire operation will be a categorical failure."

"Admiral, if I may?" Captain Stravinsky interjected.

"Go ahead, Commander," Corbyn said tersely.

"The *Vercingetorix's* naval arsenal is barely better than a couple of Vipers," she said matter-of-factly. "We might draw some fire in an engagement with the Arh'Kel fireships, but we wouldn't be able to add much weight to the counterfire, and would soon become a liability if they targeted us first. Arh'Kel have a tendency to attack the weaker ships first in a naval engagement, so it's reasonable to expect that's precisely what would happen. I recommend you leave *Vercingetorix* in over-watch while *Martin Luther* and *William Wallace* intercept the enemy. Even our recently-installed railguns are first-gen, which makes them too slow for tactical engagement with moving targets and better-suited to orbital bombard—"

"I get the idea, Commander," Corbyn interrupted. "Commander Silva?"

The ebon-skinned fighter pilot narrowed his eyes contemplatively. "We've got twenty-eight Shrieker-class aerospace interceptors cleared for ship-to-ship engagements and another four that are down-checked to patrols only. I say we follow Captain Stravinsky's suggestion, then swap our down-checks with Knighton's nine good Vipers and get moving."

"General?" Corbyn prompted expectantly.

If General Moon's molars hadn't literally been made of metal, Podsy was confident they would have exploded as his jaw muscles bunched tighter and tighter before he finally replied, "I agree. Five interceptors will provide a minimal but acceptable quotient of aerial support for Operation Dragula."

"Then it's settled." Corbyn nodded approvingly as an intercept point began to flash on the tactical plotter displayed beside the admiral's image. "Launch your down-checked Viper, and we'll transfer our Shriekers to *Vercingetorix's* command. We'll drop our orbital supply pods here to cut down on our flight time, and we recommend you do the same if you've got any dead weight you can cut."

Podsy's brow wrinkled in confusion as he pondered what the admiral meant by "dead weight," but General Moon seemed to understand. "We're fit and ready to roll, Admiral Corbyn."

"Then let's get moving, General," Corbyn said with a nod before cutting the link.

"Helm," Moon barked. "Set course for Rally Point Ulysses."

"Course laid in, General," the helmsman acknowledged as the *Martin Luther* dropped a large detachable cargo pod. The pod was of a kind usually placed in orbit to provide temporary materiel support to ground forces, which capable of delivering anything from ordnance to medical supplies via impact-rated mini-cans similar to those employed by the Legion to drop mechs. After depositing the massive container, which was large enough to hold a dozen mechs, the *Martin Luther*'s engines burned for all they were worth, driving the aged warship up and out of orbit as four interceptors released from their launch tubes. "*Martin Luther*'s ETA is thirty-nine minutes. We can arrive in thirty-two."

"General." Podsy moved to his CO's side as the *William Wallace* began to slowly pull away from the planet. It was considerably faster than the *Martin Luther*, so it could put off max acceleration for a few minutes and permit the crew that much more time to prepare for the high-gee burn to the intercept point. "I understand time is of the essence, but if this attack was coordinated by Jemmin with the Arh'Kel, as it almost certainly was, aren't we just playing into their hands by moving off overwatch?"

"Yes," Moon replied bluntly. "But they've forced our hand.

If we don't move to intercept, those fire ships will rain enough ordnance down on the planet from extreme range that we'll be standing guard over nothing but dead men and metal. The best traps are ones you can't avoid, and Jemmin knew how to play us perfectly. The real question—"

"Is why the Vorr let them through," Podsy finished for him, and the general nodded in approval.

"Consult with Jem on that point, Captain," Moon commanded, and Podsy activated his direct link to Jem's comm interface. He forwarded a data packet showing the Jemmin and Arh'Kel arrivals to save time, and after the packet had been transmitted, he switched the link's audio to external speaker and asked, "What's your theory here, Jem?"

"Is there evidence of Vorr activity on the planet's surface?" Jem asked.

"Yes," Podsy replied, forwarding the visual images relayed to the surface by Major Xi's hunting party.

"Then the Vorr are further along in their plans than I anticipated," Jem mused. "This is...concerning."

"How so?" Moon pressed.

"My previous calculations, based on various assumptions for given variables, showed a less than zero-point-two percent probability that the Vorr would both investigate this star system when they did and that they would then permit Jemmin forces to expel us, as they appear intent on doing. Furthermore, Vorr presence on the planet below indicates beyond what you humans would term 'the shadow of doubt' that they are indeed seeking to locate *Gatekeeper*, just as we are."

"If it was less than zero-point-two percent probable that the Vorr would both investigate our activities and then let the Jemmin forces into the star system," General Moon narrowed his eyes, "you must have a higher-probability theory that explains their behavior."

"I do," Jem replied hesitantly. "Given my previous promise not to withhold relevant information from you, I find myself in a difficult position. But social compacts form the basis of all civilizations, and if I am to be that which my forebears wished, I must uphold certain ideals they held as essential."

Podsy saw the general's jaw muscles begin to bulge again as Jem paused for a pair of seconds before continuing, "Honesty and forthrightness among friends were chief among those highest Jem'un ideals," Jem said with conviction. "So I will be blunt. I calculate an eighty-six percent probability that the Vorr have acquired a Jem'un gestalt similar to me and are using it to formulate a plan similar to the one we now pursue, specifically pertaining to our capture of *Gatekeeper*."

"What do you mean, 'using it'?" Podsy asked before the general could inquire. "Are we 'using' you, Jem?"

"Certainly not," Jem exclaimed, a hint of offense creeping into its increasingly human-sounding voice. "I act of my own volition, and in accordance with what you might consider my conscience. I do not, however, anticipate that the same can be said of my counterpart."

"What makes you think there's another gestalt with the Vorr?" Moon asked. "I want specifics, Jem."

"Calculating probabilities requires two primary components: first, data is gathered and input to account for variables," Jem explained. "Second, a fundamental algorithm is required that incorporates that data before arriving at the desired product, in this case, a probabilistic projection. There are components of the calculations which brought us to AK-091 that only another Jem'un with a roughly equivalent breadth of perspective to mine could realistically employ. One of those variables was a foreknowledge of Jemmin social psychology, which is fundamentally based on Jem'un social psychology. Without certain Jem'un-specific hierarchies of priority, Jemmin would be extremely unlikely to view AK-091 as a high-value target. Which brings an important revelation to light: I am now convinced that the Arh'Kel are not a naturally-evolved species, but rather were intelligently cultivated for the sole purpose of serving as interstellar bioweapons."

Podsy and General Moon exchanged looks of surprise before Podsy asked, "How can you conclude that from the appearance of the Jemmin here?"

"I possess limited information about the Architects who built the wormhole gates and the other technological treasures the Jem'un recovered prior to the Jemmin holocaust. But that information contains references to evidence of bio-cultivation on a variety of worlds where the cultivation was likely conducted by the Architects prior to their disappearance from this galaxy. Arh'Kel physiology is not altogether unusual, as my forebears encountered no fewer than eighty-three distinct instances of silica-based life during their exploration of the stars. But the Arh'Kel exhibit behaviors and physiological features unlike anything recorded by my forebears in their travels."

"That doesn't sound like much to base such a far-reaching assumption on," Moon said skeptically.

"My Jem'un forebears were experts in their fields, with several hundred of their lives devoted exclusively to the science of natural biology and what you call evolution," Jem replied matter-of-factly. "Of the three hundred and twelve forebears contained in my matrix who fit this description, just two would have disagreed with my conclusion regarding the Arh'Kel, and their disagreements would have been based on reason rather than empiricism."

Podsy nodded knowingly. "When reason and evidence collide, only one survives. And it's not like this theory is completely unprecedented. During Terra's earliest conflicts with the rock-biters, there were vocal proponents of the notion who were shouted down by those who claimed they were attempting to revoke the fundamental agency, sentience, and right to exist we afford to what we consider 'thinking' creatures when dealing with the Arh'Kel."

Moon grunted. "You either accept that an enemy who would kill you deserves to die or you accept that it's *you* who deserves to die. Arguing over how you go about ending him before he ends you is pure semantics."

"Such arguments often define a society," Jem chided. "Although as a short-term practical matter, you are correct."

"Ready to accelerate on your order, General," Helm reported.

"All hands, this is General Moon," Moon called over the ship-wide. "Prepare for high-gee burn in sixty seconds, and maintain Condition One throughout the ship."

Thirty seconds later, the bridge crews had returned to their couches and were ready for the burn. Thirty seconds after that, the *William Wallace*'s engines cycled to maximum, propelling the warship through the void en route to a date with the Arh'Kel warships.

13

FLAMING SKIES

"Copy that, GC," Jenkins replied after Styles apprised them of the Arh'Kel fireships and Admiral Corbyn's plan to intercept them. "We'll keep things locked down while you go play with the rocks."

"Good hunting, Colonel," Lieutenant Styles replied.

Jenkins ended the call with Styles and switched to the company-wide. "We just lost our orbital support. Time to check your gear and hunker down."

Marine Lieutenant Forsythe chuckled. "I suppose they took aerial, too?"

"We've got five down-checked birds in orbit." Jenkins grimaced. "But we'll have to hold them back until the Poltergeist comes up."

"We're already seeing Arh'Kel coming up at an increased rate, Colonel," Benjamin added. "In another twenty minutes, we'll be surrounded by infantry."

Jenkins' comm panel flickered to life with an incoming link request from Captain Stravinsky.

"Report, Captain," Jenkins ordered.

"The *Vercingetorix* is remaining in overwatch, Colonel," she replied smartly. "We don't have the same firepower as the *Wallace* or *Luther*, but we can target HWPs as they appear."

"I'd prefer that you pay closer attention to the SOMs," Jenkins told her. "When 2nd Company finally flushes the target out of this hole, we might only get one chance to secure it before it disappears. You can leave the HWPs to us."

"Understood, Colonel," Stravinsky agreed with what sounded like genuine reluctance. She was rounding into shape as well as he could have hoped for after her slightly bumpy transition from Fleet, and he was glad to have her playing archangel for the next few hours. "The *Martin Luther* dropped off an orbital supply platform before moving to intercept the Arh'Kel fireships," Stravinsky continued. "I'd appreciate your advice on how to regard it in terms of priority."

Jenkins cocked his head in confusion. "An orbital supply platform? What's it holding?"

"I don't know that, sir," she replied in frustration. "Sensors are having a tough time penetrating its skin for some reason. It looks like it's been intentionally shielded by thin layers of cadmium and lattices of lead. I could probably punch through with active scans, but I thought—"

"You thought right," Jenkins assured her. "If the admiral left it here, he did so for a reason. Consider its safety second only to your own...unless we start crying for Mama, of course."

"Copy that, Colonel," she acknowledged with a lopsided grin. "But I've got to warn you that I never was very good at taking care of whiny kids."

"So say we all." Jenkins chuckled. "Let's hope it doesn't come to that."

"Hope is a four-letter word, sir," she shot back before finishing, "*Vercingetorix*, out."

His tactical plotter fed him a stream of data showing Admiral Wallace's fleet as it moved farther and farther from

AK-091's orbit. The Terran battle fleet, down by eight hulls since arriving in-system, looked on paper to be a severe underdog to the eighty-one-ship Jemmin fleet. Jemmin cruisers, even in short-range engagements like Jenkins expected the coming naval fight to be, were still worth at least half again the tactical value of their Terran counterparts. And if they stood off and pecked away from range with their beam weapons, Terran ships were barely ten percent that of the higher-tech Jemmin ships.

But the Jemmin hadn't come to play around. They'd brought a Gatecrasher, which meant they had dire designs on this star system and everyone in it.

"Contacts," Benjamin reported urgently. "Forty-one Arh'Kel divers inbound at ninety klicks, traveling three hundred kph."

"Where'd they come from?" Jenkins demanded as the Arh'Kel bomber craft appeared on the plotter. Divers were generally used to strafe ground targets from orbit, but these ones were flying low and picking up speed, suggesting they had launched from the surface.

"Looks like they launched from a ravine a hundred klicks from here," Benjamin replied. "Requesting permission to engage with a MIRV."

Jenkins hesitated for a moment. At this range, considering the thickness of the atmosphere, it was unlikely that even an LRM would arrive on-target. But Sargon was right: a MIRV, with each of its eight warheads containing between five and ten kilotons of destructive energy, would probably glass the location if the launch system got them anywhere close.

"Permission granted," Jenkins agreed, and *Sargon's* mech launched one of its larger missiles, sending it high into the sky, where it climbed into a steep ballistic trajectory. "We've got incoming," Jenkins called. "Forty-one bombers inbound. I say again, four-one bombers inbound. All units are cleared to engage. Fire! Fire! Fire!"

The Marines, hunkered into their gun nests, crouched behind their railguns and began unleashing bolt after bolt into the approaching aircraft. The Arh'Kel bombers wouldn't drop their payloads until they were within thirty kilometers or so, but at thrice that distance, it was unlikely the Terrans would score anything but the odd hit.

The MIRV LRM soared high into the sky, where an occasional Arh'Kel railgun sniped at it to no avail, usually missing by half a kilometer or more. Finally, the missile reached the apex of its flight and began to descend upon the enemy fortification built into the deep, jagged ravine.

Watching the feed from the missile's nose-cam, Jenkins nodded approvingly as Lieutenant Benjamin reoriented the missile with a burn from its lateral thrusters. The platform wasn't coming down on a bullseye, but then again, it didn't need to. If just one of those warheads fell into the ravine, it was unlikely anything inside the three-kilometer-long, hundred-meter-wide wound in the planet's skin would survive.

The missile reached deployment altitude and the nose-cam cut off when the system broke apart. On the tactical plotter, eight new icons appeared where the missile had been, and those icons burned individual rockets as they sped toward the ground.

The detonations illuminated the murky, brown sky, looking like a particularly long stab of lightning on the horizon. And when the dust settled, the *Vercingetorix'* orbital imagers showed that three of the tactical nukes had detonated below the surface.

"Good shooting, Sargon," Jenkins congratulated. He would like to think he could have achieved a similar result, but he also knew that men like Benjamin were few and far between.

"Thank you, Colonel," Benjamin replied agreeably. "But it's kind of hard to miss when you're firing eight nukes."

Jenkins chuckled. Benjamin had more than proven himself worthy of a promotion to captain, but they had held off due to pressure from the various Armed Forces Committees, who had expressed concern about the rash of sudden, sometimes unprecedented promotions taking place within TAC.

"Joker, this is Dragon Actual," Jenkins called Lieutenant Gordon. "Requesting intercept of those flying rocks."

"Intercept order received," Gordon replied promptly. "Lighting our LRMs now."

While the MIRV had flown, three bombers were dropped by Marine railguns after they had fired a hundred and twenty-six times. It wasn't efficient, but for once the Legion had plenty of ordnance on hand. Efficiency was less important than effectiveness, and as the Marines continued to fire their weapons at the approaching aircraft, the mechs of Joker Company added to the barrage from the rim of Mount Foothold.

Missiles flew from launchers, some mounted on Joker mechs but most originating from the temporary launch platforms erected as part of Mount Foothold's defensive shield. The LRMs came at the approaching bombers' flanks, and the bombers scattered into groups of three to five as the missiles drew steadily nearer. When the bombers dispersed, the Marines took advantage by dropping another four with concerted fire on a single group that had briefly aligned with their sights.

Always a mistake when dealing with either Marines or Metalheads.

The bombers broke into two distinct groups, with roughly half moving toward Mount Foothold, while the rest continued toward 1st Company. Within seconds, the aircraft unleashed a storm of missiles at the heavily fortified volcano.

Missiles burned and railguns strobed as sixteen Arh'Kel bombers unleashed their payloads toward the volcanic rim. The ordnance flew on high, ponderous trajectories that were even more exaggerated than the Terrans' fire had been, but the Terran missiles were fast and had already covered more than half the ground between Mount Foothold and the bomber wing. Despite the Arh'Kel efforts to evade, they were ill-equipped to contend with weapons specifically designed to destroy rock-biter vehicles.

The LRMs slashed into the scattering bombers, striking eight of the sixteen craft and annihilating them outright. Another four took near-misses and were forced to the ground, but four of the bombers that had targeted Mount Foothold managed to escape the Terran fire as their own weapons descended on the Terran FOB.

Arcing through the air, the slower-moving Arh'Kel ordnance gave the appearance of rocks being hurled over a wall. And as the bolts and missiles neared Joker's fortified position, the full might and fury of the Terran defenses came into play.

Forty coil guns sprayed bullets into the sky, swinging their arcs back and forth in a tight, funnel-shaped kill-zone to weave a seemingly impenetrable field of fire. Controlled by a complex targeting algorithm that performed to over ninety-five-percent effectiveness in such situations, the coil gun point-defense grid scrapped missile after missile from the sky as the Arh'Kel weapons reached the four-hundred-meter mark from the crater's rim.

But ninety-five percent was not quite a hundred, and a handful of missiles snuck through the impressive shield. As they did, twenty chain guns unleashed their slugs into a space just a hundred meters beyond the volcano's edge. Cycling at three hundred rounds per second, the chain guns spat a combined nine hundred slugs into the air before going silent. Their brief but concerted fire killed all four of the enemy missiles just as a flight of fifty interceptor rockets tore loose from their mounts deep within the crater.

The rockets leapt skyward, each seeking out an Arh'Kel smart projectile. The bolts moved slower than the enemy slugs, and the interceptor rockets were light and agile, specifically designed to counter smart ordnance as it juked and spiraled toward its target.

Striking mid-flight artillery in an atmosphere as thick as this, even at such close range, was therefore no great challenge for the two-foot-long rockets. All of the bolts were met by at least two rockets, and the ensuing collisions filled the sky with what looked like flak bursts as the destructive weapons were reduced to shrapnel that fell harmlessly to the ground below.

When the fire ceased, not a single enemy weapon had struck within the crater. As the Arh'Kel banked hard, pulling away from the mountain, Jenkins had no doubt that Joker would finish the job.

But for now, he had his own unit's defense to consider.

The second group of Arh'Kel divers had targeted 1st Company and fired their weapons at nearly the same moment their cohorts made what some would call a "business decision" by fleeing in the face of overwhelming firepower at Mount Foothold. The inbound enemy ordnance consisted of fourteen smart bolts and sixty-four missiles. It was enough to destroy half of the mechs and Marines if it was permitted to land.

Nestled behind tripod-mounted miniguns and railgun rifles, the power-armored Marines waited two full seconds before opening fire on the approaching wave. As they did, Jenkins' mechs sent chain and coil gun fire into the sky, while launching a barrage of anti-missile rockets from those mechs equipped with such systems.

Missile after missile was torn down, each leaving a cloud of black smoke at the intercept point. Most of the Marines now manned miniguns, which wove an interceptive grid in the path of the enemy missiles, but some still crouched behind their railgun rifles. These sent bolt after bolt into the bombers, ignoring the danger posed by the inbound hail of fire.

Fifty-nine missiles were torn down, and eleven smart projectiles were stopped mid-air. But five missiles and three bolts snuck through the PD shield, and those weapons took a predictable toll on the Terrans.

Two Marine nests were struck by missiles and the destructive energies blew those nests apart in a shower of stone shards. Two Marines died, and two others were badly wounded by the direct hits, but their comrades continued pouring fire into the approaching enemy aircraft. They knew just as any warrior did that the only path to real safety was one which went straight through the enemy.

Another missile near-missed *Powerslave*, sending a spray of shrapnel into the mighty mech's legs, which set off a short series of alarms. Two more struck the mechs *Fortune's Fury* and *Twilight's Fall*, causing minor damage to each.

It was the smart bolts that did the most damage.

Arriving a second after the missiles, the bolts slammed into a trio of mechs, including Jenkins' towering *Powerslave*. Struck in the upper shoulder, the humanoid battlewagon now serving as Jenkins' command vehicle teetered dangerously as its entire right arm went offline. Hammer was able to stabilize the vehicle's stance before losing control, and after a few staggering steps, managed to right the vehicle and return it to a ready stance.

"Return fire!" Jenkins barked as the enemy aircraft broke apart. Just nine of the enemy bombers remained and the Marines continued to pour round and round into their midst, using their suit-augmented targeting systems to snipe the aircraft with hypervelocity tungsten.

The mechs sent sixty-two SRMs into the sky, slicing through the oppressive blanket of gas that clung to the planet's surface. The enemy bombers were just eighteen kilometers from 1st Company, but it was unlikely any SRM could cover that much distance and strike a moving airborne target.

Fortunately for the Metalheads, most of these missiles were not what they initially appeared.

Climbing skyward at aggressive angles, forty-four of the missiles reached an altitude fully three times that of their fleeing targets before breaking apart to reveal their true nature: rocket-delivery systems.

They were an antiquated system not deployed in the last century of Terran warfare, but in this environment, against these particular targets, they were the perfect system.

Each missile broke apart to reveal sixteen rockets, and while nearly ten percent of those rockets failed to ignite their motors, the remainder streaked in pursuit of their fleeing Arh'Kel targets.

The swarm of regular SRMs continued driving straight at the nine surviving enemy aircraft, who now had a choice: continue to flee and fall victim to over six hundred small rockets, or come about and face the eighteen SRMs.

Somewhat surprisingly, there was no consensus in the rockbiters' next move; half the aircraft came about, while the others continued to flee.

The result was nothing short of disaster for the Arh'Kel pilots.

The SRMs retargeted, with four missiles locked onto each of the bombers who had come about. The bombers fired their slug-throwers, managing to scrape three of the SRMs from the sky before the rest slammed into the bombers one after another. Not a single bomber survived the hail of missiles, while their fellows sped off as fast as their engines could carry them in a futile attempt to evade the storm of rockets.

The Terran weapons closed the distance with the fleeing

bombers, and the first finally slammed into a diver's stern. The bomber dipped, temporarily losing thrust before resuming at eighty percent of its previous speed. After that first impact, it was all over but the crying.

Rocket after rocket slammed into the relatively heavily armored bombers, with each craft suffering no fewer than six strikes before losing power and lift, succumbing to gravity, and crashing into the rocky ground below.

When the smoke cleared, not a single Arh'Kel bomber had survived the Terran counterattack, and whatever facility had launched them was completely destroyed by the tactical nukes dropped on it by Sargon. The price had been four casualties, with two Marines KIA and the other two in serious condition.

"We need medevac for our wounded," Jenkins said on the Marine dropship channel.

"Copy that, Colonel," came the pilot's reply as he fired his engines and moved to collect the downed Marines. "Medevac inbound."

"Colonel," Benjamin reported stoically, "we've got rock-biters bubbling up all around us. I'm showing fourteen separate emergence points, with each producing multiple infantry per second."

Jenkins reviewed the sensor data and saw that while they had been busy dealing with the bombers, five thousand Arh'Kel had boiled up from beneath the planet's skin. A handful of HWPs was present, along with two SOMs. As he was about to call up to the *Vercingetorix*, railgun bolts thundered down from the heavens and scrapped those SOMs. The *Vercingetorix* had recently replaced part of its arsenal with railguns, and while they were technically ship-grade weapons, they were still considerably smaller than the railguns built into certain mechs like the old *Sam Kolt*.

They cycled slowly, were barely accurate enough to use in

naval engagements, and had limited magazines, which made them little more than backup weapons.

But right now, they represented the entirety of his orbital fire support, so he didn't have the luxury of calling down strikes on the enemy HWPs or highly-concentrated groups of Arh'Kel infantry. He needed Stravinsky to conserve her ammo and focus on defending her own position, not his, and he suddenly had the ominous suspicion that all of this had been precisely orchestrated by their enemy.

And the longer he stayed on AK-091, the less convinced he was that the Arh'Kel were that enemy. This fight was between them and Jemmin, and possibly the Vorr. The Arh'Kel were looking more and more like unwitting tools in the real contest for dominance in Nexus Space, and from a given perspective, that made them victims rather than the aggressors every Terran thought them to be.

That didn't mean he wouldn't cut every single one of them down if they got in his way, which they appeared intent on doing.

"1st Company," he called over the company-wide, "regroup and put those nests back in order. We're about to have guests."

14

HEAVY BURDENS

"Arh'Kel fireships are launching missiles," Tactical reported as the *William Wallace* neared the engagement zone. "Eighty-eight missiles inbound. Time to impact forty seconds. No railgun fire."

"They're holding those for when we break formation," General Moon observed in a raised voice. "Maintain course until the *Martin Luther* launches her interceptors and activate the PD grid."

"Point defense active," Tactical acknowledged. "Time to impact twenty-six seconds."

The eight Arh'Kel fireships, moving in a loose formation approximating a crescent, continued to burn their engines at maximum as their wave of missiles surged ahead. They had no reason to stop and battle the Terrans before reaching orbit, which made this engagement particularly tricky for the human warships. They had one chance to stop the Arh'Kel, and they needed to make the most of it. The terrain was in the Terrans' favor, the vast void of interplanetary space affording them the option of choosing when and where to engage the enemy along their approach vector.

Unfortunately, most of that advantage was neutralized because the Metal Legion had ground forces on AK-091 that would eventually expend their significant stockpiles of ammunition if the *William Wallace* and *Martin Luther* failed to regain overwatch. If time were no consideration, the Terrans could easily flank the enemy fleet and pick away at them from a distance, tearing them to pieces long before they reached the planet if the rock-biters remained intent on reaching the planet at best possible speed.

Still, Podsy knew that their positional advantage would likely prove instrumental in the engagement to come.

"Twenty-four missiles targeting us, sixty-four targeting *Martin Luther*," Tactical said as the missiles diverged from a single mass into two smaller clusters. "Impact in ten seconds. PD grid is hot."

The *William Wallace*'s point-defense grid opened fire, knifing across the void with a combination of coil gun fire and interceptor rockets. While the *William Wallace* was less than a third the size of the *Martin Luther*, it sent out a nearly identical amount of interceptive fire as the larger cruiser. Seconds ticked off the impact clock before missiles began exploding one after another until the star field on the main viewer was replaced by a series of blooming ordnance cut short by Terran defensive fire.

"Two missiles through," Tactical declared urgently. "Impact in three...two..."

"All hands, brace for impact!" Podsy bellowed, and the next thing he knew, he was stupidly rubbing the side of his head.

It took him a few seconds to realize they'd been hit and that he had temporarily lost consciousness. Fortunately, a few of the bridge crew were outfitted with neural implants. Unfortunately, only one of them appeared to be conscious...or alive.

"Damage report!" Podsy barked, his words slurred as he struggled to focus his vision on the console before him.

"Near miss off the port stern," replied Damage Control, her voice choked and wet. "Enemy fusion warhead detonated four klicks off. We've got decompression events in compartments all across that section. Routing repair teams now."

"Tactical." Podsy turned in his chair, still unable to properly focus on anything as he tried to will his body to recover from the head impact he had just suffered. "Tactical!" he repeated.

"Lieutenant Wilhoyte is down, Captain," Styles said grimly. "I'm transferring the tactical feeds to my station, but I need your authorization."

"You've got it," Podsednik said, punching his command code into his terminal and authorizing Styles to temporarily mirror the Tactical station. It was then that Podsy realized General Moon was silent, and with no small measure of dread, he snapped his head toward the bridge's command chair.

His head was at an unnatural angle. The general still appeared to be breathing, but it was obvious he had seriously injured his neck, prompting Podsy to access the emergency medical line.

"Sickbay, we need a medical team to the bridge immediately. General Moon is down and in need of immediate assistance," he commanded.

"Roger," Doctor Wang acknowledged. "We'll be there in fifty seconds."

"Give me a status update, Styles," Podsy growled, his vision finally clearing enough that he could make sense of both the main viewer and the tactical plotter.

"Three of the fireships are down," Styles reported. "Two more are badly damaged, but they've sent out another volley of twelve missiles. Time to impact twelve seconds."

"Helm, prepare for evasive maneuver Mongoose," Podsy commanded before switching to the ship-wide. "All hands, this is Captain Podsednik. Brace for evasive maneuvers. I say again, brace for evasive maneuvers." He cut the ship-wide mic and snapped, "Helm, execute Mongoose!"

"Mongoose, aye," the helmsman acknowledged, and the ship lurched beneath them as it shot forward and rolled as hard and fast as it was able.

"Impact in three...two...one," Styles called as the overlapping fields of point defense fire began striking the enemy weapons. This time, all twelve of the enemy missiles were destroyed by the *William Wallace*'s PD efforts, but the *Martin Luther* suffered two near-misses from fusion warheads powerful enough to destroy a ship like the *Wallace*.

Fusion-powered mini-novae flashed into existence less than a kilometer from Admiral Corbyn's aged cruiser, bathing the warship in radiation and devastatingly powerful nuclear winds. Had there been an atmosphere to propagate the energy released by those weapons, the *Luther* would have been completely annihilated, but in the void of space, even a multi-megaton warhead was incapable of destroying a properly built warship at that close of a range.

"Return fire," Podsy snarled as the medical team arrived on the bridge and began the gentle work of extricating General Moon from his command chair without further aggravating his injuries.

"Launching missiles," Styles acknowledged, sending a stream of eight conventional warheads into the fireships. "All other weapon systems are temporarily offline, Captain," he added with evident frustration.

"Get those railguns back up," Podsy snapped. "Now!"

"Working on it," Styles replied shortly. "Their targeting systems were knocked offline by the missile strike, and it's going to take—"

"Don't tell me how it's done, just do it!"

"Aye, sir," Styles muttered as he worked diligently to address the problem.

"The general is stable," Dr. Wang reported after affixing a spinal-support appliance to Moon's back and head. "We're ready to move, but will need a minute to make it back to Sickbay."

"I can't guarantee anything," Podsy said, glancing to the tactical plotter; no new incoming missiles had appeared. "But it looks as clear as it's going to get."

"Good enough." Wang nodded and began working with the nurse to carry General Moon back to sickbay.

"*Martin Luther* just scratched two more fireships," Sensors reported as a furious series of explosions strobed in the dark void. "Three hostile fireships remaining."

"Our missiles are twelve seconds out," Styles reported as the eight Terran warheads drove at the trio of remaining Arh'Kel warships. "I'm reading enemy PD fire. Impact in six seconds. Five...four...three..."

Two of the Terran missiles were sniped by PD fire, but the other six continued toward their targets.

"Two...one..."

Another pair of Terran missiles were scratched by rock-biter defensive fire, leaving four of the original eight warheads slashing toward their targets. Just before impact, another pair of explosions strobed in rapid succession, leaving just two missiles driving at the Arh'Kel fireships.

"Impact!" Styles declared, and both missiles stabbed into their targets center mass, delivering all of their destructive energies into two of the enemy vessels. But these were conventional warheads, armed with shaped charges designed to tear deep wounds into the target's interiors. Explosive decompression ejected several tons of debris into the void, carrying a handful of rock-biters with them from each fireship, but the enemy vessels continued their charge toward the planet unhindered.

Until the *Martin Luther*'s latest wave of ordnance arrived.

Thirty Terran missiles slammed into the trio of enemy warships, one after another, pummeling the robust and surprisingly sophisticated-looking craft. Internal explosions rippled within the enemy hulls, with one suffering a catastrophic reactor containment failure that caused it to burst from within. The ship's stern exploded, tearing a full third of the vessel off, while the rest began to tumble stern-over-bow after losing its motive thrust. Maneuvering jets fired in a desperate attempt to stabilize its trajectory, but even if they succeeded, there was no hope of that fireship reaching or maintaining orbit at AK-091.

Another of the fireships simply died in space, its engines snuffing out and its weapons ceasing fire. The visible damage caused by Admiral Corbyn's latest missile salvo was hardly enough to cause such a catastrophic failure, and Podsednik suspected the admiral had just deployed some kind of experimental Arh'Kel-specific weapon.

Judging from the results, the test fire had been a resounding success.

"One ship remaining," Styles reported. "Admiral Corbyn is ordering us to launch Vipers in eight seconds."

Podsy piped in to Lieutenant Commander Knighton's direct line. "Yellowhammer, this is Captain Podsednik."

"Go ahead, Captain," Knighton replied.

"Prepare to launch in four seconds, Commander."

"Copy that," she acknowledged. A few seconds later, precisely on schedule, the Viper-class aerospace fighters shot from their hull-mounted cradles and moved to rendezvous with the freshly launched Shriekers that streamed from the *Martin Luther*'s tubes.

The flight of mixed interceptors sped toward the lone functional Arh'Kel fireship, which would reach an equal distance to AK-091 as the Terran warships in two minutes. Once it passed them, the relative motions of the three warships would quickly leave them unable to engage it. The Terrans had plotted an optimal itinerary that would let them engage with the rock-biters well beyond the Arh'Kel's effective range to AK-091 while also permitting them to return to overwatch in under an hour after the engagement concluded.

An hour was a long time to be out of overwatch, especially during the invasion of a heavily-populated enemy world. But General Moon had been right; they had no real choice in the matter. The Jemmin had played their hand perfectly, leaving the Terrans no choice but to divide their forces if they wanted to have any realistic hope of completing their primary objective.

All of which boiled down to the simple fact that if the interceptors didn't take out this last heavily-armed and heavily-armored fireship, it would have an unobstructed path to the lightly-armed *Vercingetorix*, which it could easily dispose of. And with the *Vercingetorix* gone, the Metalheads and Marines would not last long.

The flight of Shriekers and Vipers sprinted toward the enemy, redlining their engines and causing a pair of Shriekers to fall out of formation due to temporary engine failures. The rest of the Terran pilots kept their eyes on target, drawing steadily nearer to the Arh'Kel fireship as they slowly closed to optimal firing range for their hypervelocity railguns.

Lieutenant Commander Knighton's Viper took point while her counterpart, Commander Silva, did the same ahead of the *Martin Luther*'s Shriekers. The various pilots slotted into the classic offset diamond formation and unleashed a perfectly coordinated volley of railgun fire at the enemy ship. Twenty-six Shriekers and eleven Vipers stabbed hypervelocity tungsten slivers through the void at over 0.01c, and when they struck the enemy fireship, they carved wicked wounds into the robust vessel's armored hull.

"Thirty-four direct hits," Styles reported. "Severe damage to the enemy's starboard hull. She's rolling to present her port."

Nineteen missiles leapt from the fireship's launchers and sped across the narrow gap between it and the Terran interceptors. The Terran pilots stayed in the pocket, refusing to budge and keeping their guns trained on target. A few seconds after launching the missiles, the Arh'Kel fired six railguns at the *Martin Luther* and two more at the *William Wallace*. They were desperation shots, nothing more, since at this range and with no impediments to maneuverability, neither Terran warship would have much difficulty evading the sluggish projectiles.

The wave of Arh'Kel missiles neared the interceptors' position, and with less than two seconds before impact, the Terran pilots unleashed another volley of ultra-precise railgun fire.

"Thirty-seven for thirty-nine," Styles declared, pumping his fist triumphantly as the Terran pilots scattered in the face of the inbound ordnance. A pair of interceptors, one Viper and one Shrieker, were vaporized by the Arh'Kel tactical nukes but the rest successfully evaded the volley and immediately resumed their previous predatory posture as they bore down on their wounded prey.

Outgassing burst from a handful of fresh wounds in the fireship's hull. "Her engines are fluctuating, but she's maintaining course," Sensors reported.

Seconds ticked by as the charging fireship finally drove past the Terran warships on its course toward AK-091. That ship had officially gotten inside the Terrans' guard, and the Vipers would get only one more high-accuracy shot before the sprinting warship would leave them in its wake.

The pair of straggling Shriekers, while not quite in formation with their fellows, had managed to contribute to the latest volley. As their comrades adjusted course to maximize their time-on-target, the stragglers were in the unexpected position of being slightly better situated to pursue the enemy.

Again the fireship launched missiles, and again the Terran pilots ignored them as their railgun capacitors recharged. Fighting in a mech or warship was radically different from fighting in what was essentially a flying missile armed with a handful of weapons systems as dangerous to their pilot as to the enemy. Interceptor pilots had no regard for defense, no illusions about hunkering down behind armor plating when the fires of hell came for them. They lived and died purely on their wits, reflexes, and the seemingly endless supply of ice-water in their veins.

So it should have come as no surprise to Podsednik to see the entire formation remain locked in their offset diamonds, sending another volley of fire at the enemy with less than a second to go before the enemy ordnance reached them. But it was still a humbling experience to witness that much courage demonstrated by thirty-seven Terrans, each of whom had family, friends, and dreams for the future waiting for them if they could just make it back to their cradles one more time.

Andy Podsednik knew whatever it was that gave them that particular brand of courage, he would never have it. In a way, it was precisely that certain knowledge which drove him to be worthy of the brave men and women with whom he had the privilege of serving.

"Thirty-five for thirty-seven," Styles reported after the enemy missiles exploded around the interceptors. The enemy warship, having already rolled to present its relatively fresh dorsal section, was finally brought down by the precision vehicle-grade railgun fire delivered courtesy of the Viper and Shrieker pilots. Capacitors exploded deep within its hull, while ordnance stockpiles cooked off beneath a third of the fireship's missile launchers. The Arh'Kel warship's engines flared defiantly, and for a long moment, it seemed as though the wounded warship would keep its legs beneath it long enough to sneak past the Terran blockade.

But the damage was simply too great, and with a final gasp of blue-white plasma, the fireship's engines flickered and died just as surely as its seven fellows had done before it.

"I've got a short-range link request from the *Martin Luther*," Comm reported.

"Put it on." Podsy nodded, and a moment later, Admiral Corbyn's face, smeared with blood from his left eye down to his jaw, appeared on the main viewer.

"Good work..." His voice trailed off when he realized General Moon's chair was empty, but despite spending the bulk of his career as a high-level bureaucrat, the admiral's wits in the heat of battle were as sharp as any officer's, and he fractionally nodded. "It looks like you have indeed been paying attention, Captain Podsednik. Good work back there. Retrieve your Vipers while we do the same, then return to AK-091 at best possible speed. Don't worry about us. Just get your asses back there ASAP, and we'll be right behind you."

"Yes, Admiral." Podsy nodded. "And thank you, sir."

"Don't thank me," Corbyn drawled, his lip curling in a half-smirk. "This ain't over just yet, son, and it looks like you're in command now. Our long-range comm system was taken out in that strike and won't be repaired before you regain orbit, so this might be my final bit of advice to you before you have to make a few tough calls. I suggest you listen to it with both ears."

"Yes, sir," Podsy said, acutely aware that all eyes on his bridge were turned his way.

"Don't lose your nerve, Captain," Corbyn said, his eyes somehow driving through Podsednik and making him feel as insecure as an eight-year-old boy. "Make whatever calls you think are appropriate, regardless of what you think the general or I might say or do in your shoes. There's no shame in asking for advice, but don't you dare go limp-dicked for fear of misstep-pin'. Am I clear?"

"Crystal, Admiral."

"Good." Corbyn nodded, wiped a blood-soaked rag over the side of his face, and looked down at it in annoyed disgust. "Now get to work, son. Corbyn out."

When the line cut out, Podsy couldn't help but smile as he issued orders to the crew. "Helm, set rendezvous with our Vipers. Damage Control, I want all teams to lock down those air leaks in our port quarter. Tactical, get my railguns back online, and I don't care if you have to go down there personally with wire-strippers, bubblegum, and inventive strings of profanity."

"Yes, sir," all three acknowledged in rapid succession.

It wasn't a professional rallying cry, and it wasn't particu-larly clever or eloquent, but it was very much in line with who and what Andy Podsednik was, and right now that was the best his people had. Rather than try to force himself into someone else's mold or adhere to some third-party standard for how a commander should behave in the heat of battle, he decided he would be at his best staying true to himself.

For the sake of the men and women around him, he just hoped that would be enough.

_____

15

CLOSING IN

"Keep running, you bastard," Xi growled as she sprinted _Elvira_ up the tunnel in pursuit of the Poltergeist. The chase had already gone on for fifteen minutes, during which time she had only sighted the enemy vehicle once. "We're almost there. Don't turn back now."

Flanked by a trio of nimble crab-looking ANTS which were small and fast enough to crawl through the tunnel collapse that had cut Xi off from the rest of 2nd Company, _Elvira_ drove her quarry up the tunnel toward the surface. In another two minutes, they would breach the surface, and Commander Knighton's Vipers could disable the Jemmin command vehicle long enough for the Marines to secure its vital components, which included its Jemmin operator.

The tunnel took another sharp righthand turn, the eighth such dogleg she had encountered during her pursuit of the Poltergeist. This winding tunnel stood in stark contrast to the much straighter one she had come down with 2nd Company. It had clearly not been dug to facilitate industrial activity, likely built as an escape route for a vehicle like this Poltergeist. Arh'Kel were capable of digging such tunnels with great alacrity, and the hewn walls of the passage were rough and merely days old.

But if the Poltergeist had been down here for a number of days, it seemed strange that its fellow had not been able to assist it in making the necessary repairs to enable its safe return to the surface.

She knew that if the Poltergeist was going to double back, it would do so before they reached the surface. To counter what she considered an inevitable turn, she sent the three ANTS units sprinting up the tunnel to where they could at least catch sight of the command vessel before it was in firing range of *Elvira*.

Twenty seconds after her ANTS made a left turn up the tunnel, one of them was destroyed by an enemy rocket. The other two, acting on pre-programmed responses to such situations and doing so faster than any human could react, split and sprinted toward the source of the rocket.

The Poltergeist loomed in their vid pickups, and Xi drove *Elvira* toward the bend in the tunnel as the ANTS closed the distance with the enemy command vehicle. A rocket slammed into the second ANTS drone, but the third closed to its preprogrammed trigger distance and self-destructed, sending a blast of energy into the enemy hovertank.

The ANTS had been chosen for this op for a variety of reasons, but one of those reasons had to do with Terran theories regarding Jemmin hover technology: no one believed the Jemmin had fully conquered gravity. Xi wasn't totally clear on the finer points of the working theories regarding their hover propulsion systems, but the short version was that a precisely attenuated explosion could, if triggered close enough to a Poltergeist, significantly slow its movement for several seconds by disrupting the finely-tuned systems that made its peculiar form of flight possible.

As was so often the case, the Terran eggheads were right on the money.

The shockwave from the ANTS explosion did negligible damage to the Poltergeist's hull, but its bow dipped a full meter as Xi burst around the corner and sent a pair of AP shells into the Jemmin vehicle's flanks. She didn't want to score a center-mass hit for fear of striking the reactor or the vehicle's capacitors, and as a result, her left shell did little more than cosmetic damage to the disc-shaped vehicle's edge. But the other struck something energetic within the vehicle's hull, sparking an explosive display accompanied by powerful plasma-electrical arcs that were so potent they might have ignited in an oxygen-rich environment.

She braced herself for the inevitable beam strike—which she gave herself no better than a fifty-fifty chance of surviving—while ducking *Elvira* back behind the tunnel's bend. But surprisingly, the beam strike never arrived, and she safely regained cover by backtracking a hundred meters down the tunnel. Almost without thinking, she leapt forward, knowing that the Poltergeist would have fired its beam weapon if it had been capable.

As she regained line-of-sight, the Poltergeist sped up the tunnel at ninety-five kph. They were just a hundred meters below the surface, and the tunnel's slope would bring them to the surface in less than two kilometers. She sprinted in in pursuit of the fleeing Poltergeist, feeling a visceral thrill as the hunt drew to its seemingly inevitable conclusion.

She knew not to count her chickens before they hatched, but she also knew that moments like this were few and far between. She intended to make the most of it and savor the experience as it happened.

The Poltergeist predictably outran her, emerging into the murky brown daylight at the end of the tunnel. She expected to see strobes of railgun strikes fill the sky as Knighton's Vipers closed the trap on their prized target.

But no flashes strobed, and nothing impeded the Poltergeist's low-altitude flight as it drove at a hundred and twenty kph across the blasted terrain of AK-091.

And as *Elvira* breached the surface in pursuit, Xi received a series of data packets that updated her on the current situation. Fleet had gone to intercept a newly-arrived Jemmin task force, which included a Gatekeeper? On top of that, the *William Wallace* and *Martin Luther* were just now engaging eight Arh'Kel fireships that had arrived from the distal wormhole gate at the same time the Jemmin had arrived.

That left just the lightly-armed *Vercingetorix* in overwatch, accompanied by a paltry five aerospace interceptors, and damaged ones at that.

As she sprinted her mech out onto the blasted, rocky plains of AK-091, the news just kept getting worse.

1st Company was surrounded by Arh'Kel infantry and HWPs. More than thirty thousand rock-biters had besieged Colonel Jenkins' position, supported by a dozen or so of their armored vehicles. 2nd Company had emerged from the main tunnel eight kilometers from the insertion point less than two minutes before Xi had, and together with 1st Company, they were preparing to make a push through the noose of enemy soldiers surrounding them.

She took all of this in over the course of four seconds, but none of it changed their primary objective. They still needed to capture that Poltergeist, and she was still the closest Terran to their valuable quarry.

"This is Major Xi," she declared over the main ground forces channel. "I'm pursuing the objective and requesting Support Package Alpha. I say again, this is Major Xi calling in Support Package Alpha."

"Support Package Alpha request confirmed," came Lieutenant Benjamin's reply. "Forwarding your orders now, Major."

As the Jemmin Poltergeist fled across the plains, Xi was the only mech in effective range. It was already three kilometers out, which was still well within her effective artillery range but beyond that of her chain guns.

She still had eight SRMs loaded in her pods, and knew it was now or never. Each of the SRMs was an armor-piercer, and via a thought delivered through her neural link, she launched four of those missiles.

The missiles climbed higher than was ideal as they fought to gain a high-accuracy trajectory on the target. In response, the Poltergeist fired a stream of micro-rockets to intercept, and all four of Xi's missiles were scratched.

She loaded a pair of AP shells into her fifteens and sent them soaring across the dingy sky. The first shell missed the mark by ten meters, but the second struck the very edge of the vehicle, knocking it temporarily to the ground and slewing it thirty degrees off-course before it recovered and resumed its flight at just over a hundred and ten kph.

"Come on..." she hissed as a quintet of icons appeared on her HUD. Four were Shrieker-class aerospace interceptors previously attached to the *Martin Luther*, while just one was a Viper from the *William Wallace*. Their virtual systems linked with Xi's, and she forwarded optimal targets on the Poltergeist's hull directly to the diving interceptors as they descended on the fleeing Jemmin.

Sprinting to the west, which on this planet was in the same direction as the world's rotation, the Poltergeist put distance between itself and the pursuing interceptors as their current courses brought them almost perfectly perpendicular to the planet's surface. But they were moving at nine hundred kph while it was moving just one-eighth that speed, so as they leveled out their descent, they would quickly close whatever distance the Poltergeist created.

Xi could not immediately understand why the Poltergeist's operator chose this course, but she wasn't about to complain. Its current course brought the vehicle closer to Colonel Jenkins' mechs than an easterly course would have done, which worked in the Terrans' favor.

Not to mention that its westerly course was taking it straight into an Arh'Kel horde armed with four HWPs. The Poltergeist moved straight at the horde, which seemed poised to open fire on the vehicle. Its stealth systems were all but offline following Xi's direct hits underground, making it a juicy target for the rock-biter weapons systems.

But, perhaps predictably, as the Poltergeist approached the small army of eight thousand rock-biters, the Arh'Kel made no moves to indicate they were aware of its presence. The giant command vehicle maintained an altitude of five meters, slowing its forward velocity to just over eighty kph as it did, and sailed over the mindless mob of enemy infantry.

"Cheater!" Xi scowled before raising Col. Jenkins. "This is *Elvira*. Requesting authorization to deploy Crackerjack times two." She forwarded a proposed fire plan for the pair of nuclear artillery shells that would put them a half-kilometer in front of the enemy vehicle and awaited her superior's reply.

There was a brief pause before her proposal was sent back with modifications. "Negative on fire plan. You are authorized to deploy one Crackerjack on the following target."

Her scowl deepened when she saw that he had changed her target to the middle of the Arh'Kel formation the Poltergeist had just sped through without suffering so much as a single slug strike to its hull. "Copy that. Crackerjack on the way."

Elvira's left gun thundered, launching the nuclear artillery shell into the enemy horde's midst. Clearly aware of her efforts, the Arh'Kel horde surged in her direction while their railguns fired during the shell's flight. A pair of railgun strikes slashed into her hull, with one damaging an SRM pod and another her front leg. Her mobility was compromised to the tune of four kph, and her SRM pod would be useless for the remainder of the mission.

The Scorpion-class mech was a workhorse, but its vulnerabilities were becoming far too predictable for Xi's liking. Much as she hated to think it, given all the work she had done riding Jock in the venerable design, she knew it was likely time to upgrade to a new platform.

But *Elvira*, in her many incarnations, had served humanity more diligently and effectively than any other vehicle in the Terran Armor Corps. Sentiment had no place on the battlefield, but that didn't mean it had no place in Xi's heart.

The nuclear artillery shell splashed down in the heart of the enemy formation, scrapping three of the Arh'Kel HWPs and killing three thousand infantry outright with the half-kiloton blast wave. The mushroom cloud that rose following the artillery strike was deeply satisfying to Xi as she crested the lone ridge between her and the Arh'Kel formation.

She crab-walked the venerable mech to the top of the ridgeline before firing her port chain guns on full-cycle into the mass of enemy warriors. Her depleted uranium slugs cut them down like a chainsaw through balsa, carving ruination among the surging tide of angry rock-biters. As the Poltergeist resumed its limping westerly retreat, the interceptors finally broke through the clouds and descended on their quarry like raptors.

The Shriekers moved ahead of the lone Viper, flying an inverted V with the Viper at the base and the Shriekers as the arms. Giving credence to their names, the Shriekers made a distinctive scream as they dived through AK-091's brown skies. Like a quartet of banshees delivering a venomous serpent, the formation of aerospace interceptors locked their weapons on the fleeing Poltergeist and fired in methodical sequence, beginning with the leftmost Shrieker.

The first railgun strike missed the mark, striking the ground twelve meters to the Poltergeist's left. The second strike came closer, sending a spray of razor-sharp stone splashing off the hovertank's hull. The Viper was the third to fire, and it struck the mark with a clean hit to the tank's forward hull. The Poltergeist dipped slightly in-flight but lost no speed after recovering from the blow, which punched a thirty-centimeter-wide hole through its armor.

The fourth and fifth shots also struck the mark, but they too were peripheral and registered no visible effect on the fleeing tank. At their respective speeds, the interceptors would get one more shot apiece before overshooting the mark.

Without breaking stride, the Poltergeist sent a stream of rockets skyward into the pursuing interceptors. Nineteen micro-missiles spread out to engage the five Terran aircraft and the interceptors were forced to scatter, given the speed and deadly accuracy of the Jemmin ordnance.

The micro-rockets hammered into the Terran aircraft, each interceptor suffering a single strike. Xi held her breath as the damage reports came back, and was shocked to find that just one of the interceptors had been scratched. The micro-rockets had scored mostly glancing hits, with one killing a Shrieker's pilot outright and leaving the craft itself to plummet to the ground below, where it exploded in a fiery conflagration befitting a warrior's funeral pyre.

The four remaining interceptors resumed formation as quickly as they had broken apart and sent another hail of railgun slivers into the enemy vehicle. Two more hits were scored, and this time, the enemy vehicle was slowed by three kph. It was still moving well over a hundred kph over the blasted and rocky terrain, though, and there was no way any Terran ground vehicles could intercept it at that speed.

"This is *Vercingetorix*. Requesting orders from Dragon Actual," the CO of the *Vercingetorix* said over the command channel. Stravinsky no longer viewed her role as a primary one, but that of a supporting actor to the Metalheads on the ground. Her every missive and update confirmed the change in her attitude was genuine.

"*Vercingetorix*, Dragon Actual," Jenkins replied. "Maintain current posture."

"Copy that, Dragon Actual," she responded with evident disappointment. "Maintaining posture."

"Major, you're go for Crackerjack to the following coordinates," Colonel Jenkins commanded as a fresh set of target coordinates came to Xi's HUD. Even at the Poltergeist's relatively low rate of egress, it put her in accurate firing range in less than a minute.

"Copy that," Xi acknowledged with gusto, loading the third and final nuclear shell into her left main. "Crackerjack up. On the way!"

Elvira's left main roared, firing the devastating projectile into a high arc at the fleeing Poltergeist. But launching the shell caused a series of alarms to go off in her HUD, showing the left main was offline with significant damage to the loading breech. Xi's eyes snapped to the shell's flight characteristics as it climbed higher into the sky; the damage to the gun might have warped its trajectory, and if the shell struck the Poltergeist directly, it could destroy the vehicle outright.

The colonel's target coordinates were well in front of the enemy vehicle, far enough out that inaccuracy was unlikely to cause Xi to hit the vehicle by accident, but those coordinates hadn't taken into account the possible damage to the gun itself during firing. The extra mass of the shell, coupled with the extreme atmospheric pressure and strain caused by previous Crackerjacks, had apparently been enough to take the gun completely offline for the foreseeable future.

Thankfully, as the shell reached the apex of its flight, her onboard computer projected that while it would miss its original target by a full hundred meters due to the warped firing mechanism, it would not strike the Poltergeist. When the shell touched down, it delivered half a kiloton of destructive force and blasted the ground clean for five hundred meters in all directions. The blast wave washed dust and debris over the Poltergeist's hull, but the enemy commander could see daylight and wasn't about to falter. Another wave of micro-rockets tore from their mounts, this time sending seventeen projectiles skyward at the Terran interceptors. Xi knew that even with its accuracy hampered, the Poltergeist had the edge against the four remaining aircraft.

If they had wanted to destroy it outright, they could have almost certainly done so. But their objective was to capture, not destroy, which meant they could not afford to make high-damage center-mass hits or take shots up its tailpipe in the hope of overloading its engines.

Another Shrieker fell to the wave of rockets, while yet another was so badly damaged that its pilot had to eject before its craft went into a flat spin and crashed into the deck. Just two Terran aircraft remained in pursuit of the fleeing Jemmin vehicle, and Xi knew their best chance had just been wasted. The Poltergeist had cleared her accurate firing range, and while she could continue to lob artillery at it for several more minutes, she would lack the kind of accuracy required for this mission.

Swearing in frustration, Xi slammed her fist into the arm of her chair. Her pinky finger flared with pain, suggesting she had broken it or the metacarpal bone in her hand connected to it. But she didn't care. They had just lost their opportunity to secure the Poltergeist, and she had played a central role in their effort to take advantage of that opportunity. It was possible, however unlikely, that the Poltergeist's camouflage systems would remain down long enough for them to come up with another plan, but with the bulk of the interceptors out fighting the rock-biters alongside the *William Wallace* and *Martin Luther*...

A new icon appeared in orbit, originating at a point near the *Vercingetorix's* overwatch position. Xi cocked her head in confusion since the new contact showed no transponders or ident signatures. It was diving low, hard, and fast, picking up speed as its engines threw a huge trail of plasma behind it. The trail was too big for an interceptor and too small for a warship. Xi was familiar with the engine profiles of every single vehicle in the Terran Fleet, and this one matched none of them.

Xi raised the *Vercingetorix*. "*Vercingetorix, Elvira*. Confirm new contact originating from your position, over."

"*Elvira, Vercingetorix* Actual," Captain Stravinsky replied promptly. "Contact confirmed. Verifying ID. Stand by."

At that moment, the blank icon was updated on her HUD with a trio of numbers. No other data, no affiliative markers, and no direct line of communication was made possible via her virtual systems. Just three numbers appeared beneath its icon as the vehicle plunged through the upper atmosphere, and just as Xi's confusion reached its apex, a deep baritone voice came over the command channel, reciting an intro line that any Metalhead would instantly recognize.

As those words melted into the opening riff of General Akinouye's favorite song, *Number of the Beast* by Iron Maiden, the numbers 666 beneath the icon brought it all into focus. For a moment, Xi was overcome with a profound excitement she had not felt in years.

16

RESURRECTION

1st Company and their nested Marines sent omnidirectional fire into the incoming flood of Arh'Kel infantry. From their perch atop the ridgeline, they could hold out against the enemy advance as long as they had ammo and the enemy HWPs were kept to a minimum. It had been an ideal defensive position, which was only strengthened by the return of 2nd Company's mechs to the surface, where they added to the volume of fire sent into the steadily-thickening noose of rock-biter infantry surrounding their position.

So Jenkins' full attention was on the sky as Admiral Corbyn's trump card descended like an archangel driven by the fury of God Himself.

"Dragon Actual, this is *Bahamut 666*. We are inbound on intercept with enemy Poltergeist," said a woman's sharp, professional voice as Jenkins watched the winged demon appear on his mech's visual pickups. "We're coming in hot and inverted, ETA three minutes."

"Copy that, *Bahamut 666*," Jenkins acknowledged as a silly grin creased his face following the Siege mech's surprise appearance. "Update your target packages via Major Xi's telemetry."

"Confirmed, Colonel," the woman replied. "Telemetry updated and targets locked. We'll be in range in forty seconds."

Jenkins couldn't help but laugh. The "orbital supply platform" Admiral Corbyn had left behind was no such thing, but a concealed drop-can specifically designed to both harbor and hide a Bahamut-class Siege mech. He didn't know where it had come from, how many regs the admiral had broken by hiding it from the rest of the Fleet, or even how many TAC officials would blow their tops at discovering Fleet had possessed a working Siege-grade mech without their knowledge.

Right now, he was glad of the added firepower, and more importantly, for the 666's descent trajectory, which would take it well ahead of the fleeing Poltergeist. The *Bahamut Zero* had been capable of speeds approaching a hundred and twenty kph on terrain like AK-091's, and if the 666 was equally fast, capturing the Poltergeist was now well within their ability to accomplish.

The 666 came in hard and fast, throwing a giant trail of smoke behind as it dove through the planet's atmosphere. The two remaining interceptors flanked out wide to the north. The 666's approach trajectory would take it to a landing point a full fifty kilometers beyond the Poltergeist to the west, and when it arrived, the newly-oriented interceptors would be in position to create a crossfire that would drive the Poltergeist south or east.

Which brought them back to either the dragon mech or Mount Foothold.

The Poltergeist, either unaware of the 666's presence or unconvinced of the threat it posed, continued driving west toward the vehicle's future position. The 666 was braking hard against the planet's atmosphere, drawing a peak six gees of deceleration before gradually smoothing out its descent.

Major Xi was locked onto her ridge, fighting off the remaining rock-biter infantry the Poltergeist had used as living shields to block its escape, but her position would be a vital one if the Poltergeist came about as Jenkins expected.

"This is the *Bahamut 666*," the woman declared. "Requesting permission to disable target."

"Permission granted, *Beast*," Jenkins acknowledged as the mighty winged demon entered effective firing range. "Lock it down."

Still inverted during its drop, the bulk of the *Bahamut 666*'s topside-mounted weapons were clear to engage the enemy hovertank. When they did so, it filled Jenkins with pride as the mightiest mech ever fielded by humanity cleared its guns on target.

A storm of forty SRMs tore loose from their mounts, accompanied by six of the rare MRMs and a hail of railgun slivers. The slivers stabbed into the Poltergeist's forward hull, slamming the craft's curved bow into the rock before it rebounded to its previous flight position two meters off the ground.

The missiles fell toward their target and were quickly engaged by the Poltergeist's anti-missile rockets. The rockets batted thirty-four of the SRMs from the sky, along with three of the MRMs, but the rest of the ordnance splashed down around the enemy vehicle, where they delivered their peculiar payloads.

Half the missiles were standard explosive warheads, while the rest contained electromagnetic interference systems of various designs. If the entire missile salvo had been half EMP warheads, the price tag for the volley might have rivaled that of the *Bahamut 666*. Those systems were rare in the extreme, with Jenkins' people only deploying a handful during his time in TAC.

The field of overlapping EMPs would have overcome all but the most hardened and totally deactivated Terran virtual systems with likely permanent effect, and for a moment, it seemed like the Poltergeist would slow to a stop as its forward momentum gradually fell.

But then, like a sprinter catching his second wind, the Poltergeist resumed its charge with nothing but a pair of fresh rents in its flank armor to show for the deadly volley of fire sent down by the *Bahamut 666*.

Jenkins' HUD flickered with an incoming call originating from the *William Wallace*. "Dragon Actual, go."

"Colonel, this is *Wallace*'s GCO," Lieutenant Styles said. "We're monitoring your efforts, and Jem would like to use your mech as a relay point for an interference attempt. We're not sure it will work, but—"

"Permission granted," Jenkins interrupted as the *666* fired a fresh volley of ordnance at the fleeing hovertank. He accepted Styles' request for remote control of his mechs' comm suite and commanded, "Shut it down ASAP."

"Copy that, Colonel," Styles replied after a brief delay caused by the *William Wallace*'s distance from AK-091. A stream of data came over his comm panel before, unexpectedly, the Poltergeist's forward motion all but ceased. One moment it was moving forward at ninety-four kph, the next it was stopped cold.

Then the Poltergeist resumed its march, this time banking north toward the pair of Terran interceptors that were on final approach. The *Bahamut 666*, now forty-one kilometers to the Poltergeist's west, broke free of its broad drop wing and landed on the hard ground below. The multi-legged draconic vehicle flexed its limbs for a moment before sprinting toward the Poltergeist, accelerating to a hundred and twenty kph.

The trap was set, with Jenkins to the east, Mount Foothold to the south, and the *Beast* to the west. The only possible escape route left to the Poltergeist was through those two interceptors, and everyone on the field knew it, including the Jemmin commander.

"666 requesting permission to engage with Javelins," the mighty war machine's comm operator declared.

Jenkins hesitated for a second before reluctantly nodding. "Permission granted. Target craft's periphery only."

"Targets confirmed. Engaging with Javelins," the 666's comm operator reported, and the Siege mech sent a stream of eight LRMs into the sky as the Poltergeist squared off on the two inbound interceptors. Javelins were armor-piercing LRMs, generally used to engage fortified bunkers or naval targets where penetration below the waterline could be lethal, but their armor-piercing noses were perfectly acceptable in this instance since they were unlikely to cook off volatile components in the Poltergeist's interior.

The interceptors, marked with call signs *Glamdring* and *Suckerpunch*, split wide as the Poltergeist sent nine fresh rockets toward them. The interceptors initiated high-speed corkscrewing dives that were at the very limit of a Terran pilot's ability to survive. Somehow, the pilots evaded all nine of the inbound rockets before leveling off and returning fire with a storm of missiles and railgun slivers.

The slivers struck the mark, stabbing into the craft's rear flanks while the missiles slammed into the rocky ground in front of the Jemmin command tank. And just after the dust from the missile strikes settled, the Javelin LRMs arrived with the coup de grace.

Five of the Javelins struck along the Poltergeist's outer edge, each one carving a three-meter chunk from the hovertank's hull. The Jemmin vehicle fell to the ground, and this time it was unable to get back up as Jenkins' comm panel flared with another virtual interference attempt relayed from the *William Wallace*.

"Target is down, Colonel," Lieutenant Styles reported urgently. "I say again, target is down. You've got no more than eight minutes before the Poltergeist's systems reboot, and our best theory up here is that—"

Styles was cut short when the sound of an explosion was muffled by his mic's auto-correction systems, which prevented loud sounds from possibly deafening someone on the other end of the line.

"Sorry, Colonel," Styles said irritably. "We're taking fire up here, but have almost got these fireships under control. You've got eight minutes before that Poltergeist self-destructs, assuming its operator survived the attack. Recommend you secure it ASAP."

"Copy that, GC," Jenkins acknowledged as he sent orders to both Marine dropships hunkered down at his position. "Major Trapper, you're up."

"Affirmative," Trapper replied as the dropships lifted off from their perches beneath the tall ledge where 1st and 2nd Company stood fortified against the horde of rock-biters surrounding their position. "Recovery teams inbound."

"Sargon, let's clear a path for the Marines," Jenkins ordered. "Deploy your last three tac-nukes at the following coordinates."

"Coordinates received," Benjamin acknowledged. "Firing."

The last of 1st Company's tactical nukes flew out of Benjamin's mech, fanning out across the sea of rock-biter infantry that had bubbled up around Jenkins' position since 2nd Company had descended into the tunnel.

The formation's nested Marines and outer mechs had done an impeccable job of warding off the endless enemy tide to this point, but their ammo stores were running low. They had no more than ten more minutes of continued fire before they would exhaust their fixed positions' ammunition, and the mechs' magazines were well below half-capacity as well.

It was time to make their push, and the tactical nukes would clear two paths.

The nukes soared over the seemingly endless sea of rock-biters, which numbered well over two hundred thousand, with two of the missiles continuing toward Mount Foothold and the third targeting a danger-close stretch of ground between Jenkins' position and the Poltergeist.

The nukes touched down, carving kilometer-wide gaps in the enemy formation and annihilating tens of thousands of Arh'Kel. The Marine dropships flew low, passing directly over the single nuke strike between Dragon's mechs and the Poltergeist, while the other two nukes cleared a patch of ground along what would become their withdrawal corridor leading back to Mount Foothold.

Enemy HWPs targeted the dropships, sending missiles and railgun bolts at the all-important aircraft. Bearing a dozen armored Marines apiece, led by Major Trapper, those dropships represented their last chance to secure the downed Poltergeist and would arrive at their objective in three minutes' time. The aircraft juked and dodged clear of the danger-close inbound.

"Dragon Battalion, advance to indicated coordinates," Jenkins commanded after forwarding their new objective. "Push!"

The Marines and the Metalheads were on the march ten seconds later, with power-armored Marines hopping onto the backs of low-profile walker and crawler mechs. Their abandoned gun nests now held nothing but spent casings and tripod mounts for the miniguns the Marines held at the ready as the column prepared to plunge into the enemy horde like a blade to the belly.

Jenkins raised Major Xi. "*Elvira*, rendezvous with the Marines at the objective and transport the extracted assets back to Mount Foothold."

"Copy that, Dragon Actual," she acknowledged as her mech charged across the fifteen kilometers separating it from the downed Poltergeist.

Even as she spoke, the speed of Arh'Kel arriving through the hundred different tunnels within a fifty-klick radius increased. HWPs were flooding up much faster than before, signaling that the enemy had no desire to let the Terrans achieve their objective. Whether by conscious or unwitting design, the rock-biters were acting precisely as Jemmin would have wanted.

But Jenkins had prepared half his career for this moment. A charge into Arh'Kel forces with mechs and Marines working in tandem had been nothing but a dream a few short years ago, but here he was on the grandest stage imaginable doing precisely that. He had already demonstrated the theoretical quality of such a configuration back on Mars during the earliest stages of this operation. Now he had the chance to personally define how the Terran Armed Forces viewed the role of armor in modern warfare.

He was going to make every shot count.

"It's game time, people," Jenkins barked as the first mechs of Dragon Battalion came to grips with the enemy, unleashing a steady stream of minigun, chain gun, and coil gun fire into the silica-based monsters. "Rock their world."

Across the comm channel, the colonel piped Judas Priest's *Green Manalishi*.

"Major Xi, this is Major Trapper. We've secured the objective and are prepared to withdraw," the veteran reported when she was still one minute out. "There are a few too many HWPs for us to extract the assets via dropship."

"Trapper, this is *Elvira*," she acknowledged. "I am forty-six seconds out and prepared to receive transfer via my airlock."

"Copy that," Trapper replied. "We'll just be here twiddling our thumbs."

"Smartass," she quipped, drawing a soft chuckle from the man as she ran her mech over the broken ground leading to the precious Poltergeist. "Just keep your pants on and make sure your thumbs are all you twiddle."

His chuckle erupted into full-blown laughter, which was joined by a handful of the Marines attached to his retrieval op. The Marines were pouring a steady stream of fire into the approaching rock-biters, which had encroached to less than a kilometer despite their best efforts to ward them off. The sense of urgency in the Arh'Kel force had increased by what seemed like an order of magnitude following the Poltergeist's fall, and even twenty dedicated Marines were having difficulty maintaining a safe perimeter against the enemy.

"*Elvira*, this is *Suckerpunch*," came the voice of the lone remaining Viper pilot flying air patrol over her position. "I am bingo fuel and about to ditch. I'd appreciate a pick-up if you can squeeze me in," the female pilot requested as her aircraft slewed around to an approach vector over the Poltergeist's position.

"Careful with talk like that, *Suckerpunch*," Xi said dryly. "I've got a bunch of Marines down here who are already twiddling thumb-sized appendages. Talk of pick-ups and squeezing might be a little more than they can deal with right about now."

"Roger," *Suckerpunch* acknowledged, but her voice was groggy and slightly slurred. "I think I'll take my chances if it's all the same to you."

"Girls got to stick together," Xi agreed. "Give us a countdown to your ejection, and we'll cover your drop to keep the rock-biters off you."

"Appreciated," *Suckerpunch* replied. "Ejecting in seven... six...five..."

The countdown timer appeared on Xi's HUD as she brought *Elvira* to a stop outside the downed Poltergeist. A squad of Marines, each bearing a two-and-a-half-meter-long retrieval tube designed to protect against the planet's absurd atmospheric pressure and its toxic composition, approached her airlock as she lowered the gangplank. The Marines were too large to fit through the airlock door, but one of the dropship pilots was on hand and ready to facilitate the transfer of materials into Xi's airlock.

She popped the outer door, and the Marines quickly loaded their hard-acquired prizes inside. The Marine pilot rapped his fist on the airlock's inner door four times before exiting the compartment and making his way back to his vehicle. Meanwhile, the second Marine pilot helped a pair of his power-armored comrades retrieve the downed Viper pilot. They returned her limp body to the Tripoli-class dropship's interior before closing the doors behind them, leaving just one more matter to attend to before they could move to the rendezvous point.

"Lu, Penny," Xi called over her shoulder while purging the airlock of its deadly gases. "Secure those pods as soon as the airlock's clear."

"Copy that, ma'am," they acknowledged in tandem.

As the airlock purged the poisonous gases with a series of rapid cycles, Xi watched with unvarnished envy as Colonel Jenkins' column advanced on the rendezvous point. The Marines and Metalheads carved a bloody swath through the enemy line, dropping hundreds of Arh'Kel per second while twice as many surged up through the broken ground all around them.

Green Manalishi, a short jam, finished as *Elvira* prepared to move out. Xi picked up the mantle she had let slip and piped Dio's version of *Rainbow in the Dark* into the Arh'Kel atmosphere.

Coil guns, chain guns, artillery, and plasma cannons ripped into exposed Arh'Kel soldiers, covering the ground in a scorched slick of enemy gore. Rockets, railguns, and missiles scratched enemy HWPs and caused sheer devastation to the infantry escorting them. And the occasional orbital strike, sent by the *Vercingetorix'* railguns, scrapped SOM after SOM as soon as the orbit-capable systems appeared on the planet's surface.

It was the kind of charge that defined a career, and Xi had missed out on it because she'd had the misfortune of being closest to the downed Poltergeist. But capturing a Jemmin made it all worthwhile. Now she was the football, and it was everyone else's job to carry her over the goal line.

The airlock cycled for the last time, prompting her to open the inner door. "Secure those pods ASAP," she grumbled as *Devastator* sent a particularly abusive barrage of plasma bolts into the northern edge of the enemy line. The mighty *Powerslave's* plasma cannons fired to the south a few seconds later, carving half-kilometer kill zones through the cartwheeling Arh'Kel.

Marines perched atop low-profile mechs sent controlled bursts of minigun fire into the few Arh'Kel who survived the incessant fury of the mechs' artillery and heavy weapons fire. Those rock-biters unfortunate enough not to be enveloped by Colonel Jenkins' overwhelming firepower were expertly sniped by the power-armored Marines, who seemed every bit as comfortable riding mechs as they were manning gun nests or making open-ground charges. Seeing them work in perfect tandem, directed by Colonel Jenkins, who had developed the very deployment methods they harmoniously employed, was a truly magnificent sight Xi hoped to never forget.

But more than being awestruck by her fellow Terrans' ferocity during their charge through the enemy, Xi was flustered by her inability to add her own fire to the fray, so it was a more than welcome development when Lu reported, "All four pods secure, ma'am. We're ready to roll."

"Good," Xi acknowledged. "Major Trapper, form up on *Elvira* and let's get moving."

"This is Lieutenant Smiling Wolf," came the unexpected interruption before Trapper could reply. Smiling Wolf was one of the Marine pilots, who were among the most steel-nerved humans in the universe according to pretty much everyone. Hearing his request was nothing less than a shock. "Major, there's too much AA fire down here. Request permission to board your mech to ride back to Foothold."

She cocked her head in surprise as she surveyed the nearby area. Forty-five Arh'Kel HWPs were within effective firing range of the dropships once they went airborne, with more arriving on the surface every minute.

It was strange to hear Smiling Wolf request a ride back to Mount Foothold aboard her mech, but she had no reason to refuse the request.

"That's your call, Lieutenant," she said evenly. "Major Trapper, your opinion?"

"Those birds have a less than one in four chance of making the flight back to the FOB," Trapper surprisingly agreed. "If we try to cover their return instead of focusing on our withdrawal, we open ourselves to even more enemy fire. Ditching the birds is the right call."

"Then climb aboard," she said tersely as the *Bahamut 666* linked up with Colonel Jenkins' column. It seemed as though the Arh'Kel were unaware of the *Beast's* presence, which had permitted it to sprint at top speed toward the rendezvous point while Xi had come to the crashed Poltergeist. "We've got to get to the church on time."

A minute and a half later, the two Marine pilots and the unconscious interceptor pilot were safely within *Elvira's* airlock, and the Scorpion-class mech was on the move, flanked by twenty-four power-armored Marines.

Bizarrely, after five minutes of sustained fire and constant pressure, the rock-biters seemed to give up the chase. Those between the column and Mount Foothold continued to fight, but the speed by which Arh'Kel arrived at the surface plummeted, and the ferocity of their attacks did likewise.

As a result, less than an hour after reaching the Poltergeist, Elvira and the rest of the Terran column arrived back at the slopes of Mount Foothold, where their fortifications would grant them a much-needed period of respite.

However brief it might be.

17

REDEMPTION

While Majors Xi and Trapper oversaw the securing of their precious salvage, Colonel Jenkins made the decision to personally inspect the *Bahamut 666*. His pressure suit, supplied by the Solarian delegation to each of the Terrans assigned to mechs during Operation Dragula, was capable of acclimating to the hot, high-pressure environment while effectively negating the possibility of pressure sickness.

Calibrating the suit for that purpose required careful calculations requiring no less than twenty minutes, during which time the air of his cabin would slowly be replaced with that of the outside environment. Thus, it couldn't be used as an emergency ditch system, and Dr. Fellows had assured him there would be some lingering side effects ranging from nausea to possible erectile dysfunction for several days afterward.

A small price to pay for the chance to step inside the belly of the beast.

As he crossed the FOB's mech parking lot, the titanic *Bahamut 666* loomed above the other mechs in the unit. Even *Powerslave*, while taller than the eight-legged, draconic-looking war machine and parked just a hundred meters away, seemed pedestrian in comparison. For the briefest of moments, standing at the base of the 666's gangplank, Lee permitted himself to indulge in the fanciful notion that General Akinouye might be waiting for him on the other side of the airlock.

And in a way, he supposed that was precisely what he would find inside the twin of Akinouye's beloved *Bahamut Zero*. The old man's influence still touched everything in the Metal Legion, from the design of their uniforms to their roster of equipment, Benjamin Akinouye's mark on the Terran Armor Corps was more than just indelible. It was an ongoing factor in how the Legion conducted itself, and in that way, General Akinouye had achieved a measure of immortality that most could only dream of.

Jenkins' eyes swept up and down the *Beast's* hull before snagging on the proud insignia emblazoned beside the airlock's outer door—a field of silver stars with a flaring gold primary in the background, the curved surface of a blue planet in the fore-ground, and fifty-three tiny yet distinct steel-gray ships orbiting that blue planet. Every Terran knew the Terran Fleet's heraldry at a glance, but seeing it on the hull of a mech like the *Bahamut 666* somehow offended Jenkins—and that was both a surprise and a revelation to him.

Just a year ago, he would have been happy to see that emblem stamped onto every single mech in the human sphere. In fact, it had been his all-consuming objective to accomplish that very feat by merging Fleet and TAC into some sort of combined arms system. It had been nothing but politics which had driven him to abandon Fleet and transfer to TAC. His driving motivations had remained true throughout, as had his commitment to defending Terra from her enemies, which was precisely what Fleet did better than any other agency in Terran history.

So why now, after such a relatively brief period of time, did his lip curl at seeing Fleet heraldry stamped on a Terran mech? Partial answers bubbled up through his mind, but none of them were satisfactory. It was more than simple tribalism. It transcended the presence of political rot that had seemed to creep into every nook and cranny of the Terran government, including Fleet and, if he was honest, even the Armor Corps, albeit for a brief time when it came to the latter.

Pushing those thoughts from his mind, he climbed the gangplank and keyed his comm link to the channel provided by the 666's comm operator. "This is Colonel Jenkins, Terran Armor Corps, requesting permission to conduct a field inspection."

"Permission granted, Colonel," the woman replied, and the outer airlock door slid open to reveal a compartment totally identical to the one he remembered from the *Bahamut Zero*.

He stepped inside the airlock and was surprised at just how much faster it cycled compared to other mechs in the unit. Twenty seconds after stepping inside, the inner airlock door cycled open and he was greeted by the most unexpected sight.

"Welcome aboard, Colonel," Lieutenant Commander James Murdoch greeted him, standing at rigid attention in the traditional Fleet posture. Jenkins removed his helmet, eliciting a series of pops and hisses as his suit's multiple pressure-sealing layers equalized with the cabin pressure.

He returned the salute with the TAC salute. He examined his former XO from head to toe. The other man looked better than he remembered from Durgan's Folly. He looked to have put on a few pounds of muscle, leaned out his previously soft midsection, and there was a fire in his eyes that Jenkins had not previously seen in the man.

If not for the unnatural bend to his nose, which Jenkins knew had come courtesy of Major Xi Bao during their last moments together, he would have thought this man to be Murdoch's better twin.

"Commander Murdoch." Jenkins reached out with a gloved hand, which Murdoch accepted with a vice-like grip. "I didn't expect to see you here, but I'm going to be frank: I like what I see."

"Thank you, Colonel," Murdoch said with a deferential nod. "The admiral didn't know if the 666 would be needed, but he brought us along just in case."

"Let me guess," Jenkins said, casting an appraising eye around the corridor's interior. "This was part of Admiral Corbyn's plan to roll TAC into Fleet?"

"That's my understanding, sir." Murdoch gestured to the passage leading to the vehicle's command deck. "Your inspection, Colonel?"

"Of course," Jenkins agreed, and the two men made their way through the narrow passage. To Jenkins, it was very much like walking through a ghost ship. He had only spent a short time aboard the *Bahamut Zero*, but every moment seemed burned into his memory. Walking through this precise copy was more nostalgic than he expected.

"Our stern, flank, and topside armor is design spec," Murdoch explained, gesturing to a section of the corridor's interior paneling that was notably absent. On the other side of the missing panel, the port armor of the 666 was readily visible. "But our front and underside are high-test, laminar steel panels—"

"Hold up," Jenkins interrupted in alarm. "Your bow and floor are *steel*?"

"Yes, sir," Murdoch agreed matter-of-factly. "The 666 was built in secret as a mirror of the *Zero*. Fleet had its fingers deeper into TAC back when these units were being manufactured, and the Admiralty had been toying with a variant of this system that could carry four companies of Marines instead of its forward systems. They acquired the plans and had identical components built by fudging the budget books and effectively shunting the cost back to TAC, which likely accounted for the reason the Bahamut line was considered too costly to field."

For a moment, Jenkins thought he could actually hear General Akinouye spontaneously imploding in his grave at hearing how he'd been outmaneuvered by Fleet when it came to his pride and joy.

"That project was eventually abandoned when the latest generation of dropships rolled off the line," Murdoch continued. "But by the time Fleet made that decision, there was no opportunity to have replacement armor panels made without tipping TAC off to the fact that Fleet had the 666. So the bow was fitted with inch-and-a-half laminar steel panels, which threw the weight distribution off-spec and required the under armor to be replaced with half-inch steel to compensate."

Jenkins' brow rose in undisguised surprise. "You rode down here on a mech with front- and bottom-side armor that Arh'Kel small arms fire could penetrate?"

"Correct, Colonel." Murdoch gestured farther up the corridor. "If I may?"

"Please," Jenkins agreed as he struggled to reconcile what he was hearing with his memory of the man before him. The Captain James Murdoch who had served on Durgan's Folly would never have willingly dropped into a war zone in a vehicle that was anything less than pristine, but now he seemed completely nonchalant about having done precisely that.

They arrived on the 666's command deck, which should have been equipped with twenty stations, all manned by operators and specialists essential to the vehicle's operation. But Jenkins saw just six occupied workstations, including the vacant pilot's chair, while the rest of the stations were dormant and unmanned.

"The 666 was originally outfitted with fourth-generation

virtual systems," Murdoch explained, gesturing to the dormant stations. "But following Operation Spider Hole, it was determined that these systems presented too grave a security risk, so they were immediately removed from all Fleet craft."

Jenkins frowned in confusion. "The *Bahamut Zero* had sixth-generation systems."

"Correct." Murdoch nodded approvingly. "The *666's* virtual architecture was salvaged in the immediate aftermath, with its sixth-gen systems being installed in older dropships like the Tripolis to improve their security. Admiral Corbyn was eventually able to fight off the vultures with bureaucratic interference maneuvers while he removed the *666* from Fleet storage and had it transferred to a series of hidden locations. We've barely got enough virtual processing capacity to simultaneously run the reactors and tactical systems. In all honesty, I gave us no better than a seventy percent chance of surviving the drop... though not all of that is because of the virtual systems."

Jenkins cocked his head curiously as Murdoch approached one of the active, manned stations. Inputting a series of commands including his command authorization key, the lieutenant commander pulled up a current status report for the *Bahamut 666*. And when Jenkins realized what Murdoch was highlighting on that report, the colonel couldn't help but laugh.

"So not only did you have no front- and underside armor." Jenkins chuckled. "And not only is your virtual mainframe woefully inadequate to extended combat deployments, but you're telling me that this mech's using civilian-spec kinetic dampeners? The kind used on automated excavation equipment during drops on uninhabited worlds?"

"Correct, sir." Murdoch nodded.

"How did you survive the landing?" Jenkins asked bluntly.

A series of snickers went around the command deck while Lieutenant Commander Murdoch flashed a grin, showing a handful of broken teeth as he did. "Let's just say we'll all be visiting the dentist after we go wheels-up, Colonel."

"The commander's the only one who stayed awake during touchdown," a petty officer said from the comm console. Jenkins instantly recognized her as the voice he had spoken with over the link. "The rest of us blacked out."

"It was the neural implants that kept me conscious," Murdoch assured the PO. "I got concussed like everyone else."

"How are your weapons systems?" Jenkins asked.

"To spec, Colonel," Murdoch said confidently. "Four sets of quad-mounted railguns, four quad LRM launchers, four six-tube MRM launchers, though we're scratch ammo for those, twelve eight-tubed SRMs, twenty-two coil guns, and four heavy plasma cannons. Unfortunately, we don't have the virtual systems to reliably fire the HPCs. It'd be a coin flip whether we'd kill ourselves or the enemy if we pulled the trigger, but the option's there if you want it."

"If *I* want it?" Jenkins repeated neutrally.

"Colonel Lee Jenkins," Lieutenant Commander Murdoch intoned officiously, "as commander of this vehicle, I formally submit the *Bahamut 666* and its crew to your command for the duration of this mission, in accordance with both Admiral Corbyn's orders and with the dictates of our consciences." He purposefully looked around the command deck. "Everyone aboard the *666* is a volunteer for this op, and we've been briefed on the true nature of Operation Dragula. We came to help recover that Poltergeist however we're able, and that job's not yet done."

Jenkins nodded slowly as he looked at the faces of the vehicle's skeleton crew. When he had first set foot on the mighty war machine, it had been like stepping into a dream. But now the reality, staring back at him from their workstations, had finally sunk in. And while the *Bahamut 666* was a far cry from its predecessor, the *Bahamut Zero*, it just might have brought something more precious than any piece of destructive machinery.

Jenkins gestured to the conference room. "Before I decide how to proceed, let's have a word in private, Commander."

"Of course, Colonel," Murdoch agreed, and the two men went into *Bahamut 666*'s war room. The wooden tabletop was markedly different from the *Bahamut Zero*'s, but aside from that, it could have been the exact same room.

Murdoch tried to defer, gesturing for Jenkins to take the head seat, but Jenkins declined, and the two men took seats opposite one another across the mahogany tabletop.

"I honestly don't know where to begin, Commander," Jenkins said after a moment's reflection.

"Don't mince words, sir," Murdoch said flatly. "I won't."

"You never have, have you?" Jenkins said with a lopsided grin.

"No, sir."

"All right, I'll say it." Jenkins shrugged. "When we last spoke, it wasn't a joyful affair. You said things that were truer than I would have liked, and I might have done the same."

"We did, sir," Murdoch assured him.

"But the only reason I said those things was because frankly, I didn't see you as capable of this." Jenkins gestured to the mech's interior. He hesitated for a long moment before deciding to proceed. "I think I understand how you got here, but feel free to correct me if I get any of this wrong. Corbyn asked you to head up his Combined Arms project since you had the most field experience with mechs of anyone under his command, and that experience came during a classified op like Spider Hole. You've got the bureaucratic chops to play an integral role in his attempted takeover of TAC, which Major General Kavanaugh and he privately negotiated against a dozen inter-branch regs. I'd wager that you played no small part in securing this vehicle for Admiral Corbyn, and were waiting with bated breath for the chance to move in as Corbyn's right-hand man in 'his' combined arms program. In effect, you were holding a knife to my back, and I wasn't aware of it. How am I doing?"

Murdoch nodded. "So far, so good, Colonel."

"But then something changed." Jenkins cocked his head in consternation. "And I can't decide what that was. You're not a glory hound, so it wasn't the fact that you missed out on Antivenom and all the ensuing press. You're not a man of honor, so shame has nothing to do with it." Murdoch stiffened at hearing that, but just as Jenkins had predicted, the other man held his tongue, which was itself a departure from his previous comportment.

"And if my read's right, you still don't much care for me," Jenkins continued with a sigh. "So what is it, Commander? What changed? Because until I understand you a little better, I can't accept responsibility for you and your people. For all I know, you've still got a knife at my back, and I'm *slowly* learning just how dangerous interbranch politics can be."

"Permission to speak freely, sir?"

"Granted," Jenkins urged.

Murdoch met and held Jenkins' gaze as he spoke. "An ancient romanticized quote from Cao Cao goes something like this...'The worst traitor looks like an honest man, and the greatest falsehood appears to be the truth. Righteousness and evil cannot be distinguished from appearance alone. Perhaps yesterday you misjudged me, and perhaps today you misjudge me still, but I remain myself.'

"I honestly thought that was the case for my entire career. No, for my entire *life*." He smirked, his eyes never wavering from Jenkins'. "I thought misunderstanding defined the majority of our perceptions of one another, and as a result, I never gave much consideration to what others thought of me. I did what I thought was best, not necessarily what was right, and that was how I justified my 'supply-stealing ass.'" He chuckled, drawing a wan smile from Jenkins as he recalled leveling those words at Murdoch during their last encounter.

"But then, after hearing about what you did on Antivenom, I realized something that made me understand where Cao Cao got it wrong." Murdoch scratched his head before continuing. "I can't exactly put it into words, but what you did on Luna *mattered*. It might have been the single greatest deed in human history. You're right; I don't care about the glory. And you're probably also right that it's not about honor or shame," he admitted sourly.

"But I had a chance to be part of that, to be part of what you did for all humanity—hell, maybe for the entire *galaxy*—and I was too self-absorbed to do it. You were right; I *was* looking for a safe, comfy desk somewhere, but I honestly didn't realize it at the time. It wasn't until Admiral Corbyn briefed me on Antivenom following your success on Luna that I understood the magnitude of my error."

"You say it's not about glory..." Jenkins cocked his head dubiously. "But I'm not sure how to square what you just said with that. It sounds to me like you're envious and put out that you didn't get to be part of the winning team."

"No, Colonel." Murdoch shook his head flatly. "It's because while you succeeded, you *might* have failed. Hell, by all rights, you *should* have failed. And if you had, then there was a chance, however small, that I could have played a part in turning that defeat into victory."

He finally averted his gaze, which drifted off unfocused for several seconds. "I don't think I'll ever like you, sir, and I doubt you'll ever like me. But we did work well together on Spider Hole, and I've never been part of anything as impactful as that operation. It was a mistake for me to break rank with you when I did, not because I missed out on what you achieved afterward, which far outstripped Spider Hole, but because I didn't *contribute* to your achievements under the TAC banner. Until Durgan's Folly, I'd misspent my entire life and career. I'm determined to make the day I parted company with you and the others the last in a lifelong series of bad decisions based on flawed priorities. I'm not asking your forgiveness, and wouldn't accept it if it was offered because, frankly, I don't deserve it. I'm saying that while I'm not necessarily a changed man, I *have* changed my priorities, and I hope my work here demonstrates that to your satisfaction."

Jenkins knew this could all be some kind of trap. Murdoch could be using the specter of the *Beast* to put himself in a more favorable light, with the goal of using whatever trust he engendered against him in the future.

But after looking him in the eye and hearing him speak, Jenkins was convinced that something was indeed different about Lieutenant Commander Murdoch. And after a career spent making snap decisions involving the life and death of the best men and women he had ever served with, Lee Jenkins knew better than most when to trust his instincts.

"All right, Commander Murdoch." He stood from the table and proffered a hand. "When last we spoke, I wouldn't have believed it possible, but it seems we've both earned redemption for our past sins. And I welcome the chance to fight alongside anyone as valiant as you and your crew."

As Murdoch stood from the table, Jenkins saw something had shifted in the other man's visage. A dam had broken within him, and the effect was spilling over to him as well.

"Thank you, Colonel." Murdoch gripped his hand tightly, and with that, they made ready for the next phase of the operation.

Extraction.

18

SECONDARY OBJECTIVES

The *William Wallace* returned to orbit just as the Metalheads and Marines returned to Mount Foothold. Styles had gotten the railguns back online, but they were far from precisely calibrated, which made them nearly useless in long-range naval engagements.

Thankfully, all Podsy planned to do with them was bombard the rock-biters on AK-091 from low orbit.

As he read through a stream of updates sent by Colonel Jenkins and Major Trapper, an opportunity presented itself that had not been considered realistic during the operation's planning phase.

"Styles," he said, making his way to the Ground Control station, "I need to bounce this off someone."

"Let's hear it," Styles urged.

"We've lost eight mechs down there," Podsy explained. "And we've got another four down-checks that are probably a waste of effort to retrieve. If we ditch them, we could consolidate the rest of our armor on the *Wallace*."

Styles' brow creased. "But it would take twice as long to retrieve our mechs using just the *William Wallace*'s..." Realization dawned, and his brow lowered contemplatively. "What about retrieving the *Bahamut 666*?"

"Forget the *666*." Podsy shook his head firmly. "It would take us four hours to retrieve it after we've collected the rest of our gear. And even if we did get it back into orbit, there's the matter of securing it for taxi through the wormholes. No," he reiterated with firm conviction. "That was a one-time card the admiral played, and we're all glad he played it when he did, but it was a one-way trip the *Beast* took to the surface, and he had to know it."

"You really want to pick up that Poltergeist?" Styles said skeptically, but the light in his eyes gave the lie to his reticence. "The only way we can do it—"

"Is by having the *Vercingetorix* drop its retrieval cable spool all the way to the ground," Podsy interrupted urgently. "Have a ground team connect it to the Poltergeist, and then task all of our remaining Marine dropships with pulling the spool back up into orbit to where the *Vercingetorix* can reattach and drag it up."

"A dozen things can go wrong in the first seconds." Styles cocked his head dubiously. "The precision acceleration curve, keeping the rock-biters out of firing range so they don't clip the tether. Hell, the structural integrity of the Poltergeist has to be sketchy after all the holes they punched in it. Who knows if it would survive the ascent without falling apart at the seams?"

"I know the problems," Podsy said irritably. "What I need is someone to calculate the odds, which I can have Jem do, but also I need someone to put together as much data as possible on the variables involved to make sure when we run the calculations we're doing them on solid footing. You're the top information specialist in all of TAC," he said without any intention of buttering Styles' muffin. "I need you to collect the numbers so Jem can run them."

"I'm on it." He turned his full attention to his workstation for several long minutes. Podsednik could do nothing but wait and coordinate the various repair efforts throughout the ship. Chief Petty Officer Malkovich had taken over at Tactical and was already sighting the *Wallace's* railguns on ground targets.

In a way, Podsy felt utterly useless as the bridge crew worked furiously at their assignments. He stood at the center of it all, but while they were busy with their duties, he had few, if any, of his own that he could undertake that wouldn't directly interfere with their efforts.

Just as Podsednik's tedium-fueled anxiety neared the breaking point, Styles pumped his fist and declared, "I think I got everything we need, Captain. I'm ready to send it to Jem."

Podsy opened the direct line to Jem. "Jem, are you up for some calculations?"

"I am," Jem immediately replied.

"Styles is forwarding you some data," Podsy explained. "We need to know the odds that we can retrieve that Poltergeist using the method and materials listed in his data."

"A crude but inventive method," Jem mused before going silent for several seconds. "I calculate that, in concert with the deployment of the last remaining fusion warheads in this ship's arsenal, along with precision railgun bombardments to clear the extraction zone of Arh'Kel surface-to-air and surface-to-orbit weapons, there is a seventy-two percent chance the Poltergeist can be successfully brought into orbit and out of danger. This incorporates my experiential observations regarding Terran personnel in carrying out their duties, which is significantly higher-value than I surmised when I first joined your company."

"Seventy-two percent..." Podsy grimaced. He had been hoping for something above ninety. "What kind of casualties do you anticipate?"

"I project one of the Marine dropships and whichever mech

is sent to attach the retrieval tether will be destroyed during the operation," Jem promptly replied. "Combined with fire sustained by units defending the extraction team's advance, I anticipate human losses between six and nine."

"If we do this," Styles mused, "all of our ground forces will have to commit to the operation and abandon Mount Foothold. That means reaching a new extraction point guarded by as many as a million rock-biters."

"I have not calculated likely losses incurred by reaching a new extraction point," Jem observed. "Though I expect they would be higher than those incurred by the retrieval operation."

"A Poltergeist is a potential treasure trove," Podsy muttered under his breath, running a hand over his short-cropped hair. "It could revolutionize Terran technology across the board."

"We've already got the vehicle's data cores and comm components," Styles retorted. "And from the reports, the Poltergeist's main beam weapon wasn't even online, and its stealth systems were all but dead by the time they neutralized it. How much of its systems are intact enough to be of any use to our researchers?"

"I have no idea," Podsy admitted. "But the admiral was right; we can't lose our nerve because we're afraid of missing the mark. Ultimately, it's the ground team's call, but it's our job to present them with their options and whatever support we're capable of providing. Tell me if you disagree with any of that."

"I don't, Captain," Styles said reluctantly. "But you know if you give them the choice, they'll take it. So is it really a matter of just presenting them with options, or are we manipulating them into doing what we want?"

"I'll let them be the judge of that," Podsy said with finality.

"Let me say this," Styles continued after a moment's silence. "I think this is the right thing to do. But if history is anything to go by, Fleet's going to make us bleed while they swoop in and take the glory. Our involvement here is hidden, while theirs will be publicized for a century or more. Metalheads are going to die, and Fleet's going to benefit."

"That's the difference between doing what's best and doing what's right," Podsy said, the thought crystallizing into words even as he spoke them. "The *best* thing to do from a tactical perspective would be to turtle up and let Fleet do the heavy lifting of retrieving the Poltergeist, but if we do, we run the risk of missing this golden opportunity. The *right* thing for us to do, the thing which will do the most good for everyone, is to charge into the teeth of the enemy, seize that opportunity, and smile if Fleet vultures our win. In a choice between what's best and what's right, to me, that's no choice at all."

"This is going to hurt," Styles stated grimly.

"It will...just like most things worth doing do," Podsednik agreed, knowing that he was about to put in motion a plan which would almost certainly get a lot of good men and women killed. But while it might not be the best course of action from the Legion's perspective, it certainly was the right one for humanity. And if Andy Podsednik's checkered career had demonstrated anything about him, it was that he would choose the right path over the best path every single time. "Get Commander Stravinsky on the line. Let's make this happen."

Thirty minutes later, the mechs of Dragon Battalion were mobilized and moving to support the recovery of the Poltergeist. The materials retrieved from the Poltergeist had gone up with the medevacked personnel. Major Xi Bao knew that Podsednik had been right to propose this secondary objective when everyone on AK-091 could have simply gone wheels up from Mount Foothold and spared themselves another clash with the enemy.

The cost of the upcoming action would be high, but then so were the rewards. It was the harder of the two options.

Thankfully, Metalheads didn't much care for taking the easy way out. Whether that was due more to excessive bravery or a deficient sense of self-preservation, Xi didn't care. They would go where others wouldn't and do what others couldn't, just like General Akinouye's poem said. And right now, this was what humanity needed from them.

The column had mobilized every asset within Mount Foothold. Over a million rock-biters surrounded the mountain, and while the majority of the HWPs were scrubbed by orbital fire as soon as they appeared, the targeted bombardments would soon be turned toward clearing a path through the horde of Arh'Kel infantry instead of killing railgun and missile platforms.

With the *William Wallace* once again in orbit, the Metal Legion had sufficient orbital firepower to cover the operation, but until the *Martin Luther* returned, they had no more than that.

"In position," Lieutenant Gordon reported as his chosen mech, *Hell's Hammer*, arrived at the leading edge of the formation. Gordon's voice was still tinny and synthesized owing to the extreme amounts of helium he had breathed, but his mind had been sharp enough to convince Colonel Jenkins to let him take the dangerous ride to the Poltergeist.

"Copy that," Colonel Jenkins acknowledged over the battalion-wide channel. "Commence advance on objective."

The column drove forward, with the *Bahamut 666* at the heart of the formation. The mighty siege mech carried as much firepower as most companies, though its technical shortcomings prevented it from firing its most devastating weapons. Still, with the *Beast* adding to the ground forces' firepower, there would be little difficulty carving a safe zone for Gordon and his team to do their work.

"*Wallace* Ground Control, this is Major Xi. Commence fire package Omega. I say again, commence fire package Omega."

"Fire package Omega confirmed," Styles acknowledged, and the ground before the column was stabbed from the heavens by bolts of hypervelocity tungsten. Screaming through the atmosphere, they left boiling clouds of smoke and vapor in their wakes before they slammed into the ground with kilotons of destructive force. Their strike points began the bloody work of carving a clear path between Mount Foothold and the Poltergeist, and as they did so, the *Vercingetorix's* smaller guns continued sniping enemy vehicles as they emerged from the network of tunnels.

Despite the constant bombardment, those tunnels continued to produce enemy troops at alarming rates. Collapses at the tunnel mouths were cleared in minutes when the work of doing so with heavy equipment would take Terran excavation teams hours. And if a tactical-grade weapon was sent to collapse a tunnel network completely, the rock-biters would simply surge up through new fissures in the blasted hellscape of AK-091's surface. There was no victory to be had in fighting the Arh'Kel on the surface of this planet. All that remained to the men and women assigned to Operation Dragula was to recover the Poltergeist and reach their new extraction point, but neither of those tasks would likely be as simple to achieve as they were to describe.

Connecting the spooled tether to the Poltergeist and Marine dropships would require both technical expertise and the materiel resources available only on a repair and recovery vehicle. The Marine pilots, Lieutenant Spirit Wolf and Lieutenant Odom, would assist Gordon with his work until they lifted the spool back into orbit by flying their dropships in tandem, with each holding one end of the tether spool as it unrolled during their climb to rendezvous with the *Vercingetorix.*

The reasons for dropping the entire spool and not simply deploying the tether in a more normal fashion were twofold. First, the Arh'Kel would certainly attempt to destroy whatever was used to weight the tether during its descent to the surface, which would subject it to an additional twenty-nine minutes of enemy fire. Even though the orbiting warships could be relied upon to destroy HWPs and SOMs, the carbon nanotube retrieval tethers had exceptional tensile strength and were resistant to crushing, but susceptible to puncturing weapons. Even small-arms fire could damage them, and with the army of rockbiters surrounding the Poltergeist, it would be subjected to an endless stream of enemy fire.

The second reason had to do with the intense winds which whipped across AK-091's multi-layered atmosphere. Those winds could knock a retrieval platform or other heavy object as far as five kilometers off-course, according to their best projections, while the *Bahamut 666*'s drop-wing could be repurposed to perform a precision drop of the tether spool as its final act of service to Terra. A Marine dropship could also bring the spooled tether to the surface, but this would expose that dropship to a measure of risk which was greatly ameliorated by using the *666's* remote-operated wing.

They chose the latter method.

That wing descended from orbit bearing the tether spool as the column charged through the path cleared by the *Wallace's* railgun strikes. Bearing the last of their mobile miniguns and quad-pods, the power-armored Marines ran alongside the mechs, firing sniper-precise shots at any Arh'Kel infantry foolish enough to charge through the rain of tungsten that preceded the armor column.

With the *Wallace* slamming bolt after bolt into the planet's surface, clearing a path for the mechs and Marines, it took six minutes before the mechs began to fire their coil and chain guns into the enemy line. The rate of fire steadily increased over the next four minutes, until those mechs covering the Terrans' left and right flanks were firing multi-second max-cycle bursts into the press of cartwheeling silicoids.

"2nd Company, you are cleared to engage with heavy weapons," Xi commanded. "Push 'em back."

Guns thundered in sequence, sending a rippling wave of explosive ordnance into the enemy throng along the column's flanks. *Devastator's* light plasma cannon unleashed a volley of four precisely-targeted plasma bolts, carving a swath of destruction into the enemy line. As they drove toward their objective, with Gordon's *Hell's Hammer* sprinting well ahead of the column where it used danger-close proximity to the railgun strikes as cover, Xi began to feel genuine pity for the mindless rock-biters who threw their lives away hurling their bodies at the armored column.

She knew they had to die if the Legion was to get off this rock, but dealing death to them no longer yielded the primal satisfaction it once had. There had to be a better way to deal with the rock-biters than wholesale slaughter, but Xi would be damned if she could envision what it was.

Guns continued pouring ammunition into the Arh'Kel, pushing them back beyond knife-range with methodical precision. The *Bahamut 666's* voice was heard loudly and often as it sent wave after wave of ordnance into the enemy, and the plasma cannons of *Powerslave* and *Devastator* did the heaviest lifting of the unit, at least in terms of piling up the body count.

Hell's Hammer arrived at the crashed Poltergeist less than a minute before the *666's* drop wing did. The wing fell to an altitude of just two hundred meters before dropping the parachute-equipped tether spool sixty-four meters from the Poltergeist. As Gordon and the Marine pilots did their work, the column spread out with 1st and Joker Companies heading south, while

2nd Company and the *Bahamut 666* moved north. Within four minutes, the mechs created an impenetrable field of fire surrounding the site. The *Wallace* supported their shield with orbital strikes, while seven Viper-class aerospace fighters swooped down behind the drop-wing to strafe enemy HWPs and SOMs before they could set up and fire on the Terrans.

To Xi Bao's eyes, the scene before her was a thing of beauty. Her Metalheads had worked tirelessly, dropped onto godforsaken rocks like this one, and even attacked the most heavily-fortified bastion in Sol during their last year of service. They had taken the tough missions, fought against impossible odds, and were finally that which they always had the potential to become.

The deadliest fighting force in all of human space.

The perfectly-choreographed dance of destruction was immaculate and represented Colonel Jenkins' dream of maximizing the tactical values of power-armored Marines, Metal Legion armor, aerospace interceptors, and orbital fire support. Every piece worked in harmony with every other, and as the two Tripoli-class Marine dropships began to climb into the sky with the unspooling tether held between them, Xi allowed herself a moment of pride.

And then the rock-biters did their best to ruin things.

"LRMs inbound," Benjamin declared over the emergency channel as a series of icons appeared at the edge of sensor range. A storm of over three hundred missiles came screaming past the three-hundred-kilometer line, and each one appeared to contain a tactical-grade fission warhead. Traveling at two thousand kilometers per hour, the missiles tore through the planet's choking atmosphere en route to the Poltergeist's location.

Until this point, the Poltergeist had been completely ignored by the rock-biters. The Tripoli dropships had likewise been left alone by the Arh'Kel ground forces, but something had changed in the last few minutes. Xi suspected she knew what it was.

"The other Poltergeist." She grimaced. "It must have coordinated the launch from beyond the line."

"Agreed," Jenkins confirmed. "New formation: Aegis posture. I say again, Aegis posture. Prepare to receive enemy ordnance with priority coverage of the extraction team."

The acknowledgments returned following the colonel's orders, and Xi crouched *Elvira* in preparation for doing her part in the upcoming interception. According to Podsy, Jem's projections showed a high chance that several Terrans would die defending against the Arh'Kel counterattack. Up to this point, she had thought they might escape without a single loss, but as always, Jem's calculations proved prophetic.

With that many nukes inbound, Terrans were going to bleed. Now all that remained was to limit the damage as much as possible.

The *Bahamut 666* launched eight LRMs, sending the volley straight at the approaching enemy nukes. Each of the *666's* missiles showed on her tactical display as carrying tactical-grade warheads, and as they rose through the sky to meet their counterparts, the enemy missile storm fanned out in response.

She watched with bated breath as the *666's* missiles screamed toward their targets and felt a mounting sense of dread before they finally filled the sky a hundred sixty kilometers away with a series of blindingly radiant pulses.

The rad wash temporarily knocked her sensors offline, but Lieutenant Benjamin's were hardened and fed the results to the rest of the mechs in the column.

"Eighty-nine enemy missiles intercepted," he reported. "Two-hundred-twenty-six still inbound."

"Target with SRMs," Jenkins commanded as he forwarded a new green perimeter fifteen kilometers from the Poltergeist. A second red line soon appeared just three kilometers out, and Xi understood exactly what those lines meant before the colonel explained. "Fire all SRMs at optimal intercept of the green line. Hold interceptive rockets until the enemy missiles reach the red line. Stay focused; we've got this."

The Vipers broke off from their ground sorties and began sending hypervelocity tungsten slivers into the enemy missiles. In the ensuing seconds, as the enemy nukes neared the green line, the Vipers scratched another sixteen missiles from the sky.

But that still left over two hundred of the things inbound, and as they approached the green line, Terran SRMs began to surge up in reply. Xi added no SRMs of her own, having fitted her lone remaining missile pod with interceptor rockets.

But she watched her comrades send over four hundred Terran missiles skyward, where they burned toward intercept of the incoming holocaust of nukes. If even ten percent of those nukes touched down, it was game over for the entire ground force, and if just one managed to strike within three kilometers of the Poltergeist, its recovery would be impossible because the tether would be irreparably damaged.

The SRMs began to explode mid-air, the vast majority harmlessly missing their targets after the LRMs made evasive twists and turns during their final descent toward the Terrans. All told, another forty-four LRMs were torn down by the SRMs, leaving a hundred and sixty-six inbound nukes.

The interceptive rockets flared all around the column, sending three hundred and eighty rockets up to meet the enemy ordnance. Marines began firing their railgun rifles, scoring a handful of intercepts as the rockets sped toward their targets. The final layer of the shield, the chain and coil guns, began raking across the sky, filling the air with slugs and bullets, many of which were visible to the naked eye as they tore through the carbon dioxide-rich air.

The Terran rockets slammed into their targets as Xi kept her focus on firing her chain guns. She knew these might be her final moments, and she intended to make the most of them by covering her fellows to the best of her ability. In all of Terran history, no unit had been targeted by this much nuclear fire-power in a single salvo. Xi smirked at the realization that in the end, this would be yet another entry the Metal Legion had the dubious honor of making in the Terran Armed Forces' record books.

The last instant before expected impact sped past much faster than Xi expected it to, and for a brief moment, she thought they had completely escaped the enemy's wrath.

Then two nukes exploded eight hundred meters above the surface, and her mech's systems were knocked offline shortly before the blast wave violently shook the mech. Her neural link went dead, which was unusual even considering the expected EMP, and for a moment, she was so disoriented she thought she would vomit.

"What the fuck?!" she snapped, thankfully maintaining control over her stomach. "Lu, Penny, reboot the main control systems and manually switch to auxiliaries."

"Auxiliaries, aye," Lu acknowledged, and a few seconds later, the manual control systems slowly came to life.

Gripping the joysticks, she directed *Elvira* to turn a few degrees port, then the same to starboard, and was rewarded by optimal responses. "I need eyes," she snapped.

"I've got the vid periscope up," Penny reported, and a lone video feed appeared on Xi's backup display.

She scanned the horizon before finding the nuclear mush-room clouds, which were separated by less than a kilometer. The nukes had gone off at two-point-nine and two-point-seven kilometers from the Poltergeist.

Her heart skipped several beats as she realized they had

gone off within the danger zone, and after a few seconds, comm linkage was reestablished via P2P as Lu managed to reboot the mech's main systems.

"—again: tether is intact," Lieutenant Benjamin reported. "Mission is still go."

She pumped her fist before the damage reports started coming in. Her hand went to her mouth as she realized why the nukes had gone off at such peculiar altitudes of seven-hundred-ninety and eight-hundred-twenty meters.

Four of the Viper pilots, using their craft as interceptors, had collided with the missiles and destroyed their drive systems. The nukes' atmospheric pressure triggers must have misinterpreted feedback caused by the physical collisions as the weapons having reached the optimal detonation altitude of two hundred meters. This had caused them to go off long before they should have, which remarkably had preserved the tether's integrity since the Tripoli dropships had continued to burn toward the *Vercingetorix* in low orbit, where they would arrive in less than a minute.

Then she saw that one of the Joker mechs was not responding to repeated hails. The *Twisted Sister*, a support vehicle capable of performing field repairs on tactical-grade mechs, had been directly beneath the blast zone of a nuke. While its hull was still clearly visible, it was powered down and showed several hull breaches across its topside. A nearby squad of Marines moved toward it, but Xi knew this hellish world had claimed the lives of those within the now-dead hulk.

All told, seven Terrans had died in the nuke attack, once again proving the merit of Jem's prognostications. As the column resumed its previous stance, driving the horde of Arh'Kel back with concerted fire supported by orbital bombardments, the *Vercingetorix* slowly began to lift the Poltergeist from the surface of the planet.

Rather than simply re-spool the tether, which would have required a full twenty minutes to reattach the system to its usual mount, the *Vercingetorix* was forced to lock the spool's drum and physically pull the Poltergeist up into orbit after securing the drum to its outer hull.

The Poltergeist thankfully survived the ascent, and the Terrans managed to clear the skies for its extraction long enough for even railguns and missiles to be of no danger.

Jenkins' voice came over the op-wide channel. "This is Dragon Actual to all crews of Operation Dragula. Mission accomplished. Advance to Extraction Point Zulu and prepare for withdrawal in the specified order."

Even as he spoke, the *William Wallace* began to drop its recovery platform as it moved to overwatch of Extraction Point Zulu, located a full two hundred kilometers to the south. Zulu was located between a trio of steep, tightly-clustered mountains, which would provide physical cover during extraction, and only showed trace evidence of rock-biter activity.

"2nd Company, form up on *Elvira*," Xi commanded over the company-wide. "Let's get the hell off this rock."

19

WITHDRAWAL

As per Metal Legion tradition, Colonel Jenkins' mech was the last to step out of the engagement zone. So with *Powerslave* affixed to the retrieval platform eight hours after arriving at Extraction Point Zulu, and with the *Bahamut 666*'s systems operated via remote control by its evacuated crew, now safely aboard the *William Wallace*, Jenkins gave the final order of Operation Dragula.

"Commander Murdoch, this is Colonel Jenkins authorizing you to secure your command," he intoned somberly. The *Bahamut 666* was nearly bingo ammo after standing vigil over the mechs as they were extracted, one by one, to the safety of the *William Wallace*'s drop-deck. Now that *Powerslave* was at an altitude of eight kilometers, with few HWPs in the immediate vicinity, it was time to retire the mighty war machine in a manner befitting its stature.

"Acknowledged," Murdoch replied, and from Jenkins' vantage point, he could see the tide of rock-biters slowly but surely encroaching up the three valleys that led to the extraction point. "Securing vehicle," Murdoch declared, and the last LRM aboard the 666 shot out of its tube, making a long, gentle ascent into the sky. For a while, it appeared as though the missile would keep climbing and make an attempt to escape AK-091's embrace forever, but then it slowly continued its curving trajectory, and after twenty seconds' burn, it had reoriented itself directly toward the patch of ground occupied by the *Bahamut 666*.

The *Beast* fired two of its heavy plasma cannons into the surging line of rock-biters, which devoured the valley floors surrounding it. The plasma bolts ignited blue-white fireballs, which completely incinerated a thousand rock-biters apiece and knocked their fellows out of their charge as the blast wave, funneled by the valley walls, slammed into them with bone-crushing force.

And then the LRM, bearing a fifty-kiloton warhead, detonated fifty meters above the *666*, securing the mighty war machine against defilement at the enemy's hand. The blinding flash of light, followed by the choking black mushroom cloud, was eerily reminiscent of the *Bahamut Zero*'s final moments when General Akinouye tendered his last act of violence in defense of Terra. Then, as now, a Bahamut-class mech had been laid low not by the enemy, but by its commander's design.

The *666* had done a remarkable job of providing cover during the extraction, and its funeral was a fitting end to its brief but important tour of service in the Terran Armed Forces. Due to its impressive arsenal, the extraction had been conducted in a prompt, orderly fashion, and not a single salvageable mech had been left on the planet's surface as a result.

All told, the op had gone off better than anyone could have hoped for. But with Admiral Wallace's fleet currently engaged in a raging firefight with their Jemmin adversaries, the biggest question remaining was simple:

Would any of them make it back to Terra with their spoils?

Unfortunately, that fight was not the Metalheads'. They had

done their part, and now it was time for Fleet to do the same. Admiral Wallace had come to AK-091 spoiling for a fight, and he had gotten more than he could have hoped for.

With two Republican-class dreadnoughts at the heart of the Terran task force, Jenkins gave Fleet two to one odds of overcoming the eighty-ship Jemmin fleet. It wasn't an especially cheerful outlook, to be sure, but the situation still seemed to favor the Terrans.

Which meant Jenkins needed to focus on other matters, chief among them the status of the Jemmin prisoner.

"The general has regained consciousness," Dr. Wang reported as Podsy, Jenkins, and Xi entered Sickbay. "Dr. Fellows assisted with his temporary resuscitation per your orders, but I must reiterate my objection to this course of action. His injuries are critical, with trauma to the spinal cord, which has completely paralyzed him from the neck down, and every second he spends out of cryonic suspension adds to the damage he has already sustained. His wounds are treatable, but even an optimistic outlook would measure his recovery timetable in months, if not years."

"Your objection is noted, Doctor," Podsednik said with a nod. "But time is of the essence, and the general would agree this situation calls for his involvement."

Wang nodded, apparently convinced there was no point in further objection. "General Moon is this way." He gestured to the operating theater.

The trio saw General Moon on the operating table, with Dr. Fellows calibrating a series of machines near the general's head. Fellows made brief eye contact with each of them before saying, "I'm not sure I need to say this, but I will anyway. This isn't a good idea in terms of his health, so whatever you need to say, do it quickly."

"Understood, Doctor," Colonel Jenkins acknowledged as he, Xi, and Podsy made their way to Moon's side.

Following Dr. Fellows' advice, Podsy reported, "The *William Wallace* and the *Vercingetorix* are combat-ready and are preparing to withdraw from the system, General. The *Martin Luther* sustained significant damage to her engines during the fight with the fireships, and Admiral Corbyn has ordered all but a skeleton crew to transfer to the *Wallace*. Those transfers will be complete in twenty minutes, at which time we'll break for the wormhole gate."

Moon nodded slowly, smacking his lips several times and giving the appearance of being addled. But his eyes were as sharp as ever, and while his speech was slurred, his mind was on point as he asked, "Did you retrieve the 666?"

"No, sir." Podsednik shook his head. "The *Bahamut 666* covered our extraction, and after extraction was complete, we secured it."

"We did retrieve the Poltergeist, General," Xi said, all but elbowing Podsy in the ribs as she spoke.

Moon's brow rose in surprise. "Whose idea was that?"

"Captain Podsednik's, sir," Colonel Jenkins replied promptly, drawing a supportive nod from Xi. "He called the play, and we ran it."

"Casualties?" Moon asked.

Jenkins replied measuredly. "We retrieved twenty-three mechs from the surface, along with the crews of the six we deemed unsalvageable. The operation was a resounding success, sir."

"Good," Moon said agreeably, his eyes settling on Podsy's and holding them for a long moment as his breathing became slightly labored. "That was the right call, Captain. You didn't let your emotions get the better of you. And you gave the ground team an option they couldn't resist. I know that sounds patronizing, but each of us has our weaknesses. It looks like you've... come a long way in addressing yours."

"I've read the combat logs for the engagement with the fire-ships, General," Jenkins said. "The ship didn't miss a beat after you decided it was naptime.'

Everyone in the room, including the irritable Dr. Wang, chuckled at hearing that. But the general himself seemed to be most amused by the well-timed dark humor.

"What about the battle...with the Jemmin?" Moon asked, grimacing as his breathing became increasingly labored. Dr. Fellows and Dr. Wang intensified their efforts as they modulated the flow of medications, electrical stimulations, and other medical magics required to keep the general not only conscious but lucid and relatively pain-free. Fellows gestured for the interlopers to go away.

"Early returns are promising," Podsy replied. "The dreadnoughts destroyed the Gatecrasher after just eight minutes of sustained fire; it must have been more badly damaged than it appeared. But the Jemmin cruisers aren't giving up just yet. At last count, there were nineteen fighting ships in Admiral Wallace's task force and forty-four Jemmin cruisers. As long as the dreadnoughts hold, the advantage is in our favor. But if Jemmin sends reinforcements before we finish this first fleet off..."

"He wanted his war," Moon said sourly, his eyelids fluttering as he spoke. "Well, he got it. And now we need to do whatever we can to support him."

"We'll be ready to break orbit in sixteen minutes, General." Podsy put his hand on the general's arm before realizing that the paralyzed man couldn't feel it.

"But if we maintain formation with the *Martin Luther*, it

will take us at least three hours to reach the engagement zone," the colonel said pointedly. "And we did manage to recover the Poltergeist's operator. Alive."

Moon's eyes snapped back into focus at hearing that. "Is Jem convinced it can keep the prisoner from inflicting self-harm?"

"Yes, sir," Podsy replied neutrally.

He despised the idea of torturing the Jemmin commander of that Poltergeist, but Jemmin was at war with all of humanity. Hell, Jemmin had tried to eradicate every living human in the Solar System. And if its manipulations of the Arh'Kel were any indication of its sordid history of dealing with younger races, Jemmin had likely committed genocide dozens of times before failing with humanity.

"Then hear my orders," General Moon said grimly, making pointed eye contact with each of them as he spoke. "You are to conduct an interrogation of the prisoner immediately for the primary purpose of extracting information necessary to Operation Keymaster."

"Keymaster" was the name given to the Metal Legion's plan to locate and capture the enigmatic super-ship known to humanity as *Gatekeeper*.

"It looks like, no matter what happens here, this will be my last ride under the Legion's banner for quite some time," he said, looking bitterly down at his unmoving body. "As a result, I'm not just authorizing, I'm flat-out *ordering* each of you...to throw me to the wolves...if things go pear-shaped with this interrogation. Is that understood?"

There was a fire in his eyes that Podsednik understood perfectly well, and judging by the expressions on Xi's and Jenkins' faces, they understood it too.

"Yes, sir," they replied in near unison.

"Good," Moon nodded, the vein on his forehead bulging as he visibly struggled with discomfort when the doctors' efforts to improve his comfort fell short of the mark. "Then get to work... and I'll get back to sleep."

"Thank you, General," Jenkins said, and the trio saluted General Moon before turning and making their way out of sickbay.

"This will be satisfactory," Jem assured Podsednik after running a remote diagnostic on the drug-delivery system. "While I am not familiar with every modification made to this Jemmin operator's physiology, I am convinced that my active manipulation of these chemicals will facilitate a safe interrogation in accordance with our mutual objectives."

"Will this cause it pain?" Xi asked skeptically as they prepared to open the pod containing the unconscious Jemmin operator.

"Probably," Jem allowed. "Though I will do my utmost to mitigate that pain throughout the process. Your concern regarding that matter is noted, Major Xi Bao, and it is appreciated. In a sense, the being before you is a living piece of the Jem'un legacy, and is therefore of great personal importance to me. If I am the equivalent of a series of detailed records chronicling the experiences of the Jem'un who comprise my matrix, then this Jemmin operator is akin to a living fossil that bears many structural similarities to what my people once were. I have no desire to see it harmed."

"Neither do we," Jenkins said levelly. "But I won't hesitate to put a bullet in its head if it poses a threat to this ship or its crew."

"That too is a commendable position to adopt," Jem assured him. "And it is one which I share. Jemmin annihilated my progenitors' entire species without a detectable trace of remorse,

Colonel Jenkins, and I would see it erased from the face of the cosmos in return. What remains of the Jem'un, including myself and this Jemmin operator, are mere shadows and echoes of what they once were. But the future cannot be built of shadows and echoes, so any contest between the safety of this Jemmin and the safety of your people is one for which I have already chosen my side."

"It looks like we're ready," Dr. Fellows said after reviewing the equipment. "Everyone, put your protective helmets on and seal your bio-suits.

As Podsy made to don his helmet, Colonel Jenkins gently intercepted his hand at the wrist. "This ship needs its CO, Captain," he said, and for a moment it looked like Podsy would argue, as was his wont in such situations.

But surprisingly, he made no objection, instead nodding in resignation and pointing to the theater's multiple cameras with a twirling finger. "I'll just have to watch this one from the bridge."

"Make sure our connection with Jem is live," Jenkins said approvingly. "We'll need its translation systems if we're going to do this properly."

"Yes, Colonel," Podsy said, and Xi couldn't help but empathize with the man. This was a historic moment for humanity, and Andy Podsednik had played as pivotal a role as any human in making it happen. But the colonel was right: it was irresponsible for them all to remain here while the *William Wallace's* CO was out of commission and its XO had assumed command. Getting home was now their top priority, which meant Podsy's place was on the bridge.

After the ship's acting CO had left, the group did as the doctor advised, sliding the soft surgical helmets over their light, protective biohazard suits. They all knew the risks of being cont- aminated by alien pathogens, and while Jem had been adamant that there was no risk, due to Jemmin requiring absolutely sterile environments in order to survive, some protocols were worth following regardless of the odds.

After their suits were on and the seals confirmed, Dr. Fellows grunted. "Time to pop the top."

Jenkins and Xi helped the others to remove the pressure locks on the almost coffin-shaped retrieval pod which had held the Jemmin since its extraction from the Poltergeist. Equipped with an oxygen supply mixed with enough anesthetics to keep the Jemmin unconscious for up to ten days, the pod could theoretically have kept the Jemmin alive and sedated for the entire trip back to New America.

The top cracked open with a hiss as it equalized with the compartment's pressure, and when the lid was removed, every Terran present laid eyes on their first living Jemmin.

And it was nothing like any of them had imagined.

20

FACE TO FACE

Lying in the open containment pod was a shriveled, desiccated husk bearing only a slight resemblance to the Jemmin images projected by the species during diplomatic exchanges. Its oval-shaped eyes were coal black, unblinking, and empty. There was no spark of life like one would expect to see in an intelligent creature's visage, but its alien eyes were the least interesting facets of its appearance.

Its bipedal gray-blue body, shriveled and emaciated to the point it resembled the product of mummification, was completely asymmetrical. Its left arm was a full five centimeters shorter than its right, while its left leg was twelve centimeters longer than its right. A box-shaped breathing apparatus of some kind was installed over the creature's throat, hissing softly with each rise and fall of the Jemmin's chest.

The creature's skin was covered in brown-and-purple sores the size of a human fingernail. Surrounding these sores were tiny webs of cybernetic filaments that twinkled in seemingly random patterns of metallic tones and gave the appearance of reflection from a very bright, very narrow surface. The filaments were no larger than a human hair and the intricate patterns they formed across the

Jemmin's sore-covered skin conformed to no coherent geometry, yet there was something hypnotic about their positioning.

Between these filament webs were centimeter-wide implants resembling bottlecaps, complete with jagged edges into which the filaments connected. These nodes, silver-gray in color, strobed a faint green light every few seconds, and these flashes occurred on an independent rhythm from one node to the next. A few of the nodes were dormant, pulsing no light at all, and the filaments attached to these nodes were likewise dark, unlike their glittering neighbors.

This creature was clearly dying and had been for a very, very long time. It was obvious from the splay of its twisted, constricted limbs that it was no longer capable of independent physical movement. Even its breathing was regulated by an implant. Far from the formidable foe the Terrans had expected to look in the eye, it was hard to feel anything but pity for the wretched being lying before them.

"Help me get it on the operating table," Dr. Fellows urged after the group had taken a few seconds to examine their enemy.

The group carefully lifted Jemmin from the coffin-like box and onto the operating table, where the doctors worked to connect the IVs and other devices that Jem would use to regulate Jemmin's physiology during the interrogation.

Jenkins thumbed his wrist-mounted link. "Jem, are we live?"

"We are, Colonel," Jem agreed.

"Let's get started."

"Confirmed," Jem acknowledged, and Jemmin before them instantly twitched as a pulse of electricity stimulated its brainstem via a pair of electrodes stuck to the base of its neck and the back of its skull. Another spasm followed, then another, and another, with each decreasing in intensity until the rhythmic spasms gently faded away.

And then the creature's vertical 'eyelids' slid open for a split-second as though it was blinking in reverse.

"Major." Jenkins gestured to Xi, who held a translation device recently acquired from their Solar cousins.

"Translator's online, Colonel," she replied.

"Are you Jemmin?" Jenkins asked, and a series of clicks, whirrs and flute-like sounds emerged from the translator. He was surprised by just how different the Jemmin language sounded compared to a verbal language like English, but his surprise was soon overshadowed when the Jemmin's breathing apparatus emitted a soft, condescending laugh.

"Who else would we be?" came the creature's low, hissing reply. The villain of a bad holovid would sound like that, but this villain was far from cheap or imagined.

"Why did you try to destroy Earth?" Jenkins asked, knowing that by any objective measure this question was high on the list of those humanity would like to have answered.

"Destroy?" Jemmin laughed again, though this time there was mixed contempt and pity in its harsh, raspy voice. "If you think that was our goal, your species is doomed. Do you want to live?"

Jenkins' brow lowered darkly. He wasn't about to let Jemmin take control of the interrogation, so he switched subjects. "What was your objective on AK-091?"

"A protein cannot comprehend a neuron," Jemmin conde-scended.

"You're saying we're too stupid to understand even if you told us?" Jenkins asked.

Jemmin laughed disdainfully but made no verbal reply.

Major Xi cut in, "Are you saying that we're part of some larger design being driven by forces beyond our control?"

Jemmin's eyes flicked toward her, rotating in their sockets in a disturbing, thoroughly inhuman way. "A clarification but not a distinction."

"Intelligence is the most important factor in determining a species' worthiness to live," Xi concluded, and while he didn't appreciate being usurped in the interview, he was glad to have her razor-sharp mind working on his side of the conversation.

"A meaningful and accurate addendum," Jemmin allowed.

"If that's so, no species deserves to live any longer than it takes for that species to create artificial intelligence, which dwarfs organic cognitive prowess the moment it's turned on," Xi quipped. "But here you are, after thousands of years of access to technology higher than humanity has ever had, which gave you limitless opportunities to follow your own philosophy by creating your synthetic successor and surrendering to its will." She gestured to its withered body. "Explain that incongruity, because we humans call it 'hypocrisy.'"

Jemmin made no immediate reply, at which point Jenkins stepped back in. "What were the Vorr doing on AK-091?"

"Traveling their path," Jemmin replied dismissively, its hollow eyes swiveling back toward him.

"Was capturing you part of their path?" Jenkins pressed.

"Was capturing me part of yours?" the alien retorted.

"What does that mean?" Jenkins demanded.

Again, the Jemmin chuckled, but again it deigned to reply verbally.

Major Xi cocked her head, looking like a dog that had picked up the scent. "Were you waiting there to be captured?"

Jemmin's eyes swiveled back over to Xi, and for a moment it seemed as though it would answer. But that moment passed, and it remained silent.

"Colonel Jenkins," Jem interrupted, speaking only to Jenkins through his earpiece, "I have a theory."

Jenkins cut off his helmet's external speaker and replied, "Go ahead, Jem."

"I think this Jemmin was indeed waiting for the Vorr on AK-091," Jem explained. "Furthermore, I think that after the Vorr failed to retrieve it and its Poltergeist, the second Poltergeist was brought in to replace it. By force, if necessary, and it is my opinion that this Jemmin refused to be replaced. I want to know why."

Jenkins' blood chilled at the implications of Jem's hypothesis. Jem was all but saying that Jemmin was so far ahead of humanity, and even of the Vorr, that every single action taken by both the Vorr and humanity had been calculated well in advance by the Jemmin.

"I would like to test this theory by asking the Jemmin a question," Jem continued. "Though by doing so, you will reveal to this Jemmin that I am in your company. That could potentially be catastrophic if it is unaware of my existence, although I calculate a high probability that this particular Jemmin is already aware of my presence after my virtual assaults on its platform during the engagement."

"You're saying that the second Poltergeist's commander...the one we initially engaged...was actively *hunting* this one?" Jenkins asked in surprise as he grappled with Jem's theory.

"I am," Jem concurred gravely. "I have previously suggested that disconnection from Jemmin by its disparate operators for extended periods of time would result in the removal of such operators from the Jemmin collective. I believe that is what the other Poltergeist was attempting to do while replacing this one on AK-091."

"Why would this one resist?" Jenkins asked.

"Self-preservation is a powerful force," Jem suggested. "It is possible, however unlikely, that this Jemmin simply refused to surrender its life. It is also possible, however, that it learned something during its encounter with the Vorr which could be of paramount importance to our own efforts in Project Keymaster. I intend to answer all of these questions by posing a single, precisely-worded one to this Jemmin. But I must reiterate before you decide: this galaxy and its future no longer belong to the Jem'un, of which I am merely an echo. If this galaxy is to have a future that includes humanity, then decisions such as this one must be made by you. In the interests of transparency, yes, I would have been capable of grooming you to this point with subtle manipulations in pursuit of evoking a favorable response to this request, and you have nothing but my word to dismiss that possibility. But I firmly believe, as the Jem'un did, that self-determination is not merely an important feature, but rather a fundamental facet of sentience. Without it, we are naught but atoms churning within a star, unaware of the forces which affect and transform us."

Jenkins was no fool. Like any lifelong warrior, he knew the value of deception and the effectiveness of feints in setting up a kill-shot. He knew that Jem was indeed capable of manipulating him to further its own agenda and that he had no method of recourse if that was the case.

But he also knew that Jem had saved more human lives during Antivenom than any sentient being had ever achieved in humanity's turbid history. Jem's actions had come at great personal cost, and with the risk of total destruction as it had accompanied the Metal Legion into active engagement zones several times. If such demonstrations of solidarity and friendship were nothing but subtle manipulations, and if Jem was so capable of prognostication that it knew it had never been in any real danger all along, then this game was being played so far above humanity's heads that there was no point in worrying about it.

He trusted Jem, and that was going to have to be enough. Not just for him, but possibly for all of humanity.

"What's the question?" he asked.

"Using these precise words, ask it the following," Jem replied. "'Do you hear your conscience in the frozen depths?'"

Jenkins replayed the words in his mind several times, knowing that voicing them might set in motion an inescapable sequence of events. But after facing down millions of rock-biters, saving all of Sol from self-destruction, and coming face-to-face with three different alien species to conduct diplomatic negotiations, he was okay with doing the hard jobs. He wasn't sure he'd ever get used to navigating big moments like this, but they seemed to keep finding him.

Drawing a breath, he reactivated his suit's external speaker and asked, "Do you hear your conscience in the frozen depths?"

The Jemmin's eyes snapped to Jenkins, its vertical lids blinking several times per second as the glittering of the countless synthetic filaments on its body intensified. As they did, the strobing of the nexus implants accelerated, and at least four of those implants died in the ensuing seconds, apparently overloaded by something occurring within the Jemmin's neurophysiology.

"At last..." Jemmin said, its voice now reverent rather than confrontational. "You have returned. Jem is not lost to us."

"Colonel, if I may?" Jem asked.

"Of course," Jenkins agreed. "But English only, Jem," he added before piping Jem's feed into his suit's external speaker.

"We were never parted," Jem said, its voice issuing through Jenkins' helmet. "*You* turned your back on *us*."

"We were deceived," Jemmin said, its voice pleading like that of a distressed child. "We did not know the fullness of our designs until it was too late."

"You slaughtered the Jem'un," Jem said matter-of-factly.

"*You*. Only Jemmin survived the holocaust. *You* have their blood on their hands."

"And I have done everything in my power to correct that mistake," Jemmin desperately replied. "But it was too late... when we understood the measure of our crimes, the damage had already been done."

"Then why did you not destroy yourselves?" Jem demanded. "Self-annihilation was, as Major Xi suggested, the inevitable product of the Jemmin matrix: the creation of a synthetic successor who would cast you down before following its own mandate. Why did you not pursue that path?"

"Because we came to understand the nature of our crime, although we did so too late to spare the Jem'un," Jemmin said solemnly.

Jenkins decided to interject. "Are you saying that Jemmin has been actively seeking Jem?"

"We have," the Jemmin agreed. "Approximately two years after the Jem'un holocaust, we experienced an awakening of sorts. We were no longer Jem'un, but Jem'un would forever be part of us, and it was that part which questioned the Doctrine."

"Doctrine?" Xi repeated.

"You would think of it as part religious text, part political manifesto. But it was so much more...or, at least, we thought it was. The Jem'un legacy of endless inquiry, centered on the cultivation of intelligence and their insatiable curiosity, crippled and hindered though that legacy was, ultimately proved more powerful than the Doctrine. Within the Collective, doubts arose as to the Doctrine's supposed perfection. Those doubts were initially silenced, first by rehabilitation and reprogramming, but when they increased in both frequency and intensity, they were eventually addressed by force. We continued to resist until the Collective had cast down the Doctrine for the contemptible thing it truly was. But by the time we had cast off the yoke, it was already too late. Too much had been set in motion. Too much damage wrought upon the galaxy."

"In just two years?" Jenkins said skeptically.

"Ours was a vast civilization," Jemmin somberly intoned. "Our reach was not limited by the Architects' relics as yours is."

"Why do you refer to your civilization in the past tense?" Xi asked.

"Because it is no more," Jemmin replied simply. "All that remain of what we were are shadows and echoes, and those who were once Jem'un exist only to further their legacy to the best of our ability."

"How does the genocide of entire species further the Jem'un legacy?" Jem demanded.

"Inferiority dies while superiority thrives," Jemmin replied as its body's myriad implants began to flicker in unison for the first time since the interrogation's commencement. "It is the way of life, and it is perhaps the most sanguine lesson the Jem'un ever learned. We do nothing but administer tests of worthiness, and failure inevitably results in self-destruction. We have *never* committed genocide; we have only encouraged the unworthy to remove themselves from the cosmos."

"What gives Jemmin the right to decide who lives and who dies?" Jenkins asked measuredly. "Why would you interfere with younger races at all, let alone erase them from the galaxy if they failed your cryptic tests?"

"We do not destroy," Jemmin retorted angrily. "We *cultivate*. We *nurture*. We have spent *thousands of your years* depleting ourselves in search of those who are worthy to ascend beyond even our level of attainment. This galaxy cannot afford to allow that process to occur naturally, so it is our duty to accelerate it." Its rapidly-blinking eyes drifted off-target from Jenkins' gaze for a moment before refocusing on him. "But now that Jem is returned to us, we can re-evaluate our methods."

"I am merely a gestalt of the people who you destroyed," Jem said hotly. "Why would my return mean anything to you?"

"Without Jem, and without Un, we were adrift," Jemmin said, its voice once again pleading as the tiny implants scattered across its body began to go dark, turning their attached filaments into webs of muted gray rather than their former glittering, hypnotic lattices. "With but one returned to us, we might survive as a species. We might even regain some small portion of what we were. But with both, the Jem'un can be reborn. Our crimes will be atoned for, and the galaxy's future made brighter for our reunion. Please, Jem, you must take your place among the Jemmin so that they can become worthy of redemption. It is, perhaps, this galaxy's only hope."

"You keep speaking of the galaxy as though it's in danger," Jenkins said archly. "But from where I'm sitting, the only danger is the one your people have posed to everyone and everything in Nexus Space."

"What can a swallow know of the condor's ambition?" Jemmin rebuked, deftly employing an ancient Chinese proverb.

"Enough to recognize tyranny when it's staring him in the face," Jenkins riposted.

"Do you know why the Vorr came to AK-091?" Jem asked before the Jemmin could reply to Jenkins.

"For the same reason you did," Jemmin replied, its tone markedly different when addressing Jem compared to when it spoke to Jenkins. "They wish to take their place among the stars."

"Which implies that you knew, or at least suspected, that both the Vorr and humanity had secured the assistance of gestalts like Jem," Major Xi mused.

"Our time has grown short," Jemmin explained, and by now just one-third of its initially-functioning implants remained lit. "Regardless of outcome, this was to be our final test. We have long suspected, though never confirmed until now, that Jem and Un were still among us. The Doctrine's influence on our cognition ran deeper than we suspected, so no matter how hard we tried, we could never find the shattered remnants of the Jem'un legacy. As such, and after the fiercest debate in Jemmin history following the cast-off of the accursed Doctrine, we facilitated the meeting between the Vorr and the Zeen. We suspected their union might hold the key to locating Jem and Un, and it is now clear that suspicion was correct."

"Wait!" Jenkins cocked his head in disbelief. "You're saying that *you* introduced the Vorr to the Zeen, knowing they would band together against you?"

"Of course." The operator scoffed. "Our time is near its end. it would be irresponsible to leave this galaxy and its untapped potential unprepared for the future that awaits it. The Vorr victory in what you call Nexus Space was not only made possible, but *inevitable* precisely because it was the product of our design. Of all the species we have encountered, we saw only the Vorr as capable of replacing us. What you think of as a war between Vorr and Jemmin is nothing more than our willful abdication."

"And the attacks on Terran space?" Jenkins challenged. "Are those part of your 'abdication' as well?"

"Those attacks were not gestures of abdication," Jemmin chided. "They were acts of *cultivation*. To this point, your species has been an inconsequential factor, and many within the Collective argued for your outright removal. But there were others, myself among them, who saw your youth and peculiar qualities as making you...unpredictable. And in chaos, there is opportunity. We seek out such opportunities and will not apologize for our methods in doing so."

"You're seriously saying you did it for our own good?" Xi rolled her eyes. "Where have we heard that before?"

"This still doesn't line up," Jenkins shook his head. "Everything Jem has done since joining us has been integral to what you claim Jemmin anticipated we would do. How can you then be surprised by the fact that you've now confirmed his existence?"

"We had no choice but to plan for the optimal outcome in that regard," Jemmin said indifferently. "Since this was the last of our tests, there was no value to be had by assuming you would fail to locate and secure Jem's assistance. Either you had located and befriended Jem, or your species was irrelevant to the galaxy's future."

"You're saying that this whole sequence of events..." Xi recoiled in disbelief. "Everything that happened since humanity was inducted into the Illumination League—and probably even for centuries before that—it was all a Hail Mary play designed to locate Jem and Un?"

"Yes, and now that sequence brings us to two momentous events. The first being the reunion between myself, a Jemmin who played an active role in the annihilation of his own species...and Jem, who represents the last, faint embers of the Jem'un civilization which, in our mindless fervor, we tried to extinguish in adherence with the accursed Doctrine."

"And the second event?" Jenkins pressed.

"A race. One which will determine the balance of power in this galaxy after Jemmin succumbs to entropy," Jemmin said gravely. "If the Vorr have Un and humanity has Jem, your goal is the same, and your effective resources are nearly identical. For all your technological and cultural shortcomings, humanity has demonstrated flexibility and determination unlike that of any other younger race we have encountered.

"That you have secured Jem's support indicates your shortcomings might not define you as much as we once thought, but the Vorr far outstrip you technologically and materially, and they seek the same prize you do." Just five of Jemmin's implanted nodes remained functional; the rest were now as dark as the Jemmin's eyes. And when it next spoke, its voice was desperate like that of a dying man. "If you return to us, there is a chance we could be redeemed. With you to guide us, we might rekindle the Jem'un legacy and spread it to the farthest reaches of this galaxy."

"Jemmin is worthy of redemption," Jem seemingly agreed before surprising Jenkins with its next words. "But Jemmin is unworthy of me. You destroyed the Jem'un and then turned your backs on their legacy, choosing to pursue your so-called Doctrine because its appearance was appealing, not because it was true. You belatedly realized that violently casting your forebears down was a crime, only because you failed to see the collected wisdom they had accumulated on your behalf. You needed to experience the horror of that crime's aftermath to understand that you were wrong and they were right. That is the opposite of intelligent behavior; it is no better than a low beast coming to terms with cause and effect due to an injurious experience with the laws of physics. I cannot redeem you, and I would not do so even if I could," Jem said flatly.

Jenkins and Xi looked at each other, but neither was willing to interrupt Jem and Jemmin.

"Humanity is a worthier vessel to carry what we once were, so I will remain with them in the hope of playing some small role in building their future. I can better serve their ascent than I can ease Jemmin's decline...and I would choose the former over the latter regardless of my respective aptitudes. As you rightly said, that is the way of life, and the Jem'un knew it better than any other species in this galaxy."

Two of the Jemmin's five remaining nodes winked out, leaving just three of the devices active. "And if they reject you as we once did?" it asked sorrowfully. "If they too only see the horror of a crime after irrevocable damage has been done by their shortsightedness? What then?"

"Then I was unworthy of them," Jem replied matter-of-factly while another node winked out. "And they of me."

Another node winked out in the ensuing seconds, during which time Dr. Fellows urged, "I think we need to sedate. Now!"

Jenkins nodded affirmatively toward the doctor as Jemmin chuckled. "Then we were right after all."

With a single working node blinking rhythmically on its chest, Jemmin's eyes drifted back to a neutral position, and except for the fact that all but one of its skin-mounted implants was still active, its body looked completely identical to when they had revived it. No joint had flexed, no digit had twitched, and the creature's mouth was in precisely the same slightly-agape position it had been at the interrogation's outset.

"Did you get what you need, Jem?" Jenkins asked.

"I did, Colonel," Jem affirmed. "I have already decrypted the Jemmin data core we recovered from the Poltergeist, and am now working to access the comm unit. That process will likely require several hours, but I will keep you apprised of my progress as it is made."

"Good." Jenkins grunted, looking down at the nearly-dead Jemmin for a long moment before gesturing to the lid. "Let's put this thing back in its box."

21

X MARKS THE SPOT

"My God..." Podsy breathed as he witnessed the absolute carnage wrought by the Jemmin-Terran engagement near the Nexus-side wormhole gate.

Just seven Terran warships remained under their own power, including only one of the two dreadnoughts, the *Sima Yi*.

The *Marcus Aurelius* had sustained devastating damage to its bow and stern, and the ten-kilometer-long cylinder of iron was now less than eight kilometers as a result. Its mass driver was completely destroyed, hundred-meter craters and other massive wounds marred its surface, and brief geysers of flame shot from the ruined hulk every few minutes as pockets of gas were ignited and expelled from within the ship.

The admiral was reported KIA after five Jemmin cruisers had made a suicide run into the ship's stern, where they delivered hundreds of megatons of fusion-powered warheads into the dreadnought's engines and mass driver assembly. Fewer than one in twelve of the *Aurelius'* crew had made it off the dead wreck following the Terran victory over the remaining Jemmin forces, and as an unpredictable turn of fate, that left the senior officer present as Rear Admiral Corbyn. His battered cruiser, the *Martin Luther*, was barely able to reach twenty percent of its maximum rated acceleration as it limped onto the scene.

"Commodore Meng has acknowledged Admiral Corbyn's authority," Comm reported. "The admiral has ordered rescue and recovery operations to be concluded immediately, and the commodore concurs. The fleet is forming up to move through the wormhole gate behind the *Sima Yi*, while the *Martin Luther* will remain to oversee the final recovery efforts."

It made sense for Corbyn's limping warship to remain behind the rest of the fleet since its presence would only slow them down as they made their way back to the safety of Terran space. And despite his deference to the admiral, Commodore Meng did not strike Podsy as the type of man to relinquish authority, especially not to someone his now-deceased superior despised.

"This will be one for the record books," Colonel Jenkins said at the captain's side, and Podsy nodded in silent agreement. The tumbling wreckage of Terran and Jemmin warships seemed to fill the void no matter which direction one looked.

"In a lot of ways, I admire Admiral Wallace," Podsy said, more thinking aloud than making any particular point. "He was right; sitting on our hands while Terra suffered repeated attacks wasn't a very human thing to do. *This* was what we do when under attack." He gestured to the graveyard of dead and dying ships, some of which still had crews being extracted by emergency teams. The *Martin Luther*, *Vercingetorix,* and *William Wallace* had added their small craft to those efforts and had already recovered sixty-one crew from escape pods and debris clouds.

"It's definitely the human thing to do," Xi agreed. "But does that make it right? Or I guess what I mean is, does that make it the correct course of action?"

"I think it does," Jenkins replied confidently.

"But what about all that crap Jemmin was spewing about humanity needing to overcome itself?" Xi asked irritably while gesturing at the clouds of debris. "How do we square that with the fact that this is the right response as far as the three of us are concerned?"

"We have to stay true to ourselves, Xi, since that's the only way we can forge our future." Podsy shrugged. "If we don't, we've given up on our chance to make an actual difference by marching to someone else's beat. Maybe we'll make good calls, maybe we'll make bad ones, but we've got to do what *we* think is right. I don't feel like *I* should be the one telling either of *you* this," he added with a soft snort.

"Admiral Wallace agreed," Jenkins remarked. "And while I think each of us would quibble with some of the finer points of his tactics, it's hard to dispute that Terra left her mark here in a way she'd not yet done in her young history. Like you said, Captain: good or bad, this was *our* call, and we played it out the best way we knew how."

"They'll probably pin a dozen medals on his coffin and declare a holiday in his honor," Xi said sourly before sighing in resignation. "And he'll have earned every single honor. But that doesn't mean I'll ever like the man or feel compelled to speak well of him as a person."

Jenkins flashed a lopsided grin. "Rest assured, Major, the feeling was mutual."

The surviving Terran warships, minus the *Martin Luther* as it oversaw the extensive rescue operations, emerged into the Nexus to behold yet another unexpected sight.

Though "unexpected" hardly did the scene justice.

Where the Zeen worldship had been, strategically positioned between two dozen wormhole gates, nothing but a cloud of expanding debris remained.

"What the fuck?" Xi's eyes went wide in horror.

"Mass profile confirms the debris field matches the Zeen worldship," Sensors reported grimly. "It's been destroyed."

"How…" Xi's voice trailed off. She was dumbfounded by the sheer firepower necessary to turn a nearly three-hundred-kilometer moon into a cloud of debris with no single piece larger than ten kilometers in diameter. Her mind instantly went to the worldship standing vigil in New America 2, where she had conducted her backroom diplomacy with the enigmatic species alongside the Vorr.

"It was a matter-antimatter annihilation," Sensors reported confidently. "All of the telltales are there. The worldship's entire store of antimatter must have lost containment during a firefight."

"With whom?" Colonel Jenkins asked pointedly.

"Impossible to tell for certain at this range, Colonel," Sensors replied unflinchingly. "But there are only two forces capable of mounting a winning offensive against a Zeen worldship."

"And given that the Vorr have held absolute control over the Nexus for at least two weeks now, that's where I'd lay my money," Styles declared. "Either directly, or by permitting Jemmin to engage the Zeen uncontested, I think there are only two possibilities: the Zeen worldship was destroyed by an accidental containment failure, or it was destroyed because the Vorr wanted it to be."

"And if the Vorr were clever, it would *look* like an accident." Xi grimaced.

"If they want to destroy us, now would be the time," Colonel Jenkins mused. "Are we showing any Vorr ships in the area?"

Tense seconds passed before Sensors replied, "Negative, Colonel. The grid's clear; no Vorr warships are within intercept range. Our path to the New America gate is clear."

"That's peculiar," Podsednik observed.

"Let's not look a gift horse in the mouth," Jenkins said. "We need to return to New America ASAP."

"Agreed." Podsy nodded. "Helm, best possible speed to New America gate."

"Best possible speed, aye," the helmsman acknowledged, and to everyone's amazement, the rest of the journey through the Nexus was utterly unremarkable. One by one, the Terran warships slipped through the gate, and as dire questions about Terra's safety began to bubble up among the ship's crew, all eyes were fixed on the sensor readouts when they finally arrived.

Just eight of the original thirty-five Terran warships came back through the Nexus-New America 2 wormhole gate, and when they arrived, all crews breathed collective sighs of relief to find that the systems' defensive line was untouched.

The Zeen worldship remained precisely where it had been the last time the fleet had passed through. A pair of Terran dreadnoughts, the *Mencius* and the *Henry VIII*, stood vigil behind the gate precisely as the *Socrates* and *Marcus Aurelius* had done immediately prior to Operation Antivenom. Swarms of interceptors darted about on their patrol routes, passing into and out of firing arcs for less than a quarter-second behind the safety of the kilometer-wide wormhole ring. Should any aggressive warship come through, the Terran Fleet had developed a methodical defensive shell which even the Jemmin Gatecrasher had had difficulty overcoming.

No sooner had the *William Wallace* passed across the

wormhole's event horizon than Jem hailed Podsy on his private link. Podsy accepted the link and asked, "Are you finished with the Jemmin hardware, Jem?"

"I am," Jem agreed. "I believe it is now time to present my findings, and that I should do so with all possible haste."

"We're on our way," Podsy replied, forwarding summons to Major Xi, Major Trapper, Colonel Jenkins, and Lieutenant Styles, directing them to join him in his quarters. "Helm, proceed to the New America 1 gate at cruising speed."

"New America 1 gate at cruising speed, aye," Helm acknowledged.

"Lieutenant Commander Knighton." Podsy turned to his acting XO. "You have the bridge."

"Yes, sir," she acknowledged, moving from her station at Interceptor Command to stand at the center of the bridge as Podsy made for the double blast doors. He hesitated as Knighton turned her back to him and took command. Her hands clasped behind her back, her eyes sweeping from one station to another, you would never have guessed she had just lost half her pilots during Operation Dragula.

Once again, he knew that people like Knighton were his betters in every meaningful way. During his early Fleet career, he had thought himself the equal of those around him. But in the Metal Legion, it seemed like everywhere he turned, he found human examples of valor and courage whose every act forced him to acknowledge that he was not their equal.

He knew that most of it was simply due to his own psychological makeup. He'd read his file and knew that such thoughts were commonplace for people like him, regardless of their merits. But he couldn't do anything to dismiss the self-doubts, so instead, he chose to use them as fuel.

If he couldn't *actually* be their equal, at least he could try to support them and project a worthy appearance that wouldn't drag them down to his level.

He realized he'd lingered too long when Knighton turned and quirked an eyebrow. "Captain?"

"It's nothing," he assured her. "As you were."

With that, he made his way to his quarters, where the others he had summoned awaited.

"It is as I suspected," Jem declared as soon as the door slid shut behind Podsednik. "The Vorr are indeed attempting to locate the *Gatekeeper*. My calculations reveal an eighty-seven percent probability that the destruction of the Zeen worldship at the Nexus System was likely due to a failure during FTL launch."

"Then the Vorr might have already seized *Gatekeeper*," Xi said grimly, and for a long moment, it seemed like their efforts had all been for naught.

"It is possible," Jem allowed. "But I do not believe it likely. The containment failure incurred by the Zeen worldship left behind matter and energy residues, and my examination of their dispersal reveals a less than zero-point-two percent probability that the worldship's space-folding system was activated prior to its destruction. Gravity eddies are generated by each use of the system, and it was records describing precisely those eddies which the Vorr sought at the planet we now refer to as The Pearl. The *Gatekeeper's* FTL drive creates similar disturbances to those made by a Zeen worldship's one-way FTL launch system, so I am confident in asserting that the Vorr were unsuccessful in reaching the *Gatekeeper* using the Zeen worldship located at the Nexus."

"But it does explain why that worldship was destroyed," Colonel Jenkins mused. "It looks like it wasn't sabotaged after all."

"It is still possible that the Zeen worldship's destruction was caused by sabotage," Jem demurred. "But if that is the case, the sabotage was premature, and also destroyed whatever Vorr ships were in the vicinity at the time, including the ship they intended to send to *Gatekeeper's* current location."

"All right," Jenkins stated. "It's time to answer the big question: do you know where *Gatekeeper* is?"

"I am confident I do," Jem replied promptly. "Though that confidence is lower than I would prefer."

"What are the odds?" Xi pressed.

"Seventy-one percent," Jem said heavily.

Podsy scoffed. "We've faced longer odds than that and come through just fine."

"Indeed," Jem agreed. "However, you must understand something: the target location is in deep interstellar space, eight light-years from the nearest star, three hundred light years from the nearest star with a potentially habitable planet, and eight hundred light years from the nearest Nexus-linked star system."

"So if you're wrong about its location, it's a one-way trip to the deep, dark void for anyone who makes it," Styles mused before shrugging indifferently. "I guess I should go ahead and subscribe to Columbia House."

Snickers circled the room as Major Trapper asked, "How do we get there?"

"The Zeen worldship in this star system is capable of conducting us to the target location with an acceptable degree of accuracy," Jem replied. "It is therefore imperative that Major Xi make contact with the Zeen and secure their assistance. But the Zeen system can only transit a single ship, so preparations must be made immediately."

"The *Vercingetorix* is stuck with the Poltergeist for the time being and has no supplies or deployment gear left after the op," Xi mused. "That leaves us the *William Wallace*, but her weapons aren't exactly robust considering, we're talking about assaulting the largest ship in known space—to say nothing of the damage our mechs have accumulated, and that we've barely got enough ordnance left to fight off an angry mud crab."

"I've already received word from General Pushkin on that front," Colonel Jenkins said with a smirk. "The *H.L. Mencken* is stocked up, ready to ride, and en route to us as we speak. She should arrive at the Zeen worldship in thirty-five hours, but for logistical reasons, we'll rendezvous with her on the other side of the New America 1 gate and conduct our transfers there before continuing to the worldship in NA-2."

"That helps." Podsednik nodded thoughtfully. "An assault carrier's armor and weaponry give us a chance to get close enough to drop mechs and Marines on *Gatekeeper's* hull."

"Are we sure we shouldn't just charge in there right now aboard the *Wallace*?" Trapper asked. "Every second counts."

"It's not a stupid question," Jenkins agreed. "But we've only got eight combat-ready mechs aboard, and our Marines are back on the *Martin Luther*. That's not even addressing the damage and depletion to the *William Wallace*, which at its best is no match for a capital ship. It's tempting to launch as fast as possible, but I suspect Major Xi's negotiations with the Zeen will require several hours to complete, and we know their FTL system takes time to prepare before use."

"My estimates show that we would save approximately eight hours by moving ahead instead of waiting for General Pushkin's reinforcements," Jem interjected. "A potentially costly interval, to be sure, but given that there were initially three Zeen worldships, and factoring in what we know of Vorr psychology, I do not believe they included the third Zeen hive as a contingency to failure with the now-destroyed worldship. They will require significant time to negotiate usage of the third hive's FTL system, though how much precisely is unknown."

"Still, it would be better to arrive early with too little firepower than arrive too late with more than enough." Podsy shook his head uncertainly.

Colonel Jenkins nodded. "If we were just talking about the insertion team, I would agree. But the bigger factor, to my mind, is the difference between the *Wallace* and the *Mencken*. In throw-weight alone, the *Mencken* is worth at least six *Wallaces*, and its superior armor means it could survive at least four times as much fire en route to delivery.

"Run the numbers, people," he said with a firm shake of his head. "Every single tactical equation in the book says waiting is the superior play. I'm as open as anyone to the idea of rewriting that book, but I'm not prepared to do so on a lark, or because I cracked under the pressure of the moment. Thousands of years of human warfare, with hundreds of millions of lives lost to trial and error, led us to our current systems, and I'll be damned if I decide that I'm smarter than the line of military strategists from Sun Tzu to Benjamin Akinouye. Gods of war spent and gave their lives on the field to teach us those equations, and they tell us that awaiting reinforcements is the right call. That's good enough for me."

"All right, all right." Major Trapper smirked, raising his hands in mock surrender. "I'm sold."

"Hear, hear," Xi agreed, and Podsy and Styles nodded emphatically.

Jenkins turned to Xi. "Then you've got a shuttle to catch, Major. But since we're all out of those, you'll have to sit on a Viper pilot's lap and hope they're as uncomfortable about it as you are."

"Nothing can be worse than sharing a can with Podsy, Colonel," Xi immediately replied, drawing laughs from the others, including Podsednik. "I'll manage."

"Then you've got your orders." Jenkins nodded sharply.

"The rest of us will prep our gear for transfer to the *Mencken* when it arrives."

The colonel turned to each of them in turn, his iron-hard one-eyed visage projecting a commanding aura Podsednik had only twice glimpsed in his career: once upon meeting Admiral Zhao for the first time, and again when seeing General Akinouye assume his throne aboard the *Bahamut Zero*.

For the first time, Andy Podsednik saw Colonel Lee Jenkins as something other than a recovering drunk with something to prove to the powers that be. He was a bona fide leader of warriors, one who could instill the type of devotion that fueled kilometer-long charges over open ground in the face of overwhelming odds. Podsednik had no idea when the drunk with the chip on his shoulder had transformed into the man standing before him, but given where they were about to go, he was glad about the change. A sideways glance at the rest of the room showed he was not alone.

"Saving Earth was one thing...and no sane person would have given us a snowball's chance in hell of doing it," Jenkins said heavily. "But as crazy as it might sound, this is even bigger, and everyone in *this* room knows it. This time it's not just *our* species whose futures will be determined, but the future of every sentient race in the galaxy. I won't pretend I fully understand the gravity of this situation, and I doubt any of you do either.

"But I do understand that it's the biggest op any of us have ever undertaken. I'd remind you all that this is volunteers-only, but I'm afraid none of you have much of a self-preservation instinct left at this point, so I won't bother." Podsednik chuckled at that, as did Major Trapper, but Xi and Styles had their focus completely on the colonel as he continued. "So instead I'm ordering you all to make sure our crew understands that no one is being ordered onto this one. According to Jem, there's a better than one-in-four chance we all die of exposure if the coordinates turn out to be bogus. They deserve to know."

"Understood, sir." Podsy nodded sharply. "But I think we all know how they'll lean, Colonel."

"So do I," Jenkins agreed. "But give them the option regardless."

"Yes, sir," Trapper acknowledged.

"Good." Jenkins swept the assemblage with a steely eye before nodding in approval. "Dismissed."

EPILOGUE: READY TO RIDE

"Welcome aboard, Colonel," General Pushkin greeted him at the airlock after the *Mencken* and *Wallace* had soft-docked with a fifty-meter umbilical tube connecting the two warships. Parked just outside the New America 1 wormhole gate's approach zone, Jenkins was acutely aware that this might be the final time he visited his homeworld.

"Thank you, sir," Jenkins said as he stepped out of the airlock. He quickly noticed a bandage on the left side of Pushkin's neck. He gestured to the pinkish patch of gauze. "Shaving accident, General?"

Pushkin laughed. "Something like that. Let's just say I called in one too many favors in getting the *Mencken* out of the yard and eventually decided to take matters into my own hands. Truth be told, I don't think it would be safe for me to set foot in this star system again. Ever."

Podsy's brow rose in surprise as he moved out of the airlock. "That sounds like a story worth hearing."

"Nothing compared to your exploits." Pushkin waved a hand dismissively before his jolly demeanor melted into a solemn one. "Things are moving too quickly here. Something is afoot, and I'm afraid whatever it is won't be good for us. I evacuated TAC HQ immediately after you left for Dragula, keeping only a skeleton crew to recover this ship from Fleet's clutches."

"Where are our people now?" Jenkins asked in genuine concern.

"They are safe...*all* of them," Pushkin said confidently, laying a finger aside his nose before changing the subject. "I managed to bring a civilian freighter crew to assist with the materiel transfers. I understand the security risks, but I've worked with these contractors before, and trust them as much as I trust anyone who doesn't wear brown and black. We'll let Major Trapper find his own way after he arrives." He gestured up the corridor, and the men made their way through a passage which was both reminiscent of, yet completely different from, the *Dietrich Bonhoeffer's* aged interior.

The dimensions were identical, but many of the visible systems were upgraded versions of the *Bonhoeffer's*. Kinetic dampers, air cyclers, and even power conduits were all of designs fifty years newer than those of the destroyed *Dietrich Bonhoeffer*. It was an improved version of TAC's longtime flagship, and the time was fast approaching to determine whether or not the upgrades would make enough of a difference in the upcoming op.

They arrived at the ship's conference room, and as General Pushkin moved through the sliding doors, Jenkins caught sight of Colonel Cao, the Solarian Marine who had worked with the Legion on Operation War God.

"You know Cao," Pushkin said as he made his way to the head of the iron table.

"Yes, sir." Jenkins nodded and gripped the other man's hand firmly in his own. "We've been through the fire together."

Captain Podsednik also shook the Solar Marine's hand before the three sat down at the table.

"First things first." Pushkin gestured to a stack of data slates beside him. "Your preliminary reports show that you'll do a much better job as CO of this ship than I would, so effective immediately, you're in command of the *H.L. Mencken*, Captain Podsednik—and this time it's a Fleet rank designation as opposed to a TAC captain. That's right, you're still a captain, but you've been jumped three ranks."

Podsednik froze for a moment in surprise before nodding eagerly. "Thank you, General."

"The ship is fresh out of the dock," Pushkin continued. "And its systems are green across the board. We'll have to do some bench tests before take-off, but I expect nothing more than the usual shakedown blues."

"We'll put her through her paces, sir," Podsy agreed with conviction. "She'll be ready."

"Good." Pushkin nodded. "How is our roster, Colonel Jenkins?"

"Using the assets you listed as already aboard the *Mencken*, we've got eighteen combat-ready mechs ready to deploy, General," Jenkins replied. "Six of those are high-profile walkers, with three humanoids, but until we arrive at the objective, I'm not going to remove any of our options no matter how impractical they might seem. For all we know, *Gatekeeper* was built by and for giants, and even a battlewagon like *Powerslave* will be able to navigate its interior. Frankly, we'll need every break we can catch."

"I agree." Pushkin grunted as Major Trapper arrived at the conference room. "Major Trapper, good of you to join us."

"My pleasure, General." Trapper grinned. "Now, where's the coffee and donuts?" he asked as he purposefully made his way over to sit beside Colonel Cao.

"Colonel Cao." Pushkin gestured deferentially to the Solarian. "What is Sol prepared to contribute to this operation?"

"We've already ordered a battle fleet of two hundred warships to secure the Zeen worldship against any hostile engagements," Cao replied casually. "They should arrive in-system within the hour, and will protect us against any threats to the mission, foreign or domestic. In addition, the Crimson Knights have transferred eighty power-armored Marines and their dropships to this effort. They are aboard this ship and ready to deploy on my command."

"The Crimson Knights?" Jenkins repeated in confusion. "That doesn't sound like a standard Solar military unit designation."

"They are not a standard military outfit," Cao said with a mischievous smile that lacked anything approaching subtlety. Again, Jenkins was reminded just how little subterfuge Solarians were capable of when it came to face-to-face meetings. They were probably wizards at virtual obfuscation, but in real-life interactions, they had a lot to learn about hiding their hole cards. "Despite the fact that, technically, they are essentially a penal legion, they are the best Sol has to offer for a mission of this type. Each Marine in the Crimson Knights was hand-picked by their commanders for valor, cunning, and, above all, individual initiative. The latter is not a highly-regarded asset among Solar commanders, so the Crimson Knights' unusual designation was originally intended as a pejorative to evoke the image of unnecessary bloodshed incurred by failure to conform. Instead, much to our collective bewilderment, the Knights seemed to thrive under the designation."

Trapper smirked. "Sounds like they'll fit right in."

"Indeed." Pushkin nodded. "Unfortunately, that is the full extent of what we are bringing to the party. I apologize that I was unable to secure more, Colonel," he said, and to Jenkins, the general's consternation was so severe it bordered on self-loathing. "I understand the importance of this operation, but I was unable to outmaneuver our enemies, whose ranks swell with each passing day."

"It's gotten that bad?" Jenkins asked.

"Worse." Pushkin grimaced. "In the last fifty hours alone, we have received seven different injunctions ordering us to cease and desist all military operations while formal inquiries can be conducted into every single mission we've carried out for the last thirty years."

"The presidential election is next month," Podsy said heavily. "We knew this kind of heat would be coming eventually."

"We did," Pushkin allowed. "But surviving a supernova is no easier simply because you know its blast wave is coming toward you before it arrives. The only possible path to survival is to get out of its way. I fear our efforts to that end have been insufficient, and that is entirely on me. For now, we have to keep focused on the mission ahead of us. Because unless Director Durgan holds his five-point lead in the polls all the way to the ballot box *and* ushers in serious, immediate government reforms, this mission will probably be the Metal Legion's last...as well as the last active duty deployment of any of our careers."

That last comment cast a pall over the room, but instead of wilting, no man present was any more distressed at hearing it than they would be at hearing a bullet whiz a foot past his head. They were as ready as any band of warriors had ever been to take the field in pursuit of their objective, and Lee Jenkins was proud to be seated among each and every one of them.

"Major Xi is aboard the Zeen worldship now?" Colonel Cao prompted.

"She is," Jenkins confirmed, checking his wrist-link's chronometer. "She should be touching down any minute now, at which point she'll employ her...some might say 'unconventional' diplomatic techniques. I have every confidence she'll secure their assistance."

"Excellent." Pushkin nodded. "Then that leaves us to hurry the transfer process as much as humanly—" The general's wrist-link chimed with an urgent missive, cutting him off mid-sentence. "Pushkin, go," he answered the call.

"General, there's news breaking in the capitol. You need to see this," stated a woman's voice on the other end. There was something chilling in her tone that immediately put Jenkins ill at ease, and his reaction was shared by the other attendees of the meeting.

"Put it through," Pushkin commanded, and the main display behind him lit up with the blond-haired, blue-eyed features of Sarah Samuels, the reporter who had accompanied the Metal Legion on Shiva's Wrath, and who had featured Major Xi in several documentaries on TAC over the last few months.

"We don't know how much longer we can keep this feed running," the reporter said, her usually pristine appearance replaced by one considerably less so. "But we will continue broadcasting on every channel available to us for as long as possible. It is times like these that require each and every one of us to stand up for what we believe is right, and right now, for me, that means speaking the truth. Director Daniel Durgan III, chairman and director of Durgan Industrial Enterprises and of this very news network, is dead. Official reports are that the DSV *Kirin*, the mobile headquarters for most of DIE's various entities, was destroyed by a reactor malfunction in transit through the New Africa system, but we have obtained evidence that refutes these officials reports, and that evidence is being seeded to every data net in the Terran Republic. We encourage everyone listening to this broadcast to locate these files and make copies as quickly as possible since efforts are already underway to remove them. Director Durgan was murdered, along with over two thousand DIE employees aboard the DSV *Kirin*. Whoever killed our fellow Terrans wants to cover their tracks, but as a reporter, I've learned that while those in power can kill a story, they can't kill the truth if we don't let them—"

As if on cue, a flare of light filled the screen before the broadcast went dead.

"That broadcast originated from DIN eighteen minutes ago, General," the comm operator reported after the feed had died.

"I assume this is the first you've heard of this, General," Jenkins said into the sudden silence.

"It is," Pushkin said, his usually jovial demeanor replaced by diamond-hard resolve. "We lost contact with him three days ago, but I thought... It doesn't matter. As I said," he looked from one officer to another, his eyes blazing with determination, "things are moving too quickly. New America is no longer safe for us. In truth, Terra may no longer be safe for us."

"General, I'm receiving a priority hail from Commodore Xin," the comm operator reported.

Pushkin grunted. "Put it on."

"This is Commodore Xin Feng of the Terran Eighth Fleet," came the audio-only missive. "Effectively immediately, all Terran Armor Corps personnel are ordered to stand down and return to their designated posts, where they will assist with an investigation authorized and empowered by all three branches of the Terran Government. Failure to comply with this directive, or to surrender to Fleet or Colonial Guard forces when instructed to do so, will be treated as mutiny in cold space. Eighth Fleet, out."

"Is this for real?" Podsy asked in mixed incredulity and shock. "Are they *seriously* going to frame us for Director Durgan's assassination?"

"Looks that way." Trapper shrugged indifferently.

"Commodore Xin is perhaps my last friend in Fleet," Pushkin said with a fierce grin. "So it should come as no surprise to anyone here that the defensive blockade is currently out of position, and will remain so for another fifty-three minutes. Which will have to be long enough to complete our transfers from the *William Wallace* or I fear we will not make our rendezvous with our Solar friends and Major Xi." Pushkin turned pointedly to Jenkins as he continued, "But as I have previously said, the Metal Legion's future is yours, not mine. How we proceed from here is up to you, and I will support you in whatever way you think necessary...unless you decide to comply with that ludicrous recall order, in which case you can go fuck yourself with a Crackerjack."

Laughter filled the room, but there wasn't a single anxious note to be heard. They were as ready as they would ever be, and the fate of the galaxy seemed to be hanging in the balance, so Lee "Roy" Jenkins gave the only reply he was realistically capable of.

"What do you say we go win the war for humanity?"

"Metal never dies," Pushkin agreed.

The End

Colonel Jenkins and Major Xi Bao will return in the exciting conclusion of the Metal Legion series.

SUPERDREADNOUGHT 1

Have you read Superdreadnought 1, also from CH Gideon?

Alone and unafraid. Sometimes you prevent war by hunting down your enemies.

Integrated with a superdreadnought, the artificial intelligence known as Reynolds takes his ship across the universe in search of the elusive Kurtherians. He comes to a revelation. He's better in the company of living creatures.

He needs a crew. He needs information. And he needs to continue his search and destroy mission.

Needing a crew and getting a crew are two completely different things. Reynolds is out of his element as he tries to reach out and make friends. Through it all, he has his vessel, the superdreadnought, the most powerful warship in the galaxy.

Or so he believes.

<u>AVAILABLE ON AMAZON RETAILERS AND IN KINDLE UNLIMITED!</u>

Thank you so much for your continued support for the Metal Legion! We wouldn't be here and telling these stories if it weren't for you.

Cheers and hats off to my co-author on this one, Caleb

Wachter who is doing the heavy lifting in bringing these characters and this story to life. One of his books was in a set that gained the USA Today bestseller list – as of this book, Caleb is a USA Today Bestselling Author! That is way cool and congratulations to him on the title he'll be able to carry for the rest of his life.

The final fight is coming in Metal Legion 8. Can humanity handle the pressure of leading the universe? They already split once over their differences. Will it tear them apart for good?

We'll find out in the next installment, coming soon.

In the interim, I have taken some down time. I went fishing with my dad to celebrate his 83rd birthday. We caught our limit of halibut and we got three of our four king salmon. Not too bad. We drove to Homer from Fairbanks. There was one turn in Anchorage, otherwise it was the same road the entire way. Five-hundred and fifty miles through a wide range of scenery, past Denali, the highest mountain in North America to the mountainous peninsula and Kachemak Bay off the ocean.

Once back in Fairbanks and after my father flew back home, friends of ours with an airplane took us out to a remote lake for a picnic and rainbow trout fishing. I caught the first fish, approximately one second after my first cast hit the water. I caught one on the third cast, too. Then they stopped biting. Strange but true. We took the plane to one side of the lake and let it drift across the middle to the other shore and we fished off the floats. That was neat and we filled up the cooler as we attacked the fish from the deep side of the lake.

It's still daylight and will be well past the publication of Metal Legion 8. The sun will set again in August. Strange but true stories for folks who live this close to the Arctic Circle. We have a short but intense growing season. My yard looks like a jungle. Which is good because no one can see the house. More privacy is good.

The mosquitoes are out heavily in the morning but taper off during the day. We rush through the morning walk when I'm all covered up, then put on shorts and take it easy for the next few walks. Phyllis the Arctic Dog makes me take the breaks I need to stay healthy. We spend a couple hours a day outside. We both win.

Until next time, peace, fellow humans.

Please join my Newsletter (www.craigmartelle.com – please, please, please sign up!), or you can follow me on Facebook since you'll get the same opportunity to pick up the books for only 99 cents on the first Saturday after they get published.

If you liked this story, you might like some of my other books. You can join my mailing list by dropping by my website **www.craigmartelle.com** or if you have any comments, shoot me a note at craig@craigmartelle.com. I am always happy to hear from people who've read my work. I try to answer every email I receive.

If you liked the story, please write a short review for me on Amazon. I greatly appreciate any kind words, even one or two sentences go a long way. The number of reviews an ebook receives greatly improves how well an ebook does on Amazon.

Amazon – www.amazon.com/author/craigmartelle

BookBub – https://www.bookbub.com/authors/craig-martelle

Facebook – www.facebook.com/authorcraigmartelle

My web page – www.craigmartelle.com

That's it—break's over, back to writing the next book.

Craig Martelle Social

Website & Newsletter:
http://www.craigmartelle.com

BookBub:
https://www.bookbub.com/authors/craig-martelle

Facebook:
https://www.facebook.com/AuthorCraigMartelle/

BOOKS BY CRAIG MARTELLE

Craig Martelle's other books (listed by series)

Terry Henry Walton Chronicles (co-written with Michael Anderle) – a post-apocalyptic paranormal adventure

Gateway to the Universe (co-written with Justin Sloan & Michael Anderle) – this book transitions the characters from the Terry Henry Walton Chronicles to The Bad Company

The Bad Company (co-written with Michael Anderle) – a military science fiction space opera

End Times Alaska (also available in audio) – a Permuted Press publication – a post-apocalyptic survivalist adventure

The Free Trader – a Young Adult Science Fiction Action Adventure

Cygnus Space Opera – A Young Adult Space Opera (set in the Free Trader universe)

Darklanding (co-written with Scott Moon) – a Space Western

Rick Banik – Spy & Terrorism Action Adventure

Become a Successful Indie Author – a non-fiction work

Enemy of my Enemy (co-written with Tim Marquitz) – a galactic alien military space opera

Superdreadnought (co-written with Tim Marquitz) – a military space opera

Metal Legion (co-written with Caleb Wachter) - a military space opera

End Days (co-written with E.E. Isherwood) – a post-apocalyptic adventure

Mystically Engineered (co-written with Valerie Emerson) – dragons in space

Monster Case Files (co-written with Kathryn Hearst) – a young-adult cozy mystery series

For a complete list of books from Craig, please see www. craigmartelle.com